I0612321

KILLSTREAK: BOOK TWO

HEAVY ARMOR

AN EPIC FANTASY LITRPG

STUART THAMAN

NEF HOUSE PUBLISHING

Killstreak: Book Two
Heavy Armor

Copyright © 2019 Stuart Thaman
Nef House Publishing
www.stuartthamanbooks.com

ISBN: 978-1-937979-59-1

Cover by J Caleb Clark (www.jcalebdesign.com)
Interior layout by Bodie D Dykstra (www.bdediting.com)

ALSO BY STUART THAMAN

Micah, Shane, Zac & Seth
You guys are the best

CHAPTER 1

"**W**hat do you think?" Estelle held the half-eaten remnants of a peach tart on the end of her fork. She smiled, a strand of her wavy hair dislodging from her ear and dangling in front of her eye. She tucked it back into place with a soft giggle, then popped the last half of the tart into her mouth, savoring the flavor for a few moments.

"It isn't bad," Kadorax replied honestly. He snatched another tart, a cherry one, from Estelle's plate. "I used to eat sweets like these all the time at the office back on Earth. We'd have donuts almost every single day in the break room."

Estelle reached across the small table and squeezed his upper arm. "Not here," she said.

Kadorax flexed under her grip. He toyed with the idea of activating a talent, perhaps something to enhance his reflexes or his *Strength*, but he knew he didn't need to. The cords of iron-like muscle beneath his skin were impressive

1

enough. As a level thirty-eight assassin, he'd trained for years to turn his body into the toned machine of war that it was.

"What was your favorite food back home?" he asked.

Estelle thought for a moment as she pushed an errant wisp of pale-yellow cream from the side of her lips and into her mouth. "I traveled to New York City once when I was a girl. There were so many new foods, things I'd never had before, but the one I remember most—"

"Cheesecake?" Kadorax interrupted, vividly remembering the taste of New York cheesecake after a huge steak dinner.

"Hot dogs," Estelle corrected with a laugh. "I know it's stupid, but I loved the street hot dogs from the vendors. The smells, the sounds of the city, they all combined into those hot dogs. I know I was just a little girl, but that's what I remember the best."

"Of all the foods in New York, you liked the hot dogs the best?" Finishing the last cherry tart, Kadorax waved his empty ale mug toward the waiter.

"What was your favorite food?" she asked him, her eyes narrowing as she wore a devilish grin.

Kadorax had to think for a moment before answering. "Maybe ice cream, but mostly because no one in Agglor has come up with it yet."

"Oh, come on," Estelle playfully scoffed. "You sound like a child. Ice cream?"

The waiter stopped by and refilled Kadorax's mug from a large pitcher wrapped in a scarlet cloth. They weren't in one of Agglor's better restaurants, nothing like one of the fine establishments on the upper tiers of Kingsgate, where the nobility was served by hordes of attendants and paid their bills in gold, but it wasn't a lowly sort of place, either.

Kadorax nodded to the waiter and took a long drink, enjoying the thick, warm ale as it coursed down his throat.

"Well, if I have to pick something else, perhaps my favorite would be cold beer. Really cold. I don't mind the warm stuff here, but I'll buy a thousand kegs for the first man in Agglor to invent refrigeration." He took another long swig before setting the now half-full mug on the table. Across from his drink, Estelle held a dainty glass—real, clear glass—with a few ounces of sweet white wine left in the bottom.

"Now you sound like a drunken college boy," she countered.

Kadorax sighed. A few pieces of seared fish remained on his plate, though they had gone cold as the conversation progressed, and he no longer had any desire to finish his meal. "Well, if I have to pick something more to your liking, Estelle, then a warm, juicy steak it is."

She smiled, her expression warm. "That's more like it," she said. "Though you can get steaks here at almost any inn or tavern, so it doesn't *really* count."

"Not like back home," Kadorax went on. "Sure, there are a few places in Kingsgate where you can get beef that isn't cooked beyond recognition, but it still doesn't compare. And for the record, I think I'd still take a pitcher of ice-cold beer over a steak, if I could."

Estelle finished the last of her wine and leaned back in her chair. "You boys are all the same," she purred over the rim of her glass.

"How many have you dated?" Kadorax chanced to ask. The beautiful woman's facial expression hid everything. She was inscrutable, her emotions as masked as any of Kadorax's Blackened Blades out on a job.

Waving her index finger back and forth in front of her eyes, Estelle looked away, toward the corners of the room.

"I've told you before, my love, that I'm not interested in talking about those things." She stood from her chair, rubbing a sore spot on her back. "Come, let us talk . . . more privately . . . upstairs, shall we?"

Kadorax fetched a small handful of silver from his pocket and set the stack down neatly at the edge of the table. It was more than the meal was worth by far, but he didn't particularly care. Estelle brought out his magnanimous side, assuming he actually had one—or maybe that was just what he liked to tell himself. The enchanted dagger at his side served as a constant reminder of his grim business in Agglor.

Estelle led him to the staircase, then reached behind her to take Kadorax's hand.

"Not yet," the assassin said, tugging her back. "I can't go up yet."

When she frowned, Kadorax shifted his eyes to the man in the lobby, the one he had been hired to escort. Estelle didn't know the nature of Kadorax's contract, but she understood the less than subtle gesture for what it was. She turned to continue up the stairs, offering him a sly wink and pulling ever so slightly at the edge of her dress to give Kadorax a tantalizing hint of a view as she ascended. "Don't be too long."

Trying hard not to blush, Kadorax clenched a fist at his side to take his mind from the dark places Estelle had so effortlessly lured it. He made his way through the grid of tables to the bar situated across the room, taking the stool all the way at the left end so he could casually turn and keep his eye on his mark as long as he needed to.

The man under Kadorax's protection was seated at a large circular table near the center of the room, dining and conversing with two other diplomats whose names Kadorax did not know, nor would he have given them much thought had he ever learned them.

Not wanting to give himself away too blatantly—though it would not matter since all the traveling nobility of Agglor hired protection in some form or another—Kadorax ordered another mug of ale and began to sip it casually.

The other diplomats' guards were similarly posted not too far away across the restaurant. There were three of them, all well trained and older than Kadorax, veterans by the looks of their scars, though not a single one was higher in level than the assassin. As the evening droned onward, Kadorax's armed counterparts behaved in much the same way as he did. They languidly sipped ale, kept their eyes firmly locked on their mark and the door, and no more than one of them at a time ever went out to piss.

The diplomat was agonizingly slow in concluding his business. Hours passed, and Kadorax's ale remained roughly half full until deep into the night. Finally, gracelessly, the diplomat moved his considerable bulk from his chair. The wood beneath his mass creaked in protest, and then the diplomat was standing and shaking hands with the others, exchanging the final pleasantries of the night with his equally distinguished and rotund guests.

Kadorax waited only a few moments before tossing a copper piece to the bartender and following his mark up the stairs to a long hallway containing a dozen doors all leading to secure rooms. The diplomat was in the seventh room, and he had left the door slightly ajar.

Silently, Kadorax stepped inside and offered a gracious bow. The diplomat was already busy unfastening the buttons of his waistcoat, and the garment appeared thankful for the relief. In truth, Kadorax wasn't sure how the thread had been strong enough to survive the night's meal without bursting apart. "You are well, my lord?" the assassin asked.

"Bah, my damned feet hurt, my head's awash with wine, and there's a fucking piece of gristle stuck between two of my teeth," the older man announced as he continued to wrestle with his finery, casting the expensive articles to the floor without a hint of care for their value. The entire ensemble, intricately embroidered with gold thread at the sleeves and collar, with still more gold patterned into the back of both the shirt and coat, probably cost just as much as the inn.

Kadorax bit one of the knuckles on his right hand to keep from laughing at the diplomat. "Well, I'm not sure I can help with any of that," he said, turning back for the hallway. "I'll be sleeping outside your door, my lord. Any noise before dawn, and I'll be at your side without hesitation."

The diplomat flashed a meek smile as he collapsed onto the room's large mattress. "I'll trudge lightly if I happen to wake before sunrise," he muttered.

Kadorax had almost left the room when he remembered to check the window. The single square of glass to the right of the bed wasn't large enough for a man to sneak through, but it would offer a view of the bed, albeit at a rather extreme angle, for a deft crossbowman to take a shot should the glass be broken. Kadorax inspected it carefully, activating *Detect Trap: Rank 5* just to be sure.

Having found nothing out of the ordinary, Kadorax pulled open the door. "Sleep well, my lord. Just call out, and I'll come rushing."

"Yes, yes," the portly man said as he waved him off. His eyes were already closed, and Kadorax suspected the wine was getting to his head a little more than the diplomat had let on.

Once more in the hallway, Kadorax paced to the end of the rooms, stopping at each door to listen for any unusual activity. He liked the way the floorboards creaked under the blue carpet at his feet. Loud floors meant tougher jobs for his ilk, though he didn't expect any trouble in the first place. The job was a routine one: escort an aging, miserable, over-weight diplomat from one city to the next while ensuring no one with a blade came within a dozen feet of him. Kado-rax had, as a matter more of principle than anything else, stopped accepting such contracts back when he was only level twenty. Unless a fair amount of combat was expected, the experience yield would simply be too low to excite his interest.

But Estelle had insisted. She had tired of living her life in the bleak halls of Darkarrow, and the escort quest was the only contract with a bit of travel on the board when she had made her plea to Kadorax for a bit of a journey. The dip-lomat's journey would take them from Darkarrow, up the coast east of Kingsgate, and then back to Oscine City and the Boneridge Mountains. It would last several weeks, and Kado-rax didn't know how much patience he had for haughty tav-erns and formal meetings.

When he was confident there were no overt threats lin-gering behind the other doors of the inn, Kadorax let him-self relax a little as he sat down outside the diplomat's door, his back against the cool wood. He scrolled through his list of abilities until he found the several talents he had taken that helped with guarding and vigilance, then activated *Peer-less Resolve: Rank 3*. The ability would last twelve hours, al-lowing him to stay alert—albeit not entirely awake until he earned more ranks—and ready to spring into action at the briefest indication of trouble.

Estelle was behind the fourth door to Kadorax's right, and he positioned himself, dagger in hand behind his back, his head facing her direction. He wasn't worried for her safety, since she had no enemies, but he longed to be in her bed. The wooden wall and thin carpet would wreak havoc on his back. He knew he'd awake sore and still tired, not to mention more than a little lonely. Having Estelle so close and yet so far out of reach tugged painfully on his heartstrings. Though he sometimes hated to admit it, Kadorax had fallen in love with her. She was like him. From Earth. If there was anyone who could steal his thoughts so effortlessly, it was her.

With images of Estelle, her body framed in an enticing silk gown—a sleeveless, deep teal dress Kadorax had spent a month's worth of contracts to purchase—fluttering through his head, the assassin closed his eyes.

Hours after midnight, in the deep black of predawn, Estelle eased open her door. The hinges had been recently oiled, and they only made small, insignificant sounds as they moved. Walking on her toes, she crept down the hall toward Kadorax's sleeping form. The man was hunched over, his chin resting against his chest, his dark hair hanging down in unkempt strands on his forehead.

She was lightly clothed, wearing a thin nightgown woven from simple cotton. It barely fell far enough to cover even an inch of her upper thighs. Stealing a glance down the other direction of the hallway to ensure no embarrassing encounters with other patrons, she padded along the edge of the carpet, where it met the wall. A devious, lusty smile crossed her face when she reached Kadorax without him waking. The talent he had activated would alert him to danger, she knew, but it would do nothing when confronted with the kind of desires playing in her mind.

Mercifully, the floorboards at the edge of the hallway hadn't made a single noise under her diminutive weight, and her own breathing had been easily lost among the diplomat's loud snoring. In the deep silence of night, she considered herself lucky.

Estelle held her breath as she reached out a hand to Kadorax's shoulder. She pulled back her touch less than an inch from his shirt. Her loose gown had drifted forward as she'd leaned down, and part of her plan involved filling Kadorax's gaze with the most pleasant view she could offer when he awoke. She straightened her back and pulled the gown down, fitting it tightly to the curves of her breasts. She leaned in once more, confident that her appearance offered no doubt as to her carnal desire, and gently shook the man awake.

"My lov—"

Kadorax's poisoned dagger was buried to the hilt in her chest.

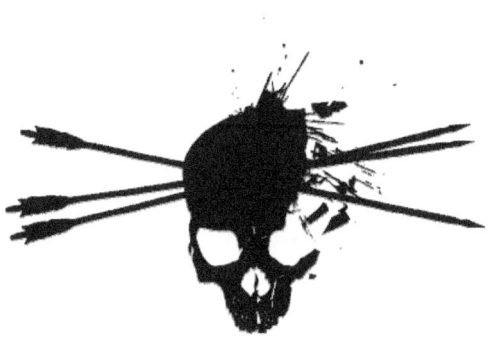

CHAPTER 2

The sounds of every Oscine City citizen panicking all at once were nearly deafening. Kadorax, Brinna, and Syzak had to fight off a wave of screaming commoners pressing against them as though their very lives depended on running toward the sea—which was most certainly the case . . . if the sea could offer any safe harbor at all.

Across the chaotic street, a small regiment of armored knights held fast in front of a building, looking around for one of the leaders to issue a command. Kadorax pushed his way to the nearest of the group and grabbed the man's breastplate to jerk him backward and get his attention. "Find the prior!" he yelled into the knight's bewildered face.

The Gar'kesh coming toward them was getting closer, rampaging within a hundred yards of the huddled knights. The end of the civilian horde was in sight, just barely a few steps ahead of the creature's heavy, swinging arms. A trail of dead bodies marked where the Gar'kesh had been.

Nodding, the man tore himself from Kadorax's grasp and began yelling to his comrades, leaving the bastion to weave his way through the panic and back to his own companions. "Let's go," he announced, turning to move with the swarm. The others followed closely on his heels.

A few streets away from all the destruction, the prior was easy to spot. He stood among a huge contingent of his knights, a great helm under his arm. He barked orders to the gathered soldiers, and they were eager to comply. The sound of metal and leather pounding against stone filled Kadorax's ears.

Kadorax couldn't make out any distinct words from the prior's mouth until he was close enough for the old man to inadvertently spit on him. "You have the warlock?" Kadorax shouted above the din.

The prior looked his way for a second, shook his head, then went back to his own charges. "You four! Head east along the waterfront! Find the prior! Find Ammon! Tell her to join me at once!" A terrified look in their eyes, the four remaining knights hurried toward the docks as quickly as their steel would allow.

Finally, the prior turned to regard the new arrivals with something more than a glance. "Atticus is being fetched at this moment, but he isn't here yet," the man stated. There was a touch of sorrow in his voice.

"What will Atticus do?" Kadorax asked. He thought of all the fire and death the Grim Sleeper had wrought—and she had been far weaker than Atticus was certain to be.

"There's no time," the prior yelled back, sweeping the three up in his wake as he spun toward the Gar'kesh, his blue and gold cloak flapping about behind him. "Follow me. There's a horde of jackals, and I don't know where your damned leader is. Until Elise can be found, you three are best suited to hunt the jackal leaders. My knights will never catch them, not without horses."

Kadorax nodded. Ahead of him, the prior sped off to organize a line of his men holding back the very first of the jackals. The horde had arrived, and they were tearing at the knights with wild abandon, showing nothing even approximating a desire to survive the fight—only a desire to overrun the city. The way the horde fought with such recklessness spoke volumes to its sheer numbers. The jackals didn't value their individual lives at all. Total victory was all that mattered.

"Come on," the bastion said, steeling himself as he drew his new sword and tightened his grip around the hilt. "Through the buildings." He stole one last glance at the shield wall the prior was trying to organize, then shouldered into the nearest building. "We'll go around them. We can find their leaders and take them out. If the knights hold, there's a chance. All we can do is hope."

When Kadorax cleared enough adrenaline from his mind to realize what he'd walked into, he found himself standing face to face with what looked to be a hundred or more civilians crowded on top of each other in a small basket shop. None of the terrified citizens said a word. They just stared, most of them slack-jawed, and followed his movements with their eyes.

"Is there an exit in the back?" Kadorax demanded, pushing against a young boy who had collided with his legs.

No one answered.

Kadorax lifted his sword high to push through the mob. He stopped after making it only a few feet. "Damn it all. Back to the street!" Syzak and Brinna more or less tumbled through the door, taking Kadorax along with them. Outside, the knights' position had held, but there weren't enough of them to completely stretch from one side of the street to the other. A gap in the line at least six men wide provided ample room for the jackals to scamper by unharmed and flood Oscine City as quickly as they could.

Brinna slashed at one of the jackals as it ran past, drawing a long line of blood down its flank. The creature didn't let up. In fact, Kadorax wasn't sure it noticed the wound.

What are they after? the bastion wondered, but his thoughts were drowned out by the roar of the Gar'kesh, now a mere fifty yards from where he stood.

"Time to go," Syzak hissed. The snake-man ran to his left, toward the Gar'kesh, the knot of embattled knights to his right. Ten or so paces forward, he bashed his way inside another building, then quickly turned and motioned for the others to follow.

"Sounds like they're inside," Kadorax said between breaths. The shop clearly belonged to a chandler, a prolific one, and it smelled so strongly of freshly dipped wax that the sensation almost overpowered the multitude of chaotic happenings on the other side of the door. At least it wasn't chock-full of refugees as the basket seller had been.

Brinna's head jerked toward the ceiling, following the sounds of footsteps—tons of them—going every direction all at once. Then a scream. More footsteps. A howl. Claws scraping against wood.

Sword in hand, Kadorax found the staircase in the corner of the small shop. The stairs themselves were old and worn, and they turned once ninety degrees, blocking Kadorax's view of the upstairs level. More sounds came from above. There were at least three jackals in the upstairs room, judging by the difference in voice. Perhaps it was more.

Kadorax let out a long exhale and charged, slashing

14

blindly with his sword as he reached the top of the stairs. The blade connected and sent a spurt of blood across Kadorax's face. A jackal writhed at his feet, and its experience points flashed in the bastion's vision. Two more stood behind it amidst the torn, unmoving remnants of at least one human. Kadorax couldn't see if any more beasts were waiting in the other rooms, ready to emerge and tear him limb from limb.

In the small space of the blood-strewn upper hallway, Kadorax couldn't move his sword hand back far enough to execute a proper swing without risking entanglement with the wall sconces and a large tapestry. The first jackal came on with its claws wide and a snarl plastered across its snout. Kadorax met the jackal with an activation of *Torment*, encasing his sword in deep shadows. He parried the jackal's right-hand claws and drove forward off his back foot, planting his blade deep in the creature's shoulder. Without a buckler or some other means of defense, Kadorax had to accept a shredding slice along the left side of his rib cage.

Cage of Chaos activated in response to the hit, and a blast of small, white, impossibly fast objects rocketed into the wall behind the jackal, right where the attack had come from just a second before. Another magical emanation quickly followed the first, scorching the wall with a bit of fire. Kadorax stole a glance to see what the first element had been as the jackal reeled in terror, clutching its shoulder and issuing a pain-filled howl.

Teeth? Kadorax thought, pulling his eyes back to the enemies in front of him. *Are those teeth?* The wall held a small collection of white objects roughly the size of human canines and incisors embedded in the wood. Before Kadorax could wonder further on the somewhat morbid dental expulsion, another jackal had thrown its wounded comrade out of its way and taken up the offensive.

Not eager to let the jackal have so much as a single moment's reprieve, Kadorax activated *Chaos Shock* with a shout, throwing his left hand forward, his palm facing the enemy's chest. A ghostly tendril flew through the jackal's torso. It didn't shred the flesh or rip a gaping hole in the creature as Kadorax had desperately wanted. Instead, the fragment of incorporeal energy had clearly been a fear-based attack, and the rune in *Assir's Edge* augmented the terror with a visible flash. The jackal fell backward at once, a claw digging into the wall at its side for balance, and it was out of range when the second activation of *Chaos Shock* sent a bolt of blue water swirling out of Kadorax's hand.

The jackal's eyes went wide. A bit of saliva escaped the edge of its snout, and it tried in vain to scramble backward as quickly as it could. Kadorax was on it with his sword faster than the creature could react, and it died without so much as a grunt or a growl, only frozen, silent terror.

Wearing a fine mail coat and holding a jagged fauchard in its hairy paws, a final jackal stood at the end of the hallway. The polearm was perhaps seven feet long, giving it both a significant advantage and a major hindrance in the tight quarters. Kadorax wouldn't be able to get close without risking impalement, but the jackal would only be able to thrust directly forward; it would never have the room to swing without taking down an entire wall first.

Thinking of the thousands—perhaps tens of thousands—of jackals swarming the streets of Oscine City, Kadorax knew that expending his only use of *Chaos Step* for the day would be dangerous. Without any room above his head to swing his whip, *Torment* wouldn't work, either. Struggling for an easy solution, he backed up a step to put the most room between him and the seasoned, cautious jackal as he scanned through his ninth level options once more.

Guardian of the Deep would get the job done . . . but at what cost? Kadorax wasn't sure he'd be able to take the un-earthly beast down himself once it had been loosed. *Bathed in Silence* was only a passive skill, and the last ability was the next rank of *Chaos Shock*—no easy choices. Slowly, the jackal began moving forward. It took its time, making sure not to step on the corpses in the hallway and risk losing its footing. When it was in range, it thrust its fauchard forward without putting much strength behind the movement, and Kadorax easily parried the strike.

"Testing my speed," the bastion surmised. "You've fought before. Probably higher level than me."

A sinister grin spread across the sides of the jackal's muzzle. The beast nodded ever so slightly, then exploded into action. It jabbed forward, twisting the wooden shaft of the fauchard in its grip, and the wide blade danced past Kadorax's already injured left side. Unfortunately, the jackal hadn't missed. The reverse side of the blade held a small, barbed hook maybe two inches in length, stained and pitted from heavy use. When the jackal leapt backward, it threw all of its weight into the haft of its weapon, and the spike caught Kadorax's armor right over his ribs.

Cage of Chaos activated, but it was no use; there was no enemy close enough to hit. Kadorax swung down with his sword, thinking to sever the blade of the fauchard. *Assir's Edge* smacked into the polished wood below the metal blade and clanked right off, leaving a nick in the finish and not much else. The hook ripped forward, and Kadorax knew that his *Reinforced Leather Vest* was the only thing saving him from watching his hot entrails get dragged across the floorboards. Still, the fauchard did its work.

Kadorax yelled in pain as he clutched his torn side, his sword clattering to his feet. Another strike came just as quickly as the first. Then a third followed, and two bloody gashes ran from Kadorax's collarbone down to his breastplate.

"Hel—"

The floor beneath the jackal vanished before Kadorax could finish begging for rescue. A dozen or more spikes fell through the air with the stunned jackal to the first floor where they landed in a heap. Kadorax could hear someone, likely Brinna, fighting below, but he was too weak to peer over the newly created hole in the floor to look. Then the entire structure lurched violently to the side.

"The house is coming down!" Kadorax yelled through the pain clogging his mind. He turned, all his weight on the wall and the railing, and began descending the stairs to the first floor. The house shifted again. The walls on either side narrowed by a foot or more at the top, and the stairs began to sag significantly in the middle.

A scaly hand grabbed onto Kadorax's belt and pulled him forward right as a bit of ceiling dislodged from above the staircase and came crashing down. Kadorax resisted the tug just long enough to reach out and pluck his sword from the floorboards.

"Hurry!" Syzak yelled, shifting most of Kadorax's weight onto his shoulders as he started to run. Her right hand covered in a noticeable amount of blood, Brinna joined the retreat and held the front door open long enough for them to escape.

The street was still fully engulfed in chaos. Kadorax tried to appraise the situation, but his eyes refused to focus.

"I left my staff," Syzak muttered, dropping Kadorax to the cobblestones as gingerly as he could. He glanced back at the crumbling building just once before shaking his head. "*Spike Trap* took out a pair of support beams, and the craftsmanship of the building wasn't great to begin with, I guess. Doesn't matter. Now hold still."

The snake-man held his hands above Kadorax's body and cast *Cure Minor Ailments*. At second rank, the spell was able to at least staunch the flow of blood from Kadorax's chest and shoulder, knitting much of the muscle and tendon back together, though it did little for the skin and nothing for the torn armor above it.

"You'll live," Syzak announced. He was back on his feet in an instant, hands wide and ready to cast should any of the swarming jackals stray too close. So far, all of the fight they could see was focused entirely on the knot of armored knights closer to the docks.

"The Gar'kesh," Kadorax panted, regaining his knees and stopping for a moment before standing.

"Getting closer," Syzak answered. The massive, many-armed monstrosity was less than fifty yards away. It slammed its huge fists into everything it could find: buildings, foolish knights who attempted to get near enough to attack, and more than a few cowering civilians who had been unable to flee with the others.

In front of the beast, a single figure stood like a stalwart statue, unmoving in the face of such terrible power. "Atticus is here." Syzak lifted Kadorax back to his feet.

"We should run," Brinna said. Her eyes were wide, and her breathing came in rapid bursts that she painfully struggled to control. Kadorax didn't have time to see if she'd been injured. He returned *Assir's Edge* to his belt and began hobbling away from the Gar'kesh, forcing his mind to ignore as much of the pain in his body as was possible. The others were eager to join him.

Syzak kept his head turned to watch the action as he covered their retreat. "Atticus summoned something," he muttered, a bit of fear plain in his voice. "Something dark. Maybe he can hold it back."

Kadorax didn't feel like waiting around long enough to find out. Before long, the trio was swept toward the front of a group of fleeing knights, the remnants of the prior's personal guard that had managed to escape the first wave of the jackal swarm. Everywhere he looked, Kadorax saw blood-stained armor, dented breastplates, shattered tassets, and scabbards missing their swords. The hodgepodge group was barely alive, and it had no leader telling it where to go. At the front of the little pack, Syzak led everyone as far down the street as he could without running into the back of the jackal horde, then turned left, heading east up the coast and away from Oscine City's overrun harbor.

A pair of fluttering blue pennants dotted the horizon ahead. For once in his life, Kadorax was thankful to see the trappings of the priory standing tall.

"The overland route," one of the knights at Kadorax's side said between pained breaths. The man's chest was bloodied, his mail coat torn. A large clump of matted hair clung to the side of his armor, and Kadorax thought he could see at least two shorn jackal claws still lodged in the interlocking rings.

Syzak stopped for a moment to readjust Kadorax's weight on his shoulder. "Which way?" he asked the knight who had spoken.

"There, between the crags. It'll take longer, but we won't have to climb from the ocean," he answered.

"Take us there," Syzak replied, a little dash of hope in his voice.

Somewhat reluctantly, the knight led the group a ways back to his left, toward the north—and the Gar'kesh—in order to find the subtle path that would bring them all to the priory's ornate driftwood doors.

Perhaps halfway through the long journey, they had to pass the area of the city that had been destroyed by the initial jackal invasion. There wasn't much left of the businesses and houses: mostly timbers and frames, fragments of walls strewn about, and corpses. So many corpses. The lead knight stopped for a moment as the sheer weight of the scene settled on his and everyone's minds.

"There were so many of them . . ." Brinna said under her breath. Similar murmurs spread throughout the rest of the group.

"The Gar'kesh—" Kadorax began, but a collapsing building quickly drowned out his words. Then the beast itself emerged into view, its monstrous arms flailing rapidly in front of it as though it was warding off some ranged attack that no one else could see. Its back, rippling with muscle as it pumped its arms, was turned to the group.

Syzak hissed and set his feet. "We might be able to take it down," he said with grim determination.

"It doesn't know we're here. If Atticus can keep it occupied, we have an opening," Kadorax agreed. He rubbed his chest through his armor, keenly aware of the beating he had taken not long before. He felt the still-alien coolness of the soul rod lodged in his chest. A shudder ran through his spine as he remembered what Banemaw had told him.

The knight with a pair of claws dangling from his ragged mail gasped and spat a glob of his blood onto the street.

"You . . . You can't be serious." He wiped his mouth on a piece of his blue and gold tabard. "You'll die. You can't face that thing."

Kadorax put on his most confident grin and turned to the group of knights and commoners behind him. More than a handful of them looked strong enough to still be in fighting shape. "Now's our chance!" he yelled into the sky above their heads.

No resounding roar of eagerness answered his call.

Kadorax licked his lips. "The Gar'kesh is turned, distracted. We can save Oscine City! Who's with me?"

A few of the closest knights suddenly found the flagstones at their feet to be the most interesting things they'd seen in quite some time. Those at the back of the group didn't bother feigning a lack of interest. "Suicide!" one of them called back, and many others quickly agreed.

"Well, just the two of us, then?" Syzak asked.

"Damn *Charisma* isn't high enough, I guess," Kadorax muttered. He drew his sword and spun it a few times to loosen his wrist.

The snake-man shook his head. "No, I don't think that's it. Anyone with a *Spirit* score above one would know that what you're asking is insane."

"You don't have to go," Kadorax said. He stepped a few paces ahead of the group to help clear his head. Every movement brought a fresh throb of pain to his side, poignantly reminding him that he wasn't at full strength.

Syzak stepped up beside him. "We may never get another shot," he said. Turning back to the small group, he nodded to Brinna. "Make sure everyone gets to the priory. We'll meet you there." The woman, her eyes wide and sweat glistening on her face, only nodded.

"Right." Kadorax adjusted his leather to try and find a comfortable fitting that would minimize his pain, though he wasn't successful. "You know how much experience this is going to be worth?" he laughed.

Syzak laughed as well, and then the troop behind them set off again in the direction of the shoreside priory. More than a few of their number muttered things about death wishes and respawning as they passed.

Without needing to vocalize their plan, the two lone fighters moved in perfect concert through the ruins of the street, getting closer and closer to the back of the flailing Gar'kesh. Perhaps forty yards from the lumbering giant, they could finally see what it was that had the creature so fully embattled. Atticus had summoned an elemental, a living construct of air, lightning, and driving rains all held together by sinuous cords of pure, visible magic. Normally, the control of an elemental was better suited to the classes of shaman and mystics—and sometimes wizards, though Agglor's histories were littered with tales of the frailer class attempting to control such amalgamations of magic and accidentally loosing them on unsuspecting towns in the middle of the night. Kadorax had to wonder if the old warlock had multiclassed specifically for access to such abilities. After a second or perhaps even less, he had his answer.

The lightning elemental cleaved forward with its brilliantly flashing appendages, but it wasn't just air and wind and electricity that coursed into the Gar'kesh with every blow. Fragments of red energy streaked with black joined the fray as well, battering the jackal god with the combined powers of the elements clearly augmented by demonic forces. The furious colossus was both elemental and underworldly, an abomination of different magics that would lay waste to Oscine City as surely as the Gar'kesh would.

"If Atticus can't control that thing—"

"Then we're all dead!" Kadorax said above Syzak's concern. "Whatever it is, it's part demon. I don't think Atticus multiclassed as a shaman just to summon an air elemental when warlocks get summoning of their own."

"Then what happened?" the snake-man asked, scrambling over a torn piece of building.

"I think . . ." Kadorax had to pause as he pushed himself over the same ruins. "I think Atticus used a demon to . . . eat an air elemental. Or something. All I know is that it isn't a regular elemental. That's a warlock's pet."

They stopped as close to the titanic duel as they dared, cowering about twenty yards away behind the shattered remnants of a potion shop's eastern wall. Kadorax still had his sword in his hand, and it suddenly felt like some sort of horrible joke when compared to the utterly impossible size of the beasts slugging each other in the street.

"What do we do?" Syzak asked. His legs were shaking, and it wasn't from the weight of his armor.

Kadorax had to think for a moment. He knew he didn't have much time, but he also didn't really have a plan. "If the elemental knocks it down," he began, but Syzak was already shaking his head.

"The elemental won't stop just because we're crawling over the Gar'kesh in search of a neck to slit. It'll crush us," the shaman stated.

"Then right back to level one we'd go."

"So come up with a better plan," Syzak urged.

Again, Kadorax had to duck his head behind the ruined

shelving of the destroyed store in order to think. The roar of the battle was overwhelming.

"What if—"

A giant, deafening crash ripped through the street, and a scattershot of stone debris rained down on Kadorax's back. The battling titans were too close. It wouldn't be long before their enormous feet—or hooves in the case of the Gar'kesh—would be right on top of the two adventurers, squishing their bodies into boneless pulp like grapes being pressed into wine.

"Time to pick my ninth level talent," Kadorax said, jumping to his side as another piece of debris shattered on the street. From the corner of his eye, he saw a new group of jackal warriors scampering over the ruined buildings and moving in their direction.

Syzak grabbed Kadorax strongly by the shoulders, whirling him toward the incoming jackals. The Gar'kesh was less than thirty feet away, and they could both smell the putrid stench on its breath. "Do it! Do *something*!" the snake-man yelled in Kadorax's face.

His character sheet visible in the bottom half of his vision, Kadorax knew what he had to select. He couldn't hope to bring down the Gar'kesh, and he knew he probably couldn't even distract it long enough to accomplish anything meaningful, but the pack of jackals bearing down on him was the larger concern. He focused, and *Guardian of the Deep* flashed to life before joining the other skills on his sheet.

"*Guardian of the Deep*!" Kadorax called. At first, nothing happened. Then, after a painfully long second elapsed and the jackals were nearly upon them, a little blue point of light flickered above the street. Kadorax moved his eyes, and the blue beacon followed, appearing directly in the center of the charging beasts.

Without thinking, Kadorax *willed* the guardian to summon, and the blue light disappeared altogether.

None of the rushing jackals were prepared. The ground beneath their feet split apart—erupted upward—and out came a flailing monstrosity the size of a small tavern: a combination of a water-dwelling leviathan and a grossly oversized horseshoe crab. If any of the jackal pack survived the initial explosion of flagstones, tentacles, and gore, Kadorax was certain they'd no longer consider him their prime target.

"Run!" the bastion shouted, but Syzak was already ten yards ahead, sprinting in the direction of the priory.

A rapid series of yellow numbers flashed across Kadorax's vision, telling him the jackal pack had been eliminated. He allowed himself only a brief flicker of joy at the prospect of hitting the all-import tenth level so quickly, though his elation rapidly evaporated.

"Come on!" Kadorax yelled in frustration. Another pack of jackals, maybe seven or eight of them, rushed into the street between Kadorax, Syzak, and the herd of civilians desperate to reach the safety of the priory.

"All I really have left is *Rat Trap*," the shaman said, coming to a halt and panting from the effort. They had twenty yards of street and only a couple of seconds before the new jackal pack was upon them.

Kadorax's own skill sheet was running woefully empty. He had *Riposte* and *Chaos Step*, but *Chaos Shock* and *Torment* were both still on cooldown. Setting his feet and taking what little time he could afford to try and steady his heavy breathing, Kadorax tightened his grip on *Assir's Edge*. "Be ready with the rats, Syzak," he told his companion. "See you on the other side."

The first of the jackals, three of them running side by side, were the typical rank-and-file warriors Kadorax was used to slaying. They fanned out at the last minute, and Kadorax dove at the center creature, his sword point leading the way. A wet, ragged howl came from the beast's snout as it was quickly impaled. At Kadorax's sides, the other two jackals went to work with their claws, raking sharp lines into his leather armor. Much to the bastion's dismay, Ayers had only reinforced the center of the leather jerkin with iron, not the sides.

Kadorax's blood flowed freely onto the street. Gritting his teeth, he activated *Chaos Step*, his sword still buried to the hilt in a jackal's torn chest. The beasts on either side of him reared back to slash again, and then Kadorax was gone. He appeared behind the second group of four enemies, his right hand and arm absolutely covered in doghead innards. Luckily, his sword had made the ethereal jaunt without coming free of his hand.

Two jackals in the second group fell to the ground before they even knew there was anyone behind them to cleave them apart. Kadorax watched his first two opponents continue toward his shaman companion, but he didn't have time to help. If Syzak died, he died.

The jackal to Kadorax's left sneered and activated a talent, suddenly becoming awash in green light and growing several feet in height all at once. *Giant's Strength*, Kadorax knew. It wasn't a common ability among dogheads, though it was certainly an effective one. Thankfully, the one disadvantage of the powerful enchantment was a reduction in *Agility*, and Kadorax knew exactly how to take advantage of the mismatch.

The bastion charged the huge jackal. He kept his sword high to his right side and took a semi-circuitous route, lining up the two jackals in front of one another so they couldn't both get to him at the same time. As expected, the enhanced jackal swiped downward with a big, meaty paw—a strike easily strong enough to crush Kadorax's skull without slowing.

With considerably higher *Agility*, it wasn't hard for Kadorax to meet the incoming claws with his blade and *Riposte*, and he twisted his body to the left while simultaneously moving *Assir's Edge* skyward. A split second later and Kadorax was behind the hulking jackal, completely unscathed, swinging his blade down as hard as he could into the creature's back. The doghead howled, and it spun on its mangy heels, claws out wide.

Kadorax took an enchanted claw to his chest, and it threw him backward, where he landed hard on the broken stones that had once been a gleaming boulevard. All the air was gone from his lungs. Above him, he saw the nearly cloudless afternoon sky, but it was quickly blocked out by a snout and a pair of dark, beady eyes. Before Kadorax could think clearly enough to begin setting some sort of defense in front of his exposed chest and face, the jackal jerked a few inches downward—the telltale sign of a trap being cast directly under its feet.

A small swarm of putrid, disease-ridden rats exploded from a fresh crater in the street. The jackal, completely thrown off balance by the vanishing roadway, tumbled to the ground in a heap of oversized arms, flailing claws, and grimy vermin.

Kadorax scrambled backward, ignoring the throbbing pain starting to cover every inch of his battered body. He didn't have time to see how Syzak was holding up at his end of the fight. The enchanted jackal would be busy fighting rats for a few moments at best, and there was still another enemy bearing down on Kadorax, malice glinting in its eyes.

As he got to his feet once more, Kadorax noticed *Chaos Shock* was about to come off cooldown. *Torment* would be right behind it, but he had to hold out for another minute without the benefit of a single skill or talent. "Just die already!" he shouted, accepting a nasty gash down his chest. His armor did little to dull the blow. His thoughts flickered for a moment to the soul rod he was supposed to protect, but there was no time. He grappled the doghead's shoulders, their faces only inches apart.

Shoeless on the broken pavement, the jackal was the first to give ground. It slid a few inches backward, and then its rearmost paw fell into the artificial pit created by Syzak's *Rat Trap*, making the beast lurch backward and lose its balance. Kadorax was right on top of the hole before he could pull back, but his feet planted firmly on the ground that ordinarily would have been there, his *Guardian's Enchanted Steel Spats* making him immune to the trap's effects. To an outsider, it would have looked as if Kadorax's foot was simply hovering in the air. All the bastion cared about was that it worked.

The jackal in Kadorax's grasp fell onto the back of its huge companion, and the bastion leapt atop them both to finish the job. He stabbed downward, and the smaller doghead attempted to activate a talent, likely something to enhance its speed and reflexes, but it was too slow. *Assir's Edge* sank through its neck. By the time Kadorax withdrew his blade from the fresh doghead corpse, the enchanted beast he was basically riding regained its awareness of the battle and stood. All the bastion could do was hold tight to its fur as it rose. *Giant's Strength*—a skill Kadorax recognized and knew well—made the creature roughly double its normal height. The taut muscles beneath the animal's matted fur rippled with life.

Holding on with his left hand, Kadorax pulled his sword back to strike. There wasn't enough room to turn the blade for a proper angle, so he slammed the hilt onto the back of the jackal's head. The strike didn't do much, and the jackal barely seemed to notice. Its head swung side to side, surveying the battlefield. Syzak had one jackal dead at his feet, and he was squared off against the last remaining combatant, trading swipes with his serpentine claws for slashes from the doghead's own paws.

Chaos Shock: Rank 2 flashed across the bottom of Kadorax's vision, indicating the cooldown had finished. With a grin, he activated the talent at once, and a fist-sized ball of verdant moss-green energy congealed around his hand. He shoved it forward, directly into the back of the enchanted jackal's skull, and the jade magic sank through fur and bone alike, exploding through the front of the creature's face as if an entire decade's worth of forest vegetation had suddenly grown in the blink of an eye.

Working as quickly as he could, Kadorax leapt from the body and made another fist, pulling a second random element from the chaos and throwing it forward at the doghead facing Syzak. Luckily, the second element was a more ordinary gout of orange flame, and it had just enough reach to singe the back of the jackal and distract it.

Fire dancing on the jackal's mane, Syzak grabbed the creature by the throat and ripped, spraying a torrent of hot blood across his scales.

"Finally," Kadorax panted.

Syzak, heaving in air as his forked tongue hung down his chin, shook his head. "That one's . . . just paralyzed," he said, pointing to one of the jackals at his feet. He knelt to finish the job with a claw, then stood, his hands on his knees.

"*Finally*," Kadorax repeated. His vision was blurry from an overwhelming combination of pain, exhaustion, and stinging sweat dripping into his eyes.

Torment: Rank 1 appeared in white letters, the cooldown expired.

"We have to run," Syzak said. His body sported a myriad of cuts and bruises that showed up on his scaled body in strange colors.

Kadorax nodded, his hands on his knees to catch his breath. "I only have one talent left. *Torment* came off cooldown about ten seconds ago. You're out too?"

"Nothing left in the tank," Syzak confirmed.

Behind them, the Gar'kesh crashed through another building, and it finally looked as if it was giving ground. The elemental Atticus had summoned held the advantage, raining blow after blow into the jackal god's chest with its crackling fists. No matter what the result would be, the northern half of Oscine City was already destroyed. Whatever structures hadn't been leveled by the dueling titans had been swarmed over and knocked to the ground by the horde of jackal soldiers. The watery beast Kadorax had summoned was wreaking havoc as well. It didn't know the difference between friend and foe, and its powerful tentacles hammered away at both the elemental and the Gar'kesh.

Kadorax set his feet, his eyes scanning the torn streets for any other foes. A firm hand on his shoulder turned him the other way.

"We have to retreat, Kad," Syzak told him.

Kadorax sighed and rubbed a hand across the back of his

STUART THAMAN

neck. Blood mixed with the sweat and grime that came off on his fingers. "Let's go."

The two began running down the street toward the ocean and in the ultimate direction of the priory. They had to scramble over fallen bits of debris scattered all around, and shouts of battle rose up from every direction, filling the morning air with an indecipherable cacophony.

"Look out!" Syzak shouted, but he was too late.

A falling chunk of building—the southern wall from the second story a tannery—crashed to the ground. Despite his higher *Dexterity*, Kadorax didn't see the dislodged rubble quickly enough to move his battered body. As the stone, mortar, and timber broke apart in the air, a square of it bashed into Kadorax's chest, knocking him to the ground.

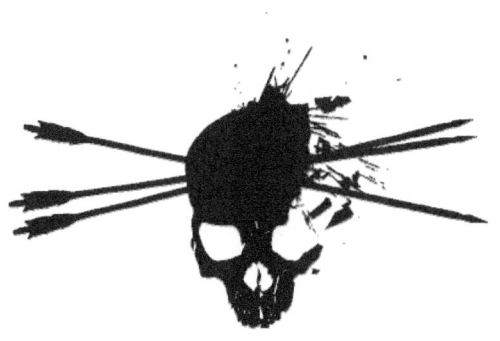

CHAPTER 3

Kadorax awoke in the chaos, but something was different. Instead of red and orange hues tinting everything in his vision, the world was dark and foreboding, steeped in shifting shadows and ominous patches of glinting black.

Ligriv stepped out of the shadows. His incorporeal body trailed a bit of silver smoke behind him as he moved. The strange man wore a frown upon his face. "What did I tell you when you first came to see me?" he asked, his voice flat and uncaring.

Pain flared in Kadorax's chest. His soul rod was the epicenter, and from there it spread to the very ends of his fingers and toes, where it continued to throb in time with his pulse. "I know . . ." he breathed. "I didn't protect the rod."

"No, Kadorax, you did not. When you died as an assassin, you were the fourth highest-level person to have ever perished on Agglor. That is why I selected you to carry the soul rod for me. It is more important than your life," Ligriv stated. He turned away and shook his head.

"What now? I'm dead for good?" Kadorax asked.

Still facing away, Ligriv sighed, and more silver filled the air like spores. "Not yet. But you need to learn a lesson. If you are to survive, you must learn an important, *painful* lesson. I will not heal you this time."

"Someone's in a bad mood."

"Hey, looks like you're coming out of it," Syzak whispered from Kadorax's side.

The bastion rubbed his eyes, then clenched them shut again as a fresh wave of pain coursed through his body. "We made it out? What happened?"

The snake-man nodded. "It's been about a day. The Priorate Knights held the city. Well, they held half of it, maybe a little less. In the north, the priory is all that's left in friendly hands."

"Ha, *friendly* might be an overstatement," Kadorax wheezed.

Syzak offered a weak smile in return. "Not this time. The old prior has thrown aside all the past conflicts, at least for now. They lost a lot of their leadership in the fight. Ammon is dead. Just the old man left to run things. If we're going to save Oscine City, it'll take all of us."

"And our friend the mayor?" the man asked.

Brinna stepped over to Kadorax's cot. "I'm here. The refugees made it. We have about a hundred. We're not sure how many others from the city have found shelter, though the fighting has stopped for now, as far as we can tell. There are probably thousands of people locked inside their cellars and waiting for rescue."

Coughing and sputtering as he tried to sit up, Kadorax finally opened his eyes to look around the room. The priory was crowded with terrified faces. People were everywhere, most of them nursing wounds, and a handful of the prior's underlings were busy seeing to them. "Looks like I'm last on the list for healing magic," he said, watching a chaplain set his hands over a civilian's arm and cast a spell.

"Ha," Syzak laughed. "One of the chaplains tried, but it didn't work. Looks like you'll be recovering the old-fashioned way on this one."

"Figures," Kadorax muttered.

"And there's something else you should see. Atticus is here," Syzak said. When he mentioned the warlock's name, his voice dropped low and his snake eyes darted all around the room.

Kadorax shifted to his side, struggling in vain to find a comfortable position. "I wouldn't mind meeting him, I suppose. What happened to the tentacle thing I summoned? And the Gar'kesh? If the fighting has stopped, I assume they're both dead."

"Yeah," Syzak answered. "That's what you should come see."

Slowly and with Brinna's help, Kadorax was able to get to his feet. They were in a room of the priory the bastion had never seen before, not that he was likely to remember it even if he had. The walls were unadorned stone, very much the opposite of the grandiose nature of the main entrance hall and other public areas. No blue and gold tapestries hung on the walls, and no towering statues dominated the corners.

Whatever the room was typically used for, it had been rather efficiently converted into a triage center to heal the wounded as they came in from the city.

Kadorax winced as he made it to a steep staircase on the edge of the room. The stairs angled downward, presumably into the side of the rocky cliff on which the priory had been built. "How big is this place?" he asked, wondering about the full extent of the complex. Like Darkarrow, there were bound to be secret places, hidden rooms, and all manner of imperceptible alcoves and chambers throughout the complex.

Syzak helped ease him onto the first stair. "Way larger than we ever thought, I think," the snake-man replied. "Atticus has a huge cavern to himself. I don't know what the Knights used it for before the warlock took over. Maybe some kind of storage area, though I guess it doesn't matter now."

They walked down the stairs at a snail's pace. Toward the bottom, the distinct scent of salt water rose to meet them, along with plenty of brilliant light reflecting off a layer of pristine sand. The staircase opened into a partially subterranean cavern poised at the edge of the glittering sea like a mouth trying to drink in the entire ocean. "It has to flood with the tides, right?" Kadorax wondered, staring at the wet, briny ceiling some thirty feet overhead. Barnacles clung to the underside of the priory.

"Magic, or so I was told," Syzak said. He grabbed Kadorax by the shoulder to manually adjust his sight. "There, take a look . . ."

In the middle of the cavern, its blood staining the white sand, lay the corpse of a Gar'kesh. Heavy metal chains had been draped over the thing's chest and head, though it was clearly dead.

"It looks . . . smaller than the one we fought," Kadorax said quietly. He pulled himself away from the others and approached, a hand cautiously held out before him as though the corpse would suddenly spring to life if he got too close.

Behind him, Syzak laughed. "You call what we did a fight? You might have *fought* a Gar'kesh, but I simply died. I've never done battle with one of those things. Not yet."

"How many are out there?" Brinna asked, her voice full of fear.

Tentatively, Kadorax put a hand against the creature's rock-hard carapace. It felt like touching the side of a castle wall. There was so much weight—so much sheer mass—under his fingers that he had to wonder how the Knights had even hauled it down to the coast in the first place. It was no wonder that they had been forced to use magic to kill it. No number of arrows or swords would ever pierce its hide.

"I'm . . . I'm not sure, no, positive . . . yes, you should not be molesting my subject there, young man," an aged, detached voice said from the other side of the gargantuan corpse.

Kadorax pulled back his hand and looked around. "Is that—"

"Allow me to introduce Atticus," Syzak said with an unenthusiastic wave of his hand.

From behind the Gar'kesh's immense, horned face hobbled a withered man that absolutely did not fit the demonic and terrifying persona of a legendary warlock. All the stories of the mighty Atticus spoke of a wild, demonic force essentially trapped within a human shell. The warlock was supposed to be the pure embodiment of power and destruction, not an old man who needed help just to walk.

"*You're* Atticus?" Kadorax nearly gasped. He stood a full head taller than the warlock, though some of the height discrepancy was clearly a result of Atticus's advanced age causing him to stoop. The man even used a cane to keep his left leg from buckling under his weight, and it dug awkwardly into the sand, threatening to spill the warlock to the ground at a moment's notice.

"Ah, the very same," the elderly Atticus went on, his rheumy eyes barely lifting high enough to look at Kadorax. "Everyone has apparently heard of me, though for what . . . I say, have you met my daughter?" He turned back to regard the Gar'kesh, and a long, painful wheeze that might have been a sigh twenty years ago escaped his mouth.

Kadorax turned to Syzak, a wild expression of bewilderment in his eyes. "That's really him?" he whispered. The shaman nodded.

"Alright . . . so the Gar'kesh is your daughter?" Kadorax asked. "What does that mean? And whatever happened to the monster I summoned? Someone tell me what the hell is going on."

For whatever reason, Atticus only laughed. He had to brace himself against the Gar'kesh's shoulder to keep from tumbling as his laughs turned into prolonged wheezes.

"No, not that," Syzak began. "Kad, what I wanted you to see—"

"Oh, but the lightning! You saw the lightning!" Atticus suddenly shouted, looking at no one in particular.

Kadorax shook his head. He brought up Atticus's character sheet just to be sure, and there was the name and class, exactly as he had expected. They didn't have the wrong person. "Is . . . Is he ever lucid?"

"I don't know," Syzak answered. "I think maybe when he fights, he's different. He's normal then. But that's a guess. Maybe he's just crazy . . ."

Brinna approached the old man and took him by the arm to steady him, a gesture that Atticus seemed to appreciate. Looking at Kadorax and Syzak, she said, "He reminds me of my grandfather. Even looks like him a little. Is there anywhere for him to sit?"

Syzak looked around the room, but there was nothing suitable, only rock walls and the sand, plus the ocean lapping at the shore about fifty feet away. Somewhere above the water, a couple seagulls were busy yelling at each other.

"Hey," Syzak said, grabbing Kadorax again by the shoulder. "Atticus is fine and all, but the thing you really—"

"Ah, there she is!" the old man shouted.

"Father, I couldn't—" Estelle stopped when she saw the trio of visitors standing with Atticus next to the corpse.

"That's what I was trying to tell you about," Syzak muttered. "I heard her voice. I knew it was her. You alright, Kad?"

Estelle, her long, dark hair bouncing as she walked, came around the side of the Gar'kesh and stopped directly in front of Kadorax. Her eyes were full of fury, but there was something else there as well: something a little closer to longing, something desperate, but something impossible for Kadorax to truly identify. Then she reeled back her arm and punched Kadorax squarely in the stomach.

Accepting the blow without offering the slightest bit of defense, Kadorax stumbled to the sand and coughed. *Cage of Chaos* reacted to the attack and fired back, launching a string of shrouded golden arrows from Kadorax's chest. They rocketed toward the woman, but every projectile stopped an inch or so short of her body, neutralized by potent magic, leaving behind only a gentle puff of water vapor.

Deep in his torso, Kadorax felt a new wave of pain emanate from his soul rod. The metal was badly damaged, and he feared it might have become dislodged, if that kind of thing was even possible. "Hey," he muttered between gasps, slowly regaining his feet and lifting his shirt. "If this thing comes out, I'll die. For real. Forever."

Estelle's eyes went wide when she saw the battered metal entombed in Kadorax's breastbone. Then, as quickly as her surprise had come, her expression reverted to one of anger. "You never went looking for me," she stated flatly.

Behind them, Brinna helped the old man back away, and Syzak also nervously retreated.

In his heart, Kadorax knew she was right. He hadn't. The thought had plagued his mind for months, perhaps years, after Estelle's death, but he hadn't actually set out to look for her. "I'm sorry," he said quietly.

"Just tell me why you didn't look for me," the woman demanded. She crossed her arms over her chest. She was wearing a light brown tunic and a weapon belt, nothing like the elegant dresses and skirts she had worn when she spent the majority of her nights sleeping in Darkarrow, curled up against a powerful and fearsome assassin. A thin wand hung from a loop of tanned leather on her belt, and it subtly pulsed with magic.

Kadorax hung his head as he searched for answers within the recesses of his own mind. *Shame*, he thought silently. After a moment, he finally summoned enough courage to speak, though his voice was faint. "I'm sorry. I didn't know where to search. I didn't know if you would forgive me."

The woman looked like she was about to say something, but she turned toward Atticus before she opened her mouth. "You need some rest, Father," she told him gently. "The Gar'kesh can wait until the afternoon. You had a busy morning."

Brinna handed off the older man without complaint.

"You," Atticus said with a sudden burst of vigor. He thrust a wobbly, crooked finger toward Kadorax's chest. "You summoned a guardian. A guardian! I can smell it on you, boy."

"What?"

Atticus turned back to Estelle, his lips spread wide to reveal a grin worn nearly toothless by age. "We've finally found a bastion, my daughter. A real bastion! Living! And in *my* cave!"

"Alright, now I'm confused," Kadorax said. "You know my class just from seeing a single ability? A class just about no one else has ever heard of?"

The man, using Estelle's hand for balance, began pacing around in tight circles in front of the corpse. "I killed a bastion many years ago. That bastard Ligriv took her corpse, though. Wouldn't let me experiment . . ."

"This guy's nuts," Brinna said under her breath.

Kadorax gave her a look that said he agreed. "You know Ligriv?" he asked the frail warlock.

The old man nodded vigorously. "He was my master several centuries ago. He brought me here. Indeed he did."

"Brought you to the priory? Or to Oscine City?" Kadorax asked. He had trouble wrapping his mind around the concept of centuries. As far as he had learned of Agglor, no one lived for an extraordinary amount of time. The dwarves and gnomes were said to live a little longer than humans, perhaps to a hundred, but never much more than that. Living for centuries had strange implications that Kadorax didn't understand. Death by old age seemed to be one of the only surefire ways of staying dead in a world dominated by respawning.

Both hands on the Gar'kesh's stony head, the warlock offered a quiet chuckle. "Ligriv brought me to Agglor," he said.

41

"From Earth. Normandy, France, to be exact. That's where I met him. Ever heard of Sword Beach, son?"

"You're from World War Two?" Syzak asked, his serpentine eyes wide. Then, in response to Kadorax's obvious surprise, he turned and explained. "You watched two different war documentaries in your room. I watched them both from my cage, remember?"

"Wow. So you're Earth-born. Alright," Kadorax stated. His eyes couldn't choose between staring at the old man and stealing glances of the long-lost woman who used to hold his heart in the palm of her hand.

"He loves his war stories," Estelle added. "Don't get him started."

Before Kadorax could ask another question, Atticus pulled a long, thin, sweet-smelling cigar from a pocket on his ragged shirt and then struck a match to light it.

"He had four cigars and the matchbook in his pocket when he arrived," Estelle said with a smile. "That's his last one. He must like you."

Kadorax didn't know what to say, so he only ran a hand through his shaggy hair, content to simply wait.

When the cigar was lit and two burnt matches were buried in the sand at the old man's feet, he went on. "Ligriv was Italian, fighting for the other side, you know? Allied with the damned Kraut. Killed him with my bayonet on Sword Beach, and then he brought me here. That was what, maybe three hundred years ago?"

So time does work differently, Kadorax thought. He wondered how much time had elapsed back home. A couple of hours? A day? A week?

Strangely and consistently lucid compared to only a few minutes ago, Atticus continued his story. "Ligriv has been bringing people here for years. He can't take many from each decade, not many at all, but he brings them just the same. People he thinks would flourish here in Agglor. People who will provide him with entertainment. Just be glad you didn't see his first world. Ha!"

Kadorax collapsed into a cross-legged position on the sand, his head in his hands. "I've met Ligriv a few times. Could he send me back? And more than one world? What the hell even is this place? *Where are we?*" he practically pleaded.

Estelle made sure the man was steady on his cane and then sat down beside her former lover. "I met Atticus not long after . . . you killed me. I'd never heard of Ligriv. Honestly, I wasn't sure I believed he existed, but if you saw him . . . Perhaps the old man is telling the truth."

"Who is he?"

"One question at a time!" Estelle laughed, rubbing Kadorax's shoulder for a second before quickly pulling back her touch. "Ever read *The Divine Comedy* back in school?" she asked.

"Oh . . ." Kadorax answered, thinking for a moment. "I get it. A palindrome. He's not just Italian. He's Roman, right? And Ligriv is Virgil, I suppose. My personal guide through hell."

She nodded. "That was the first world he made. Though Atticus thinks Ligriv is also God, the one with a capital G. He might have made Earth as well. Atticus," she said, raising her voice to recapture the warlock's attention. "Who is it that Ligriv is searching for?"

The man turned, a gleam in his ancient eyes. "Right after I killed him on Sword Beach, Ligriv told me what he was hiding." He pointed to the center of Kadorax's chest. "The soul rod. There is only one. If it is ever destroyed, all of Agglor will perish. My friend Aeneas held it first, though he did not possess the rod long enough to see it through to its final destination."

43

"Shit," Kadorax replied, still staring at the sand. "Aeneas is here? In Agglor?"

Estelle sighed. "Maybe. I hadn't read *The Aeneid* back on Earth, so Atticus had to explain it to me. Apparently, Aeneas is more of a mantle or a title than a real person. A persona, maybe. I don't really understand it all myself. Aeneas was real on Earth, but he was human. He died at some point, I guess. Ever since, Ligriv has been making worlds and stealing people from Earth, throwing them into impossible wars in an effort to find his beloved Aeneas. The levels and classes and experience points are a way for Ligriv to track everyone's progress numerically. He uses it to select who can become a bastion. As far as I can tell, the soul rod is the key to restoring Earth. Or maybe it just sends everyone back. I don't know, and Atticus has never been too clear about it."

For the first time since seeing her again, Kadorax thought to read Estelle's character sheet: *Estelle, Human, level 41 Harbinger.* Like his own class, a *Harbinger* was something he had never seen before.

Estelle smiled as she watched him read. "When I respawned, Atticus was in the tavern. He'd been waiting for someone to become his assistant—to help him find Aeneas. He made me a *Harbinger.* It's a unique class. Atticus said Andromache was a *Harbinger* as well, or maybe the class was modeled after her. His mind kind of flutters in and out as a result of his age and the things he's seen here. You've already gotten more information from him than anyone other than me. Perhaps you are the one he seeks. If you truly have *the* soul rod, I think you are."

"And what happens when I fulfill whatever it is I'm supposed to do with the soul rod?"

"Atticus?" Estelle prompted. "What happens then?"

The old man brought both of his hands to the top of his head, his cane jutting out to the side as it went along for the ride. Instead of answering, he only gritted his teeth and pulled in a noisy breath.

"I don't know," Estelle said for him. "Perhaps he knows. Perhaps not. But that's why Atticus razed the northern kingdoms so long ago. He burned their cities to the ground, challenging their greatest fighters and entire armies in search of someone who would be strong enough to be Aeneas and hold the soul rod. Whatever happens when he finds him is a mystery to me."

"And you've been helping him all this time?" Kadorax asked.

"He thinks I'm his daughter, but he wasn't married and had no children back on Earth," the woman replied. "He never died in the war, but Ligriv took him here before he ever made it back home."

"Everyone here is real, though, right?" Kadorax asked, his mind awash with thousands of questions. The frustration of the old man's jumbled mind meant he knew he wouldn't be getting many answers.

"Real, but born here," Estelle said. She looked to Brinna, who wore an expression of absolute confusion. "They're all real people. Agglor, as far as I've learned, is older than Earth. Created before our world, I think."

"I don't really understand any of this . . ." Brinna stated.

Kadorax stood, then offered a hand to help Estelle up from the sand. She didn't take it. "I'll explain as much as I can later, Brinna. There's a lot. Too much for right now," he said, looking out toward the sea. "I don't know how much will make sense to you. Maybe none of it will."

Atticus turned away on his cane and began walking around the other side of the carcass. "So much work to be done," he muttered to himself.

"And you took too many hits," Syzak reminded the bastion from his side. "We should talk to the Knights about getting you some proper armor."

Kadorax flicked his own character sheet back into his vision. "I'm level twelve, also," he said. "Lot of new decisions to be made. That was a huge fight. And I guess my guardian died?" He looked toward Atticus to try and get the man's attention one last time. "Did my guardian die? Is it still out there in the city?"

Softly muttering as he moved about on his cane, the warlock did not respond.

"Well, whatever," Kadorax sighed. He watched Estelle move back to the old man, and his heart sank a little. She didn't look back at him.

"Let's go back upstairs and find some armor. You two can talk later. There will be time tonight," Syzak told him.

"You knew her well?" Brinna asked as the trio began to move back toward the staircase that would take them into the priory once more.

Kadorax gave Estelle a final look, shaking his head and swallowing a bit of regret that had lumped itself in his throat. "Yeah. I did."

It took a conscious effort for Kadorax to be able to clear his mind enough to sit down and address his new level options. Whenever he called his character sheet to the front of his mind, memories of Estelle flooded through his mind, and he'd dismiss the sheet and close his eyes to bathe in the old scenes, replaying them over and over. Finally, sometime in the afternoon, he read through his twelfth level abilities.

To start, he had two points to distribute among his stats. Without much thought other than a strong desire to not take such a beating in every single fight, Kadorax assigned his points to *Strength* and *Spirit*:

Strength: 17
Agility: 15
Fate: 20
Spirit: 15
Charisma: 14
Bond: 7

More *Strength* meant he would have an easier time lifting and using heavier armor—something at the top of his list—and increasing his *Spirit* would hopefully help him pick his battles with a little more wisdom. Next came the abilities, and there were certainly a lot of them. Level ten marked a sort of tier in Agglor, a demarcation between someone almost completely unskilled and someone who would be a real threat in most situations. Sadly, it wouldn't be until level twenty that he would earn a class-specific *Superior Talent*. As an assassin in his previous life, Kadorax had absolutely loved the dazzling speed and deadliness of *Coup de Grâce*. It was a brutal maneuver, and he fulfilled many contracts for the Blackened Blades with a single activation.

Having achieved so many levels in the massive battle for Oscine City, Kadorax spent a few minutes reading and analyzing each new option available to him:

Radiance: Rank 1 - Channeling some of the fire native to chaos, the bastion becomes an engulfed beacon of flame, scorching and engulfing everything nearby. Lasts until canceled. Effect: moderate. Cooldown: 1 hour.

Undue Knowledge: Rank 1 - Knowing chaos begets further information regarding enemies. Character sheets of unfriendly creatures reveal more information. Additional ranks increase the visible information. Effect: minor. Passive.

A Birth of Stars: Rank 1 - Allowing another with a lower Fate score than the user to glimpse into chaos, the bastion attempts to wrangle the target's mind. A dominated creature will accept small commands that do not harm it. Effect: moderate. Cooldown: 1 hour.

Skin of Darkness: Rank 1 - When struck, the bastion's flesh partially melds with the nearest shadows, deflecting part of the blow. Effect: minor. Passive.

Guardian of the Deep: Rank 2 - The guardian, when summoned, may receive the most basic of commands. Higher ranks allow more detailed commands to be followed and for the guardian to learn more abilities. Effect: profound. Cooldown: 9 days.

The Eightfold Terror (Guardian of the Deep: Rank 1): Rank 1 - The bastion's guardian is enhanced and modified, adding a new ability it may cast. The Eightfold Terror places a mantle over the guardian, which inflicts fear and panic among all those who bear witness to it. Effect: profound. Passive.

Chaos Shock: Rank 3 - The bastion pulls two slivers of chaotic energy into the world and thrusts them forward, creating a random magical effect augmented by a second impact quickly following the first. If neither of the slivers hit an enemy, there is a small chance that Chaos Shock will not be expended. Effect: minor. Cooldown: 24 minutes.

Torment: Rank 2 - The bastion's weapon magically extends to a second target beyond the first, and Torment inflicts slightly more damage than rank 1. Torment has an increased effect when used with a whip. Effect: moderate. Cooldown: 28 minutes.

The Obsidian Well: Rank 1 - Congealing the very essences of darkness into corporeal magic, the bastion summons a well of pure obsidian from whence unknown wonders—or terrors—may be acquired. Effect: profound. Cooldown: 2 days.

Bathed in Silence: Rank 1 - Surrounded by the eternal quiet of chaos, the bastion no longer needs to announce when abilities are used, and words spoken softly cannot be heard by enemies without enhanced perception. Passive.

Sly Concealment: Rank 1 - Misdirection was born in chaos. Using a sliver of magic to create a visual obstacle, the bastion may hide one movement from enemies without enhanced perception. Effect: minor. Cooldown: 30 minutes.

Bridge the Chasm: Rank 1 - The bastion forms an ethereal, tangible connection with one willing ally nearby. Enemies struck by the bridge receive a debuff to one of their stats chosen at random. Warning: connection to an ally sometimes has adverse side effects. Effect: moderate. Cooldown: 1 hour.

With three choices to make—one for each level he had gained—Kadorax immediately selected *Bathed in Silence: Rank 1*. His next decision was a bit more difficult. More than one ability caught his attention and made his eyes linger as he struggled to decide. *Radiance* felt like it could be a little dangerous, especially without any specifically made armor to shield his companions from the heat, so he scrolled past it without giving it any further thought. *Skin of Darkness* gave him pause. On the one hand, it was a way to avoid more damage—something he desperately needed. On the other hand, the text of the ability said it would only activate if his flesh was hit, not anything he was wearing, the way *Cage of Chaos* worked, so he didn't think it would actually end up being that useful in the long run.

Looking at the offensive abilities, almost everything on

the list was enticing. Grimacing, he decided that upgrading his guardian would likely be the best route. The summon was one of the most powerful abilities he had ever seen, and if each rank reduced the cooldown by another day, it would eventually prove to be an absolute go-to talent in every big fight. Imagining the tentacle monster rampaging through entire jackal cities brought a smile to his face, and he unlocked *Guardian of the Deep: Rank 2*.

For Kadorax's final selection, he had the field of abilities narrowed down to *Undue Knowledge, A Birth of Stars, The Eightfold Terror, The Obsidian Well,* and *Bridge the Chasm*. Every single one looked useful, and he didn't know if he'd see any of them again as he continued to level.

Time continued to tick by, and Kadorax sat on a small, carved bench in one of the interior halls of the priory. Around him, handfuls of knights and healers were still busy at work, and several groups of messengers came and went through the driftwood door. Kadorax hadn't seen the prior himself since arriving. He figured the old man was off in some other part of the building, probably going over strategy with his highest-level retainers. In the prior's stead, a younger knight wearing an embroidered blue and gold tabard over his armor was directing the semi-chaotic human traffic.

Returning his thoughts to his character sheet, he tried to imagine what each of the abilities would look like in action. As an assassin, he always had others in the Blackened Blades to lead him along his path. Once he had eclipsed all of the other assassins in the guild, he then served as such a guide, helping the less experienced pick their abilities and learn to use them efficiently. He longed for someone like that to take him aside and divulge all the knowledge of the bastion class, laying out a nice, easy build for him to follow.

Unless Ligriv stepped onto the material plane to offer a hand, Kadorax knew he would have to make all of his decisions alone.

Well, not *exactly alone*, for Syzak came wandering over, a smile spread across his scaly mouth. "Have you made your picks?" the snake-man asked.

Kadorax stifled a curt laugh. "All but one," he answered.

"Check out what I unlocked," Syzak told him. The shaman's eyes drifted upward, the telltale sign that he was reading his own character sheet out of the air.

Kadorax did the same, summoning his friend's character sheet to his own vision as he had done hundreds of times before. Syzak had only progressed to level nine for his part in the battle. It was disappointing to see him leveling slower, but there wasn't anything they could do about it. For his ninth level talents, Syzak had chosen *Stitch Together: Rank 1* and *Spike Trap: Rank 2*.

"Good choices," Kadorax said, dismissing the sheet. "I remember some clerics with *Stitch Together*. A powerful ability; let's just hope you won't have to use it on me too often."

Syzak slapped him playfully on the shoulder. "I'm used to fixing you. It's the whole reason I like being a shaman. Now, let's see about some finer armor, shall we? The Priorate Knights must have some old plate or scale that they don't need."

"Hey, I'm past level ten. You know what that means," Kadorax said.

"You're going to multiclass?" Syzak replied. "We would have to find a trainer. Nothing but knights and chaplains around here, I bet."

Kadorax looked at him with a devious smile.

"No, Kad," Syzak moaned. "You can't be serious."

With a nod and a sigh, Kadorax got up from the bench and stretched his aching back. "Think about it. Knights use heavy armor. They get tons of talents related to taking hits, and that's what I need." He pulled his shirt up high enough to expose the damaged soul rod lodged in his chest. "What better way is there to protect the soul rod?"

Syzak closed his eyes and ran a hand down his scaly head in defeat. "If you had told me a year ago that you would multiclass as a knight, I would have called you a liar."

"Ha, the words would have never left my mouth a year ago," Kadorax shot back.

"Well . . ." the snake-man continued. "Should we find a high-level knight? Anyone over level thirty can do it."

Kadorax pointed to the younger knight who seemed to be in charge. "Let's ask him. He'll know."

As it turned out, the priory retained two class trainers: one for knights and the other for chaplains. They had their own area of the building, a balcony extending off the highest floor and overlooking the ocean. Fortunately for Kadorax, the knight trainer was there helping some of the newest recruits run through various drills. The chaplain trainer had been lost at some point during the fighting.

Kadorax didn't recognize the woman leading the drills, but she recognized him at once. "What do you want?" she scoffed upon seeing the former leader of the Blackened Blades ascend the staircase to her training pavilion. She looked him over, then shook her head. "Healing is downstairs. You look like you could use it."

Putting on his most disarming smile, Kadorax sauntered forward and onto the pavilion. "I heard you're the one to see about multiclassing. That so?"

The woman turned back to her handful of students, gave them another command, then stalked over to where Kadorax was standing. She had short, icy white hair and a face that said she was used to getting her way. The armor she wore, a dark leather jack of plates, looked like it had seen more than a few years of heavy use. "You expect me to simply walk into whatever trap it is you're planning?"

Kadorax lifted his shirt. "Trust me, I'm no longer the leader of the Blackened Blades. I need armor to cover . . . this . . . and becoming a knight is the quickest way to get some armor talents."

The woman scrutinized his soul rod for a moment before shaking her head. "What the hell is that?"

"Just something I need to protect. Now," Kadorax went on, "are you going to help me or not? All of Oscine City is in danger. As much as it might irk you, we're in this one together."

A hand on her chin, the trainer thought it over for a moment before acquiescing. "Fine," she said. "You know how to use that sword hanging on your side?"

Kadorax drew *Assir's Edge* from his belt and set his feet. Multiclassing always involved a trial of some sorts, anything from hunting an ancient relic and rescuing a lost practitioner of the class to solving a riddle. Fittingly, the knights' trial revolved around single combat. "I've had some practice."

"Good," the knight said with a grin. "No enhanced attacks. All other talents are fair game." She took a step toward the middle of the pavilion and waved off her students, who formed a ring along the outer edge. Laughing, she tilted her head to the sky. After uttering a line of words Kadorax wasn't close enough to hear, the knight drew a heavy mace from her belt.

"Alright, Blade," the trainer began. "Hit me three times and you'll have your multiclass."

Kadorax rubbed one of the many bruises on his chest. Weapon in hand, he took a few slow steps forward, trying to get a feel for the woman's strategy. He had fought against Priorate Knights on several occasions, but those battles and duels had been a long time ago. More recently, he'd found himself fighting on their same side, and those pitched battles hadn't revealed anything useful about how the trainer would fight. Curiously, the woman had no shield. Her left arm was cocked back, her fingers empty.

Kadorax eased closer, his sword in front of him to parry, and the knight made the first move. She lunged forward like a fencer, then pivoted off her left foot and swung her mace in a circle, using her entire body for momentum. Kadorax had plenty of time to get his crossguard into position. The resounding clang that rattled his arm was enough to knock him backward on his heels. The difference in *Strength* between them was considerable.

The trainer didn't relent. She came on with more power than technique, swinging her heavy weapon in a series of downward strikes. Kadorax successfully dodged the first two strikes, then thrust out with *Assir's Edge* toward the mace's thick head. He caught it and tried to activate *Riposte*, but his sword was bashed from his grip.

A bit of laughter from the students mingled with the sound of Kadorax's sword clattering across the stone floor. And that was all he had left—Kadorax was out of abilities that he was allowed to use.

"You'll have to do better than that," the trainer said. She turned her back and pointed her mace at *Assir's Edge*. "Pick it up."

Kadorax grabbed his sword and charged, hoping to catch the trainer with her back turned.

At the last possible moment, the knight dropped to her knees and turned, sending Kadorax stumbling over her shoulder without coming close to scoring a hit.

From his back, Kadorax groaned.

Rushing forward, her boots pounding the stone, the trainer leapt for Kadorax. Her mace crashed into the pavement where the bastion's head had been a moment before.

Kadorax rolled up to his knees and kicked. He finally caught a bit of luck; his boot connected with the trainer's jack, and she wobbled backward. *Assir's Edge* cut a fine line across the armor of her left wrist.

"That's one," Kadorax shouted. A fresh wave of adrenaline accompanied his words.

The woman took her time regaining her feet. She squared her shoulders and spat on the stones. "Commendable." Her voice was as flat as the pavilion's floor.

The two combatants met again in the middle of the pavilion, steel ringing against steel. A yellow glow enveloped the trainer—*Resolute Presence*, Kadorax knew, an ability that enhanced the knight's *Strength* and *Agility*—and her arms melded into a blur of speed. Kadorax felt the mace crash into his left shoulder, throwing him ungracefully to the side, though he managed to keep his footing as his armor helped dull the blow.

As long as the trainer had *Resolute Presence* active, Kadorax knew he'd never be able to land a strike. He needed to slow down the duel, to keep himself upright and parrying long enough for the activation ran out of energy.

Kadorax didn't know what rank the knight's *Resolute Presence* was, but it was higher than any he'd seen before. She bore down on him with a flurry of heavy, impossibly fast blows, forcing the bastion closer and closer to the crenellations at the edge of the pavilion.

I need something to counter, he thought, teeth clenched tightly together as he barely managed to parry another strike before it would have connected with his head. He still had one selection left from leveling, so he called forth the available options on his character sheet and quickly glanced through them.

A Birth of Stars wouldn't work against a target at such a higher level than he was. The rules of the engagement forbade *Chaos Shock* and *Torment*. All he really thought he'd be able to use were *The Obsidian Well* or *Sly Concealment*, neither of which felt like obvious choices—and time was running short. One more parry would put Kadorax's back against the side of the pavilion, where he'd be trapped.

Kadorax blocked a mighty overhand swing of the knight's mace with *Assir's Edge*, and instead of twisting and turning away as he'd been doing, he held his grip high, keeping the mace from coming down for another strike. He knew he'd be overpowered before long, but a couple of seconds were all he needed.

Without needing to speak the words to the ability he unlocked, Kadorax cast *The Obsidian Well*, willing the magic to appear right under the knight's back foot as he'd seen Syzak do with his shamanistic traps so many times before. The stone floor of the pavilion melted away, and in its place was a round, irregular pit of jagged obsidian crystals.

The knight yelped as she lost her balance, and Kadorax pushed her backward into the hole with all the strength he had left. As she fell, her armor crunched through dozens of gleaming crystals, shattering them into dust. She continued to yell, but a new, unsettling noise joined her cries.

Something within the cavern screeched.

Two antennae, thin and wispy like those of an over-sized insect, emerged over the fallen knight's shoulder. They didn't attack her, just tested the air for a moment. Then the rest of the creature emerged, two powerful sets of mandibles clacking around the trainer's legs.

Whatever the thing was, Kadorax had never seen anything like it before. It had the body of a crustacean, perhaps some sort of crab or lobster, and the head of a mutated insect complete with two mouths stacked on top of each other.

Leaving behind whatever honor he had taken into the duel, Kadorax jabbed out twice in rapid succession with *Assir's Edge*—not hard enough to cause any real damage, but more than was necessary for the knight to feel it.

"Two and three," he said, but he turned his attention to the obsidian crab. The creature's carapace was hard, and his sword didn't do much besides scratch the glittering surface.

Still gripped in the creature's dual maws, the trainer shrieked and dropped her mace, struggling in vain against the jagged crystals to crawl out of the well. Kadorax scooped the mace from the ground and swung, knocking away a huge chunk of the crab's crystalline hide. Luckily, the creature appeared intent on feasting, and it didn't turn to face the new threat.

Kadorax swung again and again, and on the fourth strike, he completely obliterated the monster. Bleeding from both sets of mandibles and the sharp crystals that had gouged her back and arms, the trainer collapsed to the stone of the pavilion just beyond the well. She breathed heavily, but she wasn't in any mortal danger.

"Sorry," Kadorax quietly said. He offered her a hand to help lift her to her feet, but she shook her head, her eyes still closed against the pain.

An awkward moment of silence passed. Finally, the trainer reached down to her wounds, and a blue glow replaced the yellow that had enveloped her. She was healed after a few moments of casting.

Using her mace like a cane, the knight got to her feet and bowed. "You did well," she said without a single hint of malice in her voice. "I have never seen such an ability. It will be my honor to bestow upon you a second class to augment your own. Come, follow me."

A bit surprised by the woman's complete lack of anger or sense of betrayal, Kadorax dutifully followed her to the end of the pavilion, where a wooden chest stood on stout legs. The knight opened the chest with a key, then thought for a moment before pulling out a pair of runes.

"Here, every knight receives the two runes of the priory. Receiving them will grant your multiclass, and you'll be able to immediately choose another talent as part of your new progression." She dropped the runes into Kadorax's outstretched hand with a smile. When he had earned the mystic multiclass in his previous life, it had required bathing in an enchanted pool of liquid beneath a short waterfall, and he hadn't received any items whatsoever. Getting a little bit of gear was a welcome addition to the process.

Kadorax held the runes in his hand and called up their information to his vision:

Rune of Perseverance - Allows the bearer to withstand one devastating blow per day. Passive.

Rune of the Protector - Enhances any shield worn by the user, making it weightless. Passive.

"These are perfect," Kadorax said, clutching the small runes in his palm. They were both normal runes, a tier above the minor runes that Ayers was able to make and a tier below the highest: runes that had their own rank like the *Theft of Life Rune* inside Brinna's *Talon Dagger*.

"The Priorate Knights are happy to call you one of their own, Kadorax," the trainer said.

The bastion was happy when the woman didn't also call him the Lord of Darkarrow after saying his name. Perhaps being a knight meant he'd find a little more acceptance within the priory. "Thank you," he said. "Is there somewhere here in the priory where I'd be able to get a shield?" The thought of trying to use a shield in combat—something he'd never attempted before in any life—gave him pause. But the possibility of a Gar'kesh shattering his soul rod was all the convincing he needed.

The knight ushered him back toward the pavilion's only exit. "Speak to the quartermaster, Ana. She will help you."

As the trio exited the training facility, the strange obsidian well disappeared, its magical timer expired. Most of the stones it had displaced were back in their original positions, but the flooring at the very center of where the well had been was gone. Kadorax had to shake his head at the strange magic. He had seen all manner of magic in Agglor—things that would have made him get an MRI and talk to a shrink back on Earth—but the well had been rather unique. No other class that he knew of could do what he could as a Bastion of Chaos Incarnate. All the things Atticus and Estelle had told him about the world came fluttering back to his mind. Whatever the man-apparition-thing truly was, Ligriv appeared to be in charge. But a simple search for a famed warrior? It didn't make sense. No one would go through the trouble of creating new worlds just to find one person. There had to be something more, something no one had yet discovered, and Kadorax burned to know what it was. Sadly, figuring out the core of Agglor's world was a path he would have to wait to traverse. The shred of a clue he possessed was the metal between his ribs. Whatever Ligriv wanted with Agglor, the soul rod was at the center of it.

Back inside the busy priory, the quartermaster was easy to find. She stood guard in front of an armory with a slate and several rolls of parchment, a blue and gold tabard hanging over her well-oiled plate mail.

"I need a shield," Kadorax stated.

The woman looked him over once before replying. "Supplies are running low. Everything with any value has already been taken into the field. I'll see what we have left."

Kadorax had to laugh when he considered exactly what he was doing. He'd already seen more of the Oscine City priory than he had ever thought possible as a member of the Blackened Blades, and now the very organization that had been his sworn enemy hadn't hesitated to offer him free gear.

"Help me pick a multiclass ability," Kadorax said to Syzak, calling forth his character sheet. Adding the additional class opened a new path for his build, one he hoped would further increase his survivability. Three new options presented themselves:

Shield Wall: Rank 1 - Forming up with other knights, each member of the shield wall receives a +3 bonus to Strength. Passive.

Rallying Strike: Rank 1 - The knight deals a devastating blow that marks the target, illuminating it for allies to see. Higher ranks allow the knight to accurately predict the target's movements as well. Cooldown: 1 hour.

Aura of Command: Rank 1 - Taking on the mantle of a leader, the knight bestows an aura of encouragement upon allies, allowing them to inflict more damage and sustain heavier hits. Passive.

"Well, without other knights, the choice seems pretty clear. Get *Rallying Strike*," Syzak said after he read all the options.

Agreeing, Kadorax unlocked the ability just as the quartermaster returned from the armory with a kite shield in her hands.

The metal was rough, clearly had seen extensive use, and looked heavy. Smiling, the quartermaster handed it over, and Kadorax immediately struggled with its weight. "This'll take some serious time to get used to," he said. There was a strap on the inside for his forearm and a handle for his fingers. Another length of leather was large enough for him to store the shield on his back when not in use.

"Bring death to our enemies," the quartermaster said with a nod.

Kadorax flexed and turned the shield at a couple of different angles in front of him, imagining what it would feel like to deflect a blow on its pockmarked surface. "Thanks for the gear. I just need to figure out what I'm doing with it."

"I'm sure Lady Apos would be happy to allow you into the newest class of recruits if you'd like some training," the quartermaster continued.

Fortunately for Kadorax's still-healing body, Syzak pulled him to the side. "You need rest, Kad. The Knights are planning an expedition into the city tomorrow, and if I know the Lord of Darkarrow, you'll want to join them on the front lines."

After slinging his new shield onto his back—which only eased the burden of its weight by a fraction—Kadorax agreed. "Besides," he said, "I think I have other things to address tonight."

"Other people, indeed," Syzak added.

"It's just that . . . I don't know. Seeing her here . . ." It wasn't the first time Kadorax had felt completely lost since arriving in Agglor, and he knew it wouldn't be the last. Not even close.

Brinna stepped forward and put a hand on his shoulder. "If you liked her so much, why don't you just tell her? I'm sure you have a lot of catching up to do, and you don't need to be distracted tomorrow."

"Heh, it's a lot more complicated than that," Kadorax replied.

"What happened between you two?" Brinna asked.

Syzak silently tried to get her attention and divert her line of questioning, but he was too late.

With a sigh, Kadorax simply told the truth. "I killed her," he stated. "And then I never went looking for her again, even though I knew she would have respawned. I was ashamed, and I had let the shame win for years."

"Come on," Syzak said, ushering Kadorax back to the barracks room where they could both get more rest. "We need to get you to Ayers and install those runes. I have a feeling you won't be good enough to even use the shield until that happens."

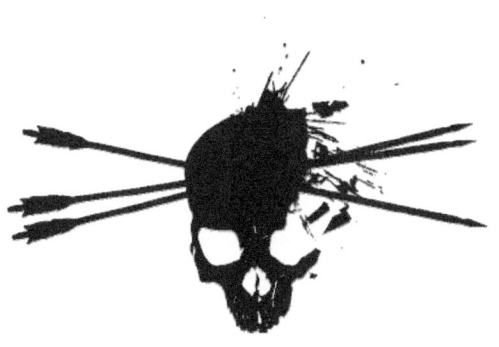

CHAPTER 4

"News of the princess!" someone shouted in the main foyer of the priory.

Kadorax awoke on his cot with a start. All around him, the rest of the barracks was rubbing the sleep from their eyes and finding their clothes. He looked to the cot on his left, but it was empty. Estelle had already moved from his side. They'd stayed up late and talked, Kadorax mostly just listening and nodding as his former lover recounted the years that had passed. He had fully expected her to greet him as he awoke. A shard of disappointment worked its way into his chest, where it settled like a cat snuggling up in a heap of blankets. Part of him had wanted to pick up where he had left off, but he knew deep down that his old life was finished.

The prior, dressed in shining armor and ready for battle, descended the steps to the barracks. "Anyone strong enough to fight, now's your chance. If you still need time to recover, there's no shame in that. Two chaplains will remain behind to continue tending to the wounded. The rest of you, assemble upstairs in five."

What had been a slowly awakening hall moments before suddenly burst into action. Almost all of the wounded were knights, and Kadorax assumed it was their rigid sense of honor that forced them out of their cots despite their aching cuts and bruises. He couldn't blame them, though; he was doing the exact same thing. Perhaps his motivations were different, but he started getting ready all the same. His chest still hurt, and his back was so sore and stiff that it popped with even the slightest of movements.

"Get your gear," Kadorax told his serpentine companion. "Let's join whatever raid they're planning. If it takes us near the docks, we can split off and find the *Grim Sleeper*. I'll need that rune installed soon if I'm ever going to use a shield in combat."

A few minutes later, the gathering of soldiers in the priory's main hall commenced with a somber tone. The fighting men and women were dressed for battle, their armor dented and covered in unwashed grime. At the front stood the prior, old but commanding in presence with two swords hanging in scabbards at his sides. Normally, the prior was the very image of Priorate Knight pomp and heraldry. Now, a cloud of unshaven stubble adorning his chin, he looked his age.

"There's news from Kingsgate," he began, his voice still booming and vibrant despite his years. "It isn't good. You should have heard by now that King Bennington's daughter was kidnapped by jackals, taken from the sea while en route to this very city. Well, she's been spotted."

A murmur spread through the gathered mass. Most of the whispered words were oaths and other commitments to personally rescue the lass—another product of Priorate honor at work. Kadorax smirked when he considered all the traps he had laid for the organization in years past. Knights would rush headlong into carefully crafted ambushes if they thought they were pursuing a boldly noble goal. In the back of his mind, Kadorax had to wonder if the upcoming mission was one such jackal gambit. The race had never been regarded as clever, but old stereotypes meant nothing now.

"Where is she?" one of the female knights near the front of the assembly shouted.

The prior calmed the growing torrent of voices with an outstretched hand. "What we know is this: one of our scouts along the docks spotted a group of high-level jackals, probably forty of them, escorting several prisoners away from the shoreline on the western part of Oscine City. That's as far from here as it can get, and the jackals hold the city. Our best estimate puts the jackal force at over a hundred thousand. Most of them are untrained, and their weaponry is far below ours in terms of quality."

"What about an army from Kingsgate?" another hopeful voice called to the prior.

The old man frowned, his face seeming to age several years in the span of only a few heartbeats. "They're organizing, but they're slow. It will take dozens of ships to move the guard from Kingsgate to Oscine City, and even then, they won't have sufficient numbers to purge the city of jackals. Right now, we're the army."

A chorus of cheers and raised fists answered the prior's well-timed platitude, easing some of the dire atmosphere of the room. "I'll be sending two groups: one along the coast, the other circling north around the city to potentially cut off the band of jackals moving the princess. We'll march heavy,

65

full arms and armor, full companies, no exceptions. I will lead the northern group personally. Lady Alexandrina Apos will lead the expedition to the docks. We move out in half an hour. Sergeants, assemble your companies!"

The roar that followed the end of the prior's speech was deafening. Every knight in the room bellowed at the top of their lungs, and the human cacophony was thoroughly augmented by a raucous din of swords smacking against shields. "The coastal group," Kadorax said to Syzak and Brinna. He had to lean down close between them just to be heard.

The next thirty minutes passed like a whirlwind of steel and enthusiasm. What was left in the armory was meted out rather quickly, leaving the priory's storeroom completely devoid of anything at all related to combat. Even the quartermaster, Ana, had gone outside to form up with the prior's company.

Kadorax approached Lady Apos and extended a hand. She took it with a smile. "You'll be joining us along the coast?" she asked.

Holding his hands out wide to indicate Brinna and Syzak as well, Kadorax nodded. "Of course. Our ship was at the docks, and I'd like to meet up with the crew if they haven't put out into the harbor for safety."

"Any chance you have a blacksmith here in the priory?" Syzak asked.

"Not right now," Alexandrina replied. "Our smith was in town getting supplies when the attack began. There's been no word from him since."

Kadorax, his new runes secure in a pocket, cursed his luck. "Sorry for your loss," he said.

The armored woman waved away his concern. "Let me introduce you to our sergeant." She pointed to a young man

66

in a polished brigandine, who was busy directing the flow of flesh and metal into something cohesive. "Sergeant Reinhardt has two decades of experience. I'll be leading us, but he'll be organizing the fights. Try to stay behind him."

Kadorax pulled up the sergeant's character sheet. The man was level forty-four, a knight multiclassed with a tactician, one of Agglor's less common classes. Tacticians didn't learn any skills to enhance their own combat, similar to the nature of a blacksmith or an alchemist, but having them around during pitched battles was a huge boon.

"How many will be in our company?" Brinna asked. Standing around all the veteran soldiers in their clanking armor, she looked nervous. Her two small daggers tucked into the tops of her boots might as well have been letter openers when compared to the refined blades carried by the Priorate Knights. Most of the knights preferred a traditional longsword to complement their familiar shields, though a handful of the soldiers had maces or axes instead—probably at least in part the result of a multiclass. Lady Apos had her heavy mace dangling at her side, and the sergeant carried two curved picks in an X on his back.

After issuing more commands to her charges, Alexandrina turned back to answer Brinna's question. "We'll march with forty. Most will be the rank and file of the priory, but each company will carry both a chaplain and a sorcerer as well. We'll teach the jackals a thing or two about war. Don't worry about that."

Kadorax thought it odd for the priory to even have sorcerers on hand, though he didn't blame them. Just because the class didn't fit with the armored ideals of the glittering knights, that didn't mean the spellcasters were anything less than useful. In fact, he felt a fair amount of the apprehension that had lodged itself between his shoulder blades lift at the thought of fighting alongside sorcerers. Still, the coming battle would be a far cry from a Blackened Blades operation—no skulking through the darkness to find a handful of specific targets among thousands. No, the incessant clanking of greaves against stone would certainly erase the possibility for stealth. Kadorax would be marching headlong into a true battle with men and women who would depend on him for their lives.

Even in Agglor, where the slain would only need a few weeks to respawn and begin anew, Kadorax knew he couldn't let down his comrades. Failure to take back the city would mean a new jackal stronghold. More importantly, failure would mean the loss of dozens of Agglor's highest-level soldiers and perhaps everyone's greatest chance of ultimate victory.

When Kadorax first learned of the world's respawn mechanic, he thought his life inconsequential. The fear of a painful death had kept him alive for a few years, but joining the Blackened Blades made him realize just how significant respawning truly was. Starting again at level one meant his organization would suffer, and their loss of standing allowed other groups to gain power. If any of Agglor's groups were in the business of tyranny—perhaps a race like the jackals, for instance—the consequences could be worse than death. Once they held the majority of Agglor's strength, they'd be insurmountable: either they would conquer the cities one by one and hold all the low-levels as slaves, or they'd simply kill everyone opposed to them. Being forced to constantly restart would prevent any resistance at all from effectively mounting. Then the jackals would control the entire world. Kadorax shuddered at the possibility.

He hoped everyone else in the troop understood the stakes as well as he did.

Finally, after the shouts of the commanders died down into the sounds of the ocean and the two companies of knights were assembled and prepared for war, Kadorax turned his attention back to the task at hand.

"Men! Women! Soldiers of the priory!" Lady Apos shouted at the front of the large assembly. She had produced a short wooden stool from somewhere, and it gave her enough height to easily command everyone's attention. The old prior of the chapter looked on from the back with an approving smile on his face. "Today we march for the king! The daughter of the realm is captive to our enemy, and we are the only remedy."

The knights shouted and clanged their weapons against their shields once before Apos regained their silence with an upraised gauntlet. "Rescuing the princess will break our enemy's back! We'll carve a path of destruction through Oscine City, freeing the trapped citizens and covering our blades with jackal blood!"

Another wave of celebration rattled through the soldiers, and Alexandrina used the moment to leap from her stool and begin the march.

At the outskirts of Oscine City, the prior's own contingent of soldiers broke off to the north, leaving Kadorax and thirty-nine others to traverse the shoreline toward the harbor. "Have you seen anything?" he asked Syzak once they had been underway for a few minutes.

The snake-man answered with a low, quiet voice. "Just some glimpses. We're being watched."

Kadorax nodded in agreement.

"Shouldn't we tell the commander?" Brinna asked, her voice loud and shaking.

"If Alexandrina is any good at her job, she knows already,"

Kadorax said, keeping his eyes forward and talking from the side of his mouth. "And keep your voice down. We don't want the jackals knowing that we've seen them."

The woman swallowed hard, her nervousness beyond obvious.

"Just follow orders when the fighting begins. You'll find a place in it all," Kadorax told her. He felt like he was back in his old training days, teaching a young rogue the ways of the darkness that he had mastered so well. The weight of the shield slung to his back reminded him that he was no longer a Blackened Blade.

Up ahead, Lady Apos held point, her mace at the ready. Behind the mass of noisy soldiers came Reinhardt, his watchful tactician's gaze constantly scanning the surroundings, no doubt planning mock battles in his mind and anticipating ambushes behind every building.

As they entered the fringes of the city proper, Kadorax was surprised by how eerily quiet everything was. Most of the buildings by the coast were still intact—the majority of the devastation had taken place in the northern quarters—but they weren't occupied. The jackals hadn't set up defenses or dug in to prevent a liberation at all. For as many dogheads as they had seen during the initial invasion, they saw no significant number of the creatures as they moved closer to the harbor.

Even worse, they didn't see any humans. None alive, at least.

There were corpses on every single street. Dead humans, most of them civilians or peasants with noncombat classes, were strewn about in a haphazard fashion. A few other non-human bodies were mixed into the morbid lot, though fallen jackals clearly numbered least among the dead.

"Where are they hiding?" Kadorax quietly asked.

Syzak kept his eyes on the streets, and his serpentine tongue flicked through the air. "A trap? Or running back north with the princess?"

"Look, the *Grim Sleeper* is still moored in the harbor," Brinna added, pointing to the ship's recognizable figurehead and bowsprit. Sure enough, the imposing ship was still at the dock, and a huddled mass of sailors mixed with Oscine City refugees waited behind a makeshift palisade where the dock met the shore.

Lady Apos turned the warband toward the docks. Easily recognizing their apparent salvation, the men and women on the docks began to cheer and pat each other on the back. Kadorax turned to watch the knights' rear flank as they headed onto the docks. Reinhardt stayed behind as well, a dark expression on his chiseled slab of a face.

"Doesn't bode well," the tactician whispered.

"No, it does not," Kadorax agreed. Beside him, Syzak and Brinna had also stopped.

"If they're planning a trap—"

"Then we're all fucked!" Reinhardt interjected. "The docks are the perfect place. Knights clad in steel from toe to nose don't often get much of a chance to go swimming. All it would take—"

Kadorax began shouting before the tactician could finish his sentence. "Get off the docks!" he screamed at the top of his lungs. Some of the soldiers in the rear of the company heard him, but there was too much confusion with the tumult of the celebrating refugees for his words to carry any significant meaning.

"A trap! Get off the docks!"

Syzak and Brinna both joined him, yelling at the top of

their lungs. Still, the revelry carried on. Somewhere in the mess of armor and smiling faces was Lord Percival.

"Get them off the damned docks!" Reinhardt roared, pushing past Kadorax and toward Lady Apos. Unfortunately, the woman had disappeared into the very center of the crowd.

"T-They're coming!" Brinna shouted. She nearly fell to the ground in her haste to catch up with Kadorax, and her outstretched hand grabbed the side of the bastion's shield slung over his back, suddenly wrenching him in the direction of the city streets.

"Oh, shit," Kadorax said, spinning on his heel.

The streets leading into the heart of the city sloped upward as they left the coastline, and the very top of them was covered in darkness. A wave of brown and black fur slowly rumbled downward, and Kadorax could not see its end.

"Now! Get off the damn—"

Before he could finish yelling at everyone to move, a magical sensation washed over him and everyone else, instantly quieting the dock-borne mass and giving Reinhardt the precious moment of silence he needed.

As the tactician began rattling off commands at a volume that probably could have made it all the way to Kingsgate on a clear day, Kadorax had to smile. He recognized the magic that had quieted the group. Lord Percival had cast *Batten the Hatches*, using the aura simply to rattle everyone enough to get them to pay attention.

Reinhardt's commands ended quickly, and then the dock exploded into action. Sailors and refugees alike started grabbing anything they could to build a rampart, moving with heightened speed and alacrity thanks to the captain's talent. Still, the defenses wouldn't be nearly enough.

Kadorax grabbed both of his companions and took off for the *Grim Sleeper*.

"The docks aren't defensible, not without more numbers," he shouted as he ran between scurrying soldiers and refugees.

"It'll take too long to cast off!" Brinna frantically yelled.

Kadorax didn't have time to explain his plan. He found Ayers and Percival near the rest of the crew. The sailors huddled along the side of the ship and looked terrified. "Let's go!" he shouted at them. Without waiting to ensure they were following, Kadorax turned back toward the city and the promise of safety.

"Wait!" Lord Percival called at his back, but no one waited to hear what he had to say.

Leading a small group of about ten, Kadorax vaulted over the western side of the rapidly growing dock barricade and veered down a street that ran parallel to the ocean.

The first wave of the jackal horde reached the docks with a resounding crash of claws against shields. One of the sailors—the galley chef, if Kadorax's memory served correctly—was too overweight to move quickly enough and get himself clear of the front lines. He took a hit to his shoulder from a passing jackal, and then three more descended on him faster than the portly cook could react—though trying to fight three enraged jackals probably wouldn't have done him any good in the first place. As deadly as it was, the butcher's cleaver in the cook's hand would be no match against the horde.

Kadorax, his shield still slung across his back, silently activated *Chaos Step*, his aim taking him directly behind the trio of jackals about to eviscerate Lord Percival's chef. *Assir's Edge* made quick work of the three mangy assailants. They had never seen Kadorax coming, and the former assassin had certainly killed enough contract targets from behind to still remember how it was done. When the three jackals—now in five different pieces—were scattered across the stones, Kadorax grabbed the chef by the arm to pull him along. The man had taken a serious blow to his upper torso, but he'd live if he could only put some speed into his legs.

Another handful of jackals broke off from the main body of their force to run down Kadorax's fleeing group. "Don't cast!" the bastion yelled to his companions. "Save your abilities!"

Chef in tow, Kadorax rejoined the rest of his small crew right as a bolstering wave of magic bathed them all in a faint blue light. Kadorax didn't recognize the spell—he'd never worked alongside a tactician before—but he could immediately feel its effects. His muscles bulged as his *Strength* score nearly doubled, and the battlefield suddenly appeared much clearer, as though the jackals moved slower than they should have. The general flow of the fledgling battle also seemed to make itself known in Kadorax's mind. He could see what was happening as if he were inspecting pieces on a gameboard. He *felt* where the jackal force would push and attack the rampart moments before it moved.

Kadorax had to assume the ability was Reinhardt's *Tactician's Superior Talent*. In addition to the visual enhancements, a palpable surge of simply *knowing what to do* flooded through the soldiers, and the entire dock leapt into action. Knights on both flanks of the bulwark shifted forward, their shield wall flashing with bloodied blades and glinting steel.

Gathering his men in his wake, Lord Percival charged back down the street and toward the docks, cutting through the jackal horde's exposed right side with all the poise and forethought of a battlefield veteran.

Kadorax's trio held back for a moment to allow Percival and his sailors to fully engage the enemy. Again relying on unnatural insights concerning the flow and mechanics of the battle, Kadorax led Brinna and Syzak into the fray on Lord Percival's left. Every time a jackal claw came sweeping down to harm a human, a perfectly timed blade was there to meet it. Before long, Kadorax's armor was doused with gore. They had carved a swath of death through the jackal army that was almost deep enough for them to reach the docks once more.

And then, as quickly as the aura had activated, the magic faded. The blue shimmer surrounding the knights and sailors evaporated into the ocean breeze. All the flawless coordination that had pervaded the movements and thoughts of the defenders descended into pure chaos.

A heavy swipe came in from Kadorax's side, one he hadn't seen coming, and his armor thankfully dulled the brunt of the force. Pivoting, Kadorax watched as *Cage of Chaos* fired a thin line of liquid fire into the attacking jackal's snout. The creature reeled back, scraping its paws along its face to extinguish the flames, and Kadorax ran *Assir's Edge* through its gut.

"Time to retreat!" he yelled at the top of his voice. The others were already falling back. One of Percival's sailors was down, and the man was quickly trampled as their little band rapidly gave up ground.

Kadorax could barely believe how quickly the battle was turning. What had begun as an outright jackal slaughter had rapidly descended into blood-splattered anarchy, and even that was about to give way to a rout. Luckily for him and for

Lord Percival's charges, the jackal horde was intent on completing its initial goal: pushing the human defenders into the sea.

To the side of the main battle, Kadorax's small band had dwindled to eight.

"What's the plan?" the beleaguered ship's captain asked, clutching a bloody spot on his left forearm.

"Uh," Kadorax stalled, his eyes frantically searching the battle for some sort of answer to pop out at him.

Syzak stepped forward and cast *Cure Minor Ailments* on one of the sailors who had received three nasty, parallel gashes across the base of his gut. "We're only eight," the serpent said. "We can't turn the tide on our own. We need to stick to the original plan: find the princess."

"And my ship?" Lord Percival asked, a heavy layer of sadness on top of his voice.

"The *Grim Sleeper* is just a ship. It can be rebuilt," Kadorax said.

The captain gave a solemn nod.

"We should run," Brinna said. She was out of breath, but she looked unharmed. A bit of fresh blood adorned the backs of her hands.

Everyone readily agreed. Ayers, standing quietly in the back of the group with a hammer in his hands, was the only one who showed any hesitation. "What about the knights who came to save us?" he said, his usually gruff voice playing out in a slightly higher register.

"Give 'em to the sea," one of the sailors offered.

"Nothin' for it," another added.

Kadorax grasped the burly smith by his shoulder. "If they survive, we'll find them. If not . . ."

"Give 'em to the sea," the first sailor said again. Nods all around confirmed the general sentiment among the *Grim Sleeper*'s crew.

Finally, Ayers rubbed his eyes and let out a sigh. "Let's get to it then," he said, turning away from the noise and the slaughter. An unmistakable sadness clung to his voice. Kadorax had to remind himself that the smith was not a soldier. Ayers had made them weapons, certainly, but he had not borne much witness to the up-close and personal brutalities of war. The cornucopia of death arrayed in front of him was taking its toll on his mind.

Offering the big man one last brotherly slap on the shoulder, Kadorax turned to lead the group away from the docks. "Keep your eyes open. There might be another ambush or we might catch a glimpse of the princess. Either way, we have to be on high alert."

He clanked along as he ran, and the grating sounds of his shield against the *Reinforced Leather Vest* he wore were so unfamiliar that he hardly believed they were his. He thought of how far he had come since his stint as the leader of the Blackened Blades—but he regretted nothing. His mind, though, drifted back to Estelle . . .

"Hold up!" one of the sailors called from the rear of the group. Kadorax stopped and whirled, his mind instantly ready for combat, and saw that he had outpaced most of the others. Lost in his thoughts despite the constant danger lurking around every corner, he hadn't realized how quickly he'd been moving. He had to remind himself that it wasn't just Ayers who was new to the idea of a pitched battle. It wasn't only adrenaline filling their veins; it was fear as well.

Kadorax and the rest stopped, the bastion taking up watch around the corner of a stone building. They were behind a row of what looked like squat businesses, and the alleyway Kadorax had chosen was clear of bodies from the invasion.

One of the sailors was doubled over to catch his breath. All in all, their little group wasn't that impressive. Kadorax and Syzak could fight, Brinna and Lord Percival weren't bad, but the others were untrained. Ayers and the three sailors were all winded already. For a moment, Kadorax thought of leaving the noncombatants behind, but he knew it wouldn't work. They'd all be slaughtered by the time they regrouped, and he already had enough death weighing on his conscience. They needed a dedicated tank to protect the untrained members of the group.

"Ayers," he called, an idea growing in his mind, "you have your blacksmith's hammer?"

The smith held up a hand as he sucked in air, then finally steadied his breathing enough to reply. "Always at my side. Never leave the ship without it."

"Perfect." Kadorax retrieved the two runes he had received from his knight multiclass and held them in the palm of his hand. "Any chance you could install these into my armor without me taking it off?"

The smith picked up the *Rune of Perseverance* and inspected it, then glanced back at Kadorax's leather. Without answering the question still lingering in the air, he pulled his hammer from his side and set it over the rune, aligning the small bit of enchanted rock with one of the slots on the leather armor he had made. A single tap later and the rune was successfully installed. Kadorax and Ayers didn't waste any more valuable time installing the second rune.

Eager to test the efficacy of the *Rune of the Protector*, Kadorax swung his shield from the back of his chest to his left side. "Weightless," he gasped, truly amazed. Having never used a shield before in his life, he hadn't considered the possibility that all the shield-bearing knights he had fought before had used the same rune. *No wonder they had never tired as I had always thought they would have*, he silently mused, half-heartedly chastising himself for never investigating the issue before.

Kadorax swung the shield side to side, then quickly jerked it above his head and jumped backward, testing how he moved with the weightless object strapped to his wrist and hand. It felt fluid, but he knew he wasn't anywhere close to proficient yet. It would still take some serious getting used to.

Before any of the sailors had truly recovered enough to take up the run once more, a small band of jackals came barreling around the nearest corner, instantly throwing themselves into the small group with little concern for their own lives. Kadorax still had his shield above his head when the combat erupted.

Slamming his newly acquired chunk of battered metal into a charging jackal's skull, Kadorax spun to take in the scene and map it in his head. Awareness of the field was something he had learned through great pain and misfortune during his first few years with the Blackened Blades. Luckily, the jackal he had slammed had fallen to the ground in a daze, affording him a few seconds to find his bearings. One of the sailors was already down basically before the fight had even commenced. Brinna and Syzak were holding off against two of the hairy beasts, and Percival was struggling to protect his downed man.

Kadorax, thinking to use a bit of space to his advantage before diving in with *Assir's Edge*, grabbed his whip from his side and set to work. The first crack was devastating against the prone, unarmored jackal five feet in front of him. A second strike ensured the beast wouldn't get back to his feet, and then a pair of the newcomers were bearing down on him from either side.

The bastion's whip cracked through the air, slicing a wide path through the cheek of the jackal bearing down on his right. He spared only a second to ensure the enemy had been staggered before turning to the creature on his left. Kadorax lifted his shield to meet the incoming, brazen charge. A loud thud told him the creature had plowed headlong into the metal. In the time it took Kadorax to lower his shield and push a step forward, he dropped his whip and drew his sword. Images of old Roman combat tactics he had seen in a couple of documentaries flickered through his mind as he moved with coordinated precision. Step, slash, push with his shield, repeat—the jackal was dead after two cycles.

Kadorax turned back, a smile spread across his face. He hadn't even activated a talent yet. The enemies were weak, he knew, far below even his modest level, likely just an errant pack that had stumbled upon his ragtag group by accident.

Relatively low skill aside, the jackals had already scored a kill. One of Percival's men was down, and he wasn't moving. Kadorax sheathed *Assir's Edge* and scooped up his whip from the ground. There were three more jackals left in the melee, and each of them had its back turned.

Kadorax slashed open the torso of the nearest unarmored jackal. It fell in a heap of screams, and it didn't take long for Brinna to finish it off with one of her daggers. The next two fell in rapid succession, Kadorax flaying their backs with his whip and the rest of his group pouncing and cutting with reckless abandon. When the brief skirmish concluded,

Lord Percival's finery was splattered with blood, as was his remaining crew. Even Ayers had seen some of the action personally, having meted out a devastating hit with his hammer.

"Everyone alright?" the bastion asked, his voice all business.

One of the sailors had his eyes tilted upward, obviously contemplating his character sheet. "I leveled," he said quietly, more to himself than to the group.

Kadorax glanced at the man's stats, then quickly looked away. A level three sailor wasn't bound to be much help in the grand scheme of things.

"Figure out your level later. We need to get moving." Kadorax turned to take up the lead once more.

Continuing north through the city, away from the slaughter in the harbor, Kadorax led the others toward some of the larger buildings where the local government had resided. If the jackals had secured a foothold in Oscine City, he figured they would have claimed the most defensible parts for themselves, and that meant the municipal complex with its walls and gates and fences.

They arrived in front of the government building without meeting any more wandering packs of enemies along the route. Kadorax knew the lack of battles along the way was a good indication of how many jackals were busy killing his compatriots down by the coast, but it was also a positive sign. If the bulk of the jackal horde was busy in a different part of the city, they would face less resistance in the government building. With such a small group, Kadorax was eager to take advantage of any benefit he could find.

"Think they're in there?" Percival asked. The man was breathing heavily, though not as badly as Ayers and the other crewmen.

"That's where I would set up a forward command post

81

if I were running the invasion," Kadorax replied. Everyone agreed.

The building, a huge structure of light-colored marble and imposing columns, was surrounded by a waist-high brick wall topped by an iron fence taller than anyone in the group. "How do we get inside?" Brinna asked. She approached the iron bars and tested them once before realizing how solid they were in their brick foundation.

"I used to be an assassin, remember?" Kadorax said. He had scaled walls, slipped past guards, and infiltrated highly defended compounds dozens of times before. A fifteen-foot barrier, unmanned and unwatched, would be nothing. "Get a couple boards from the nearby houses. It won't take much."

"Should we check first to see if anyone's inside?" Syzak asked.

Kadorax shook his head and frowned. "We don't know where the jackals have gone, and we don't have any tracks to follow to the princess's captors. If you have another idea, I'm all for it. If not, let's just be quick about it."

"We could split up," the shaman suggested.

"No, not against thousands of bloodthirsty enemies," Kadorax was quick to reply, much to the overt relief of everyone else in the group. "We'll go in together. If it looks like there's nothing inside, we'll head out and keep looking."

A few minutes later and Kadorax had constructed a makeshift ramp from the splintered and busted materials the sailors had scavenged from the nearest buildings. It wasn't much, but they didn't need a huge siege tower to beat a basic wall. Up and over they went, Kadorax leading the way and issuing commands. At the end, Percival grabbed the last board on his way over to ensure they'd at least have something handy to help them get back outside the fence. The rest of the interior ramp would have to be scavenged from the building itself unless they found a key to the only gate.

Between the fence and the main building was an expanse of thirty yards. The grass was low, spotted here and there by shrubs and small trees arranged in no discernable pattern. Much to Kadorax's dismay, the vegetation wasn't nearly thick enough to offer a good amount of cover. Anyone watching from the building would easily know they were coming. "Quickly," Kadorax told the others over his shoulder. He waved to keep everyone close by, and they sprinted across the open expanse as quickly as they could.

Kadorax searched for the nearest point of easy entry. If he were alone, he would have scaled the side of the building and entered through the roof two stories above, but he didn't think any of his burlier companions would be able to make the climb. There was only a single window on their side of the first floor. Without any other options, Kadorax bashed out the thick glass with the hilt of *Assir's Edge*.

"Brinna first," he said, ushering the woman through the newly created portal. "Stay low, look around, scream if anything goes wrong."

The nervous rogue nodded once before disappearing into the interior gloom. Crouching just below the windowsill, Kadorax and the others waited for sounds of a struggle coming from within. No such sounds met their ears. A minute later, Brinna appeared with a smile. "First room's safe. They're here. I could hear them above."

Kadorax nodded and offered a hand to help boost the rest of the party through the broken window one by one. The room was rather plain: just a holding area for Oscine City's citizens to wait before being called to meet with one of the bureaucrats who ran the government. "Where'd you hear them?" Kadorax asked quietly, keeping his eyes glued to the two doors on the interior wall across from the window.

Brinna pointed toward the front corner of the room. Scratching sounds came through the ceiling, faint and muffled, but there were a lot of them. "Jackals can probably jump and climb the fence. Could be dozens of them upstairs," Kadorax whispered.

Syzak pointed to the ceiling with his claws, a smile on his scaly face. "Want a trap? Drop them down?"

"Could be the princess," Kadorax said. "We need to find the stairs."

The group silently slipped from the room and made its way to the front of the building. The main entrance, a heavy wooden door intricately carved with various images of Oscine City life and landmarks, had been ripped from its hinges and thrown to the ground in the foyer. "Gar'kesh," Kadorax whispered. "No way jackals bashed down the door on their own."

Everyone else silently nodded their agreement. While Kadorax and Syzak appeared eager—excited even—the rest of the party shifted back and forth, their hands slick with sweat. Kadorax knew they'd be more of a liability than a boon in close-quarters combat. "Captain, keep your men here. Keep them safe."

Displaying his anxiety without a hint of shame, Lord Percival nodded and turned to his men. Kadorax didn't waste any time before heading for the nearby stairs that would take him to the second level. Syzak and Brinna, the most veteran members of the party, crept behind Kadorax.

Near the top of the stairs, Kadorax stopped for a moment to listen. There were scraping sounds like heavy paws dragged across the wooden flooring—something far different than the scampering noises that a pack of jackals would have made. He grabbed his whip, ready to crash into the fight with an activation of *Torment*, though there wasn't enough room in the cramped building to put the weapon to full effect.

Kadorax held up three fingers on his left hand. His shield was still slung behind him, and he didn't want to risk the noise of sliding it onto his forearm. He put down his fingers one at a time until he made a fist, and then he charged over the last three stairs and barreled through the flimsy door at the top.

Three jackals, each looking momentarily terrified, occupied the upstairs room. The two on the sides looked exactly as Kadorax, Brinna, and Syzak had seen so many times before: mangy, muscled dogheads with claws and crude weapons. The one in the middle, however, was something different. The creature wore a thick, bronze-colored helmet on top of an impressive array of linked metal plates. It stood a full head taller than the others, almost tall enough to scrape the ceiling with its ears, and Kadorax knew after only a momentary glance that the weapon in its hands was well made.

The armored beast standing in the center of the room snarled and raised its kanabō high, instantly ready for bloody combat like it had been waiting in the upstairs room for just such a challenger. Kadorax had seen the somewhat unique, club-like weapon several times before, namely in a shop in one of Kingsgate's affluent districts. The kanabō was one of the standard choices for Kingsgate guards and personal protectors of the royal family. Those outside the monarch's service rarely found enough necessity or even casual interest to ever purchase one.

Kadorax had also witnessed firsthand the destruction that such a heavy, brutal weapon could bring upon foes, especially lightly armored ones. A single hit against exposed flesh was almost always enough.

The bastion, first up the stairs and first in the vision of the huge armored bruiser, instantly thought to activate *Chaos Step*. The ability would send him rocketing through space to appear behind the giant, but without the proper tools to pierce the jackal's backplate, it wouldn't do him much good. He'd need a punch dagger or a stiletto to make it through in one clean, quick stroke. *Assir's Edge* wouldn't be the right tool for the job. Still, he was far from out of options, and the battle had only just commenced.

Kadorax sprinted to his left, rolling his shoulders away from a clumsy attack offered by one of the lesser beasts. "Trap!" he yelled to the shaman coming up the stairs at his heels. "Drop him below!"

He envisioned one of Syzak's *Spike Traps* appearing beneath the beast. The spikes, with nothing to anchor them in place, would clatter harmlessly to the floor below. The gargantuan mass of the armored jackal, however, would certainly be devastated. Even a ten- or twelve-foot fall was more than enough to make quick work of the battle.

Without hesitation, Syzak conjured a *Spike Trap* at the giant's feet.

An icy wall of protection shimmered into view around the armored jackal's body, and the talent was expended without effect.

"Warding!" Kadorax called. He could only hope Brinna understood the specific term, one plucked from a large lexicon of quick communications Kadorax and Syzak had developed over thirty years of fighting side by side in Agglor.

But then again, it didn't really matter if she knew the term or not. Brinna's only magic resided in a powerful dagger, and Kadorax doubted she would find the need for it against the armored behemoth and its two consorts.

The jackal squaring off against Kadorax would be easy work for the bastion, probably not even requiring a single talent activation—but he quickly saw the error of his hasty dodge, which had taken him away from the giant in the center. Syzak was only lightly armored and had no evasive abilities. Brinna was even worse, and the two of them would face the full attention of the juggernaut without Kadorax there as the more experienced fighter to help deflect the blows.

Swinging *Assir's Edge* through a simple combo—a quick feint high to the left followed by a devastating sweep from the right—Kadorax tried to eliminate his opponent as quickly as possible. Surprising them both, the jackal managed to block the brunt of the strike with its own weapon, a curved sword sporting several splotches of grayish-red rust.

At the head of the stairs, the armored giant smashed forward with its kanabō, and Syzak wasn't able to get out of the way in time. The snake-man took a heavy hit to his back and side, screaming out in pain as he fell backward into Brinna, nearly sending them both tumbling down the stairs.

Kadorax didn't have time to be patient. As an assassin, he would have waited for an opening, ensuring he struck with cruel efficiency to save every bit of combat prowess he had just in case something else needed his attention later. It had been that sense of reserved pragmatism that had seen him through more than twenty years as the head of the Blackened Blades. With his one true friend being hammered by the giant jackal, Kadorax disregarded all of his old assassin's principles.

He lunged forward, silently activated *Chaos Shock*, and

rammed his fist home into a patch of soft jackal hide. The first element the spell conjured was steam, scalding hot and filling the small space between the combatants with a hazy mist. *Assir's Edge* in his right hand, Kadorax was able to slice into the jackal's thigh before the second element activated.

When *Chaos Shock* concluded, there wasn't much left of the unarmored jackal. A deafening burst of sound and vibration had emanated from Kadorax's hand and shot directly into the chest bones of the poor beast. It hadn't erupted in a shower of gore, but the vibrations were more than strong enough to shatter bones and dislodge muscular connections. One more swipe of his sword, and Kadorax stood with a clear shot between him and the giant's back.

Kadorax knew another hit from the creature's kanabō would probably send Syzak back to a lonesome inn full of class trainers. In the tight quarters, and with another jackal still in the mix as well, there wasn't anywhere for the shaman to flee. Kadorax, grimacing at the thought of burning too many talents so early in the fight, grabbed his whip from his belt as quickly as he could.

Torment: Rank 2 landed squarely between the giant's shoulder blades—or rather, the whip cracked off a steel breastplate, though it would have scored a direct hit on the creature's spine had the armor not gotten in the way. Regardless of the physical damage inflicted, the talent imparted its fearsome energy, though only for a split second. The beast's warding, probably some anti-magic relic it wore or perhaps an enchantment that had been cast on it, stopped the full effect of the ability from reaching its brain.

Still, the giant hesitated mid-swing, giving Kadorax just enough time to grab the shield from his back and reclaim *Assir's Edge* in his main hand.

HEAVY ARMOR

I've never tanked before, the bastion thought. He had seen others, especially knights, taunting larger enemies to draw their attention, and the mere idea of getting the huge creature to focus on him was so foreign to his mind that he had to actively will a few words to his lips. "Hey!" he shouted. "Uh, come at me!"

Kadorax accented his weak taunt with a straightforward strike to the back of the hulk's legs, and the combination of annoyances threw the creature off balance. The head of its kanabō crashed noisily onto the floor, sending up a few fistfuls of wooden splinters. Luckily, it turned to face the new threat.

Roaring, the jackal monstrosity switched its focus to the bastion, and Kadorax winced as he took a hit squarely on his shield. His feet moved back several inches beneath him, and then the jackal was rearing back for another round.

Kadorax, his left arm already stinging from the first impact, knew he wouldn't be able to survive such a direct onslaught for long.

Two more heavy blows rained down on Kadorax's shield. The second was strong enough to trigger the *Rune of Perseverance* installed in his armor, and a burst of magic turned the strike into something so soft it was almost undetectable. Kadorax used the split-second reprieve to slide his shield left and stab. Against an unarmored opponent, the quick, powerful jab from *Assir's Edge* would have been enough to end the fight, spilling blood and guts at the bastion's feet.

With a loud clang, the sword deflected off the jackal's thick breastplate. Other than leaving behind a couple of inches worth of unsightly scratching, the attack had done nothing. Behind the armored giant, it looked as if Brinna and Syzak had at least mortally wounded the jackal soldier they had been fighting, and Kadorax had to thank his luck for that much.

"Sy!" he quickly called. "Find an opening! Venom!" Kadorax hoped the creature he fought wasn't skilled enough with the human language to understand the terse commands, but he had no way of knowing. Announcing his plan was a risk he didn't have much choice but to take.

The towering jackal came on again. Heavy kanabō going high and then rushing down again like a lumberjack splitting logs, it struck Kadorax's shield with all the force of a landslide. The shield buckled along the top edge, and Kadorax was forced backward, nearly off his feet. As the creature prepared another massive blow, the armor encasing its right arm fell to the ground, and Kadorax watched Brinna dance backward, a dagger in her hand. She had cut the straps, finally offering them a bit of soft flesh to go after.

Surprisingly calm for its size and jackal heritage, the creature let its arm fall to its side, the kanabō held out horizontally, and then a red shimmer came over its exposed limb and weapon.

"Run!" Kadorax yelled. So far, the beast hadn't used any talents, and he didn't want to be close enough to get caught up in whatever it was about to unleash.

In a blur of speed, the huge jackal began spinning in a tight circle, kanabō out like a fan blade, becoming a whirling tornado of death in the center of the room.

Kadorax backed against the wall. There wasn't enough space. Another few seconds and the jackal would be close enough to turn him into a bloody sack of meat and pulverized bones. Crouching low to go under the whirling kanabō wouldn't work. Looking to the ceiling, Kadorax saw no handholds or rafter beams he could grab.

"Rats, Syzak! On the wall!" he screamed as though his life depended on it—which it most certainly did.

Without hesitation, Syzak cast *Rat Trap: Rank 1* on the center of the wall against Kadorax's back. The wooden paneling fell away, and a dozen or so fetid rodents appeared in the air. The little critters scrambled for purchase, but most of them were unable to cling to the remaining wall, so they fell to the ground at Kadorax's feet, likely just seconds left before being mercilessly squished underneath the jackal's feet.

Kadorax wished he had the high *Agility* he had enjoyed as an assassin in his previous life. A raw score of fifteen, already buffed by his boots, wasn't enough to get him through the hole the trap had made before the jackal was upon him. He heard the rats trying desperately to scamper away, punctuated by a distinct squish as some of them were ground into the floorboards.

The kanabō connected with the bottom of Kadorax's boots. Pain blossomed up the entire length of his legs, but he managed to pull himself through the wall and to the other side, where he collapsed in a heap. Hand over hand, he forced himself along the ground, expending every ounce of energy he could muster to escape certain death.

Much to Kadorax's dismay, the jackal wasn't slowed by the rats or the wooden wall. Its whirlwind of pummeling force turned the already damaged wooden barrier to splinters, and then he emerged in the next room only a foot behind the struggling bastion.

Kadorax got his shield in front of him to block the incoming devastation. His teeth clenching tightly and his head behind what suddenly felt like a very thin piece of steel, he accepted two whirling blasts of force that easily would have killed him if not for his armor. From his crouched position,

Kadorax couldn't see any way to extricate himself. The room he had crawled into was nothing more than storage sparsely attired and with no exits. Even worse, it was smaller than the room the two combatants had come from.

For perhaps the first time in his three decades on Agglor, Kadorax had to rely solely on his companions. Either Syzak and Brinna would figure out a way to take down the giant armored beast, or the three of them would suffer horrible deaths at the scant mercy of its huge hands.

Kadorax winced in anticipation behind his battered shield. No strike came.

Chancing to lift his head above the shield's rim, he saw Syzak latched onto the jackal's right arm where Brinna had cut away the armor. His fangs were embedded in the flesh, no doubt pumping the jackal full of *Paralytic Envenomation*. As Kadorax watched, the jackal's arm slumped to its side, and the massive kanabō fell from its grasp.

Brinna jumped forward, a wild snarl on her face. One of her daggers landed in the meat between the jackal's shoulder and neck. The beast spun and swung at her with his still-functioning left arm, and the woman's attack was short-lived. The jackal's gauntleted fist sent her flying backward and crashing into the broken wall behind her. Luckily, Syzak had managed to hold on through the chaos, though his talent was surely finished.

Kadorax rose to his feet and let his shield fall from his left arm. He lunged forward like a fencer, keeping his body as far away from danger as possible, and struck with the tip of *Assir's Edge* against the beast's thick gorget. "Bring it on!" he screamed, allowing himself to be lost in his own rage in order to effectively taunt the beast.

The shout worked, and the jackal seemed to forget the

snake and woman harrying him from the back and sides. It swung a heavy armored fist for Kadorax's chest, and the bastion knew his opening. With a full dose of *Paralytic Envenomation* coursing through its veins, the creature's *Agility* score—what was probably already encumbered by its armor—was bound to be extremely low. Kadorax, taking *Assir's Edge* in both hands to ensure he had enough strength, met the jackal's incoming gauntlet with his blade. He turned and activated *Riposte. Assir's Edge* danced in his hands and slid upward, gliding noisily along the beast's arms until it connected with the top of its gorget.

Kadorax was close enough to smell the jackal's rancid breath. Whatever the doghead had eaten, it left a putrid stench on its teeth. Mustering all of his power, Kadorax rammed his sword directly upward, finding a small gap in the armor that gave way to flesh. The beast howled, and blood flowed freely down the deep fuller in Kadorax's sword.

Behind the interlocked combatants, Syzak used his claws to rake several bloody lines down the jackal's shoulder. The creature howled in pain, but it was not dead. It wrapped a huge arm around Kadorax's chest and squeezed.

Cage of Chaos activated through Kadorax's breastplate, sending forth a complex, visible amalgamation of gears and spinning components representing the element of time. In his grasp, Kadorax felt the jackal's writhing movements come to a grinding halt. It was stuck, suspended in air like a marionette on stationary strings while everything else continued to progress at full speed.

"Kill it!" Kadorax shouted. He tried to push himself away, but the enveloping magical snare had caught his own torso and arms as well.

Once more with her feet solidly under her body, Brinna came at the jackal from the rear. With one dagger in each hand, she jabbed both of her blades through either side of the jackal's thick neck and severed its spinal column.

Time readjusted itself as *Cage of Chaos* wore off, and the armored jackal collapsed to the ground without so much as a whimper.

"Thanks," Kadorax said to both of his companions. He rubbed his left arm, trying to take some of the sting from his battered bones.

Brinna fell backward to the ground, completely winded and still dazed from the vicious hit she had taken to her chest.

"I have both of my heals left," Syzak said between breaths. "What do you need?"

Kadorax waved off the notion. "None for me. Save them. I just need to figure out how to hold a shield and take hits without shattering my wrist."

Brinna didn't share the bastion's bravado. "I think . . . my ribs," she said.

The shaman knelt beside her and placed a hand on her chest, feeling for damage. "*Cure Minor Ailments*," he announced after a moment. A burst of magic leapt from his hand and into the woman's broken ribs, and her breathing immediately improved. "I don't think it was that bad, just a minor fracture, but it will still hurt."

"We found a trail," Lord Percival called from the first room. He and the rest of the group emerged from the stairs. None of them looked like they'd seen a fight on the lower level, Kadorax noted.

The Bastion of Chaos Incarnate wrenched Brinna's two daggers from the fallen jackal's neck and handed them back to the woman. "Well done," he said. When he had his own gear safely returned to him and properly stowed, he finally called up his character sheet to see how much experience he had earned. The jackal champion had been the difficulty of a minor dungeon boss, and splitting the points three ways wasn't too bad.

"I'm almost up to level thirteen. How'd you two do for experience points?" he asked.

Syzak and Brinna both flicked their eyes upward to their floating character sheets.

From his place in the first room—the floor had finally rematerialized after Syzak's *Spike Trap* had dissipated—Ayers gave a half-hearted grunt. "I need to stick with you lot," he said. "For how much you get into fights, I'd be level forty in no time, making legendary armor with the best enchantments you've ever seen."

"Ha," Kadorax laughed, indicating the room's obvious destruction with a wave of his hand. "You don't want any part of these kinds of fights. Stick to smithing."

"Yeah, yeah. Leave the killing to the professionals. I get it," Ayers said with a smile.

Both Syzak and Brinna were smiling as they dismissed their character sheets. "I leveled," the snake-man said. "Time to get another rank of *Cure Minor Ailments*, and I think I'll take *Remote Detonation: Rank 1* for a new trap once I level again. I never had it before, but the ability to throw a fire rune seems pretty useful, especially considering how often you seem to need saving."

"I like the choices," Kadorax said with a nod. His own character sheet showed him only a few kills from reaching thirteen, though *Riposte*, a sub-skill of *Blade Training (Light): Rank 2*, had been used enough to increase to the second rank, although the ability's text hadn't changed. In order to unlock the third rank of the ability, he would have to unlock *Blade Training (Light): Rank 3* the next time he leveled, assuming the choice would be available.

Brinna, smiling despite her arms wrapped tightly around her injured chest, said, "I jumped two levels. That jackal was worth a huge amount of experience. I'm not exactly sure what to get for level eight, though. Take a look at my sheet."

Kadorax and Syzak both pulled up the woman's information to their vision:

Sneak: Rank 3 - The rogue blends into her surroundings with veteran efficiency, becoming extremely difficult to find with any non-magical sense. Increases the rogue's Agility by 1. Higher ranks allow the rogue to bypass magical detection as well. Effect: moderate. Cooldown: 1 hour.

Dual Wielding Block: Rank 2 - When using a weapon in each hand, the rogue can block a single incoming attack. Works against enemies with less Agility than the user. A disparity of Agility of more than 4 points causes the block to become more effective. Effect: moderate. Cooldown: 50 minutes.

Treasure Hunter: Rank 1 - The rogue's Fate increases by 1, and she has an easier time finding useful items and gold pieces. Higher ranks allow the rogue to detect magically hidden items. Effect: minor. Passive.

Vile Concoction: Rank 1 - The rogue learns the ability to brew deadly poisons from easily sourced herbs and other plants. Unlocking Vile Concoctions allows the rogue to immediately learn one poison recipe. Passive.

Blade Training (Light): Rank 1 - Showing affinity for the dagger, the rogue unlocks the ability to earn several assassin talents related to shuriken, daggers, and knives. Blade Training (Light): Rank 1 also grants Hidden Ambush: Rank 1. Passive.

Serpent's Kiss: Rank 1 - A knife from an unseen angle strikes a target with devastating effect. Serpent's Kiss can only be activated when the rogue is unseen by the target. Higher ranks allow for more artful execution. Effect: moderate. Cooldown: 1 day.

Unabashed Murderer: Rank 1 - When striking a killing blow against a target that has done no harm to the rogue, an aura of fear is generated, which causes the target's nearest allies to cower. Duration: 1 minute. Effect: moderate. Passive.

"Wow," Kadorax said. "You have some good choices. *Treasure Hunter* might be really useful, especially if we're going to be delving deeper and deeper into jackal territory."

"Speaking of which, here's the necklace that denied my *Spike Trap*," Syzak said. He wasn't able to lift the magical relic from the jackal's corpse on account of the creature's enormous head, so he cut the chain and held the silver charm out in his hand.

Kadorax sent his vision to the item to see exactly what it was:

Ivory Locket - Rune Slots: 1. Allows the wearer to be easily identified by Kingsgate guards as friendly. Passive. Rune of Suppression - Prevents up to 3 ranks of magic spells used against the wearer. Cooldown: 1 day. Passive.

"I'm guessing that locket wasn't made for our friendly jackal giant here," Kadorax stated.

Syzak dropped the small charm into a pocket. "Either the princess herself had worn it, or else it belonged to one of her retinue. Either way, we're on the right track."

"I think I'm going to take *Treasure Hunter* and another rank of *Dual Wielding Block*, if you two think that's a wise plan," Brinna said. She still had her character sheet up, and her eyes were distant as she continued reading over the myriad of options.

Kadorax thought for a moment before answering. The *Blade Training* talent Brinna had unlocked would allow her to take assassin skills as she progressed, and he knew those like the back of his hand, but the woman didn't strike him as a cold-hearted killer. A certain kind of resolve was needed to wrap a bit of wire around a man's throat until he stopped kicking. Brinna could fight, and he didn't doubt her willingness to protect herself, but he wasn't sure she'd be too eager to use some of the more sinister assassin talents.

"Go for *Serpent's Kiss* instead," Kadorax told her. "As long as you have the first rank of *Dual Wielding Block*, you'll get value from it, and you'll probably be able to upgrade it later. You don't have a single offensive ability yet, and that's going to be a requirement if we keep going up against jackals like that one." He gave the dead giant a kick for good measure.

"If only the armor was smaller," Syzak lamented.

Kadorax nodded his agreement. "You're right. It would probably sell nicely as well, but we don't have time."

Stepping into the room and offering the jackal corpse a disapproving grimace, Lord Percival knocked a knuckle against Kadorax's dented shield. "We need to get moving before the trail goes cold. Come on, let's go."

"Right." Kadorax stepped over the jackal corpse and back to the stairs. The whole group descended, and one of the *Grim Sleeper*'s crew was waiting in a different room to take them to the path they had found.

"Looks like the jackals kept going north. They stopped here for a while, probably just to set up the preliminary defenses, and then they kept going. More tracks lead from one of the back rooms to another building," the crewman said.

Kadorax could easily see the tracks. "What if the tracks are just a trap? That beast upstairs was meant to slow us down. The jackals know someone will follow them. They could be leading us astray or right into an ambush."

Everyone was quiet, each person taking in Kadorax's warning in their own way. Finally, Brinna was the first to break the silence. "I'll get a third rank in *Sneak*," she offered. "I can follow the tracks on my own. If there's an ambush, we could avoid it altogether."

"Not a bad idea. Meet us here or else back at the priory. We'll follow the second path," Kadorax said.

"Just don't get yourself killed," the shaman added.

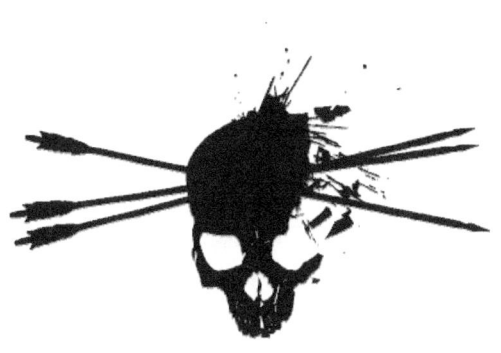

CHAPTER 5

Brinna scampered toward another set of streets to the northeast. She stuck to what little shadows were available under awnings and between fallen sections of buildings. When she was fifty or so feet away, Kadorax had trouble seeing her. The edges of her body and armor blended into her surroundings, and his mind refused to track her movements, no matter how obvious they were.

"A few more ranks of *Sneak* and she'll be good enough to join the Blackened Blades," the bastion said. With more *Spirit*, he would have been able to track her even at a distance, but her skill in stealth was outpacing his own stat increases.

The rogue turned a corner and was gone from Kadorax's sight. "Alright. Let's follow the second path," he said.

"Over here," a crewman said. He led them to an area of the governmental compound where the wall had been partially destroyed. "Look, there are prints in the dirt, but I think they tried to cover their tracks before moving on."

Kadorax knelt to inspect the evidence. "If we had a hunter or some other class that could track . . ." he said under his breath.

"If they took to the sea, I'd find them in a heartbeat," Lord Percival added cheerfully. "Ninth rank *Read the Tides* would tell me exactly where to set our heading."

"Hopefully we'll get to use it," Kadorax replied with a smirk.

Ayers stepped forward, a hand over his eyes to shield them from the sun. "There's a door in that building that isn't original. Someone put it there on purpose."

The group, numbering six with Brinna off on her own, ran toward what appeared to be a papermaker. They saw no jackals peering down from the windows or rooftops of the buildings they passed, and the lack of enemies did nothing to shake the feeling in Kadorax's gut that the path they were following was the real ambush. "The door's been reinforced, but that could have been done before or after the invasion. No way to know if there are jackals inside."

The group fell into a line to the right side of the papermaker's door, listening intently for sounds from the interior. They heard nothing.

"Whoever did it was a smith," Ayers told them. "I know the talent for that kind of barricade. Probably wasn't the jackals."

"Unless they have allies," Syzak added.

Lord Percival, holding the end of the short line, peered around the side of the building. "Nothing this direction," he whispered to the rest of the group.

"There," one of the two remaining crewmen said. He was looking away from the papermaker and pointing toward a bit of movement off in the distance.

Leading the group close to the buildings on the left side of the street, Kadorax took off in the direction of the movement. "Stay close, stay quiet," he said over his shoulder. They ran a block north, farther from the heart of Oscine City, and Kadorax saw a pair of jackal soldiers scampering away ahead of them.

He kept the group about a block and a half behind the doghead pair as he followed them around several turns. If they were being watched from the rooftops or anywhere else, there was no way to know.

Finally, when they were far enough away from the main part of Oscine City to be almost completely without cover, Kadorax saw where the jackals had led them.

"Move back," he said through clenched teeth, trying to keep his voice low enough to not be heard. The group scrambled to get behind a waist-high heap of collapsed ruins. Luckily, the two jackals they'd been following didn't turn or raise any kind of alarm.

"What is it?" Lord Percival asked.

In front of them, beyond the limits of the city and maybe a hundred yards away from the nearest structure, was something that shouldn't have been there—something that certainly had not been there a few days before the invasion. "Well . . . we found their headquarters. If the princess is still in Oscine City, that's where they've taken her."

"What about Brinna?" Syzak asked.

"She's headed right for an ambush," one of the crewmen stated, his voice low.

Kadorax shook his head. "She'll handle herself. We have bigger problems."

The two jackals they had been following stopped in front of a gate and waited for a moment before a large wooden door was opened to allow them entry. The front of the jackal fortress to either side of the gate was built entirely from stone, though the patchwork colors indicated that the building had been cobbled together from ruins, not strategically built by skilled hands. Still, the heavy blocks were solid.

"They've been busy," Ayers said. "Looks like they aren't done with the eastern wall yet. Damned jackals are probably sending work crews into the city to bring back more stones. They'll have a castle before the week is out."

"How long would that have taken?" Lord Percival asked.

The smith thought it over for a moment before responding. "With only jackals? Would have been at least a couple weeks, I'd guess."

"Doesn't make sense." Kadorax dropped behind the rubble where they were hiding as movement along the top of the outer wall caught his attention. His eyes barely visible above the barrier, he caught sight of something distinctly non-jackal.

"There's our answer," Syzak said with disgust.

Two dwarves sporting mining gear appeared above the stone gateway. One had a brass spyglass in its hands.

"Down," Kadorax said, though he hadn't needed to issue the warning. Everyone dropped below the ruins.

"Miners' Union?" Percival scoffed.

Ayers nodded. "That would explain the rapid construction. They probably had the majority of the fortress already made and waiting in the Boneridge Mountains. Then they brought it down behind the invading force. All that's left to do now is reinforce the outer walls with as much heavy material from the city as they can salvage."

Plausible as the smith's explanation was, it still didn't make a whole lot of sense to Kadorax. "Why bother setting up a fortress here? Jackals control most of northern Agglor already. Why wouldn't they just take the princess deep into their own territory?"

"When was the last time someone went into the north and came back to tell everyone what was there?" Syzak answered. "Maybe something happened that drove them out."

"Or maybe there's something they need to find in the city," a crewman added.

Kadorax ventured another quick look over the ruins. The two dwarves were still at the top of the wall, and one of them was sweeping the area with his spyglass. "At least we know now that the jackals have allies. We can worry about whatever they're doing in Oscine City later. Our best chance to rescue the princess will be right now. They don't expect an attack, and they aren't fully prepared."

"Aye," the captain said. "The longer we wait, the more entrenched they'll become."

"We don't even know what we're up against," a crewman said, shaking his head and pushing himself a little farther away from the fortress.

Kadorax turned to his lifelong companion with a sinister smile. "Just the two of us? Like old times?"

"I don't—"

"Like hell," Lord Percival cut in. "I had to stand by and watch my crew and my ship get sent to the bottom of the damned sea. I'm not waiting here like a coward while you two run off to get killed."

Kadorax had to admit that he was surprised by the captain's sudden courage, and he welcomed the determined ally. "Alright. Anyone who wants to stay back, go to the meeting point and wait for Brinna. When she arrives, take her to the priory. Tell the Knights what we've found."

The crewman who had voiced his concern before

swallowed hard. "I'm not a fighter," he said. "I'm just a sailor. I'll . . . go wait for Brinna."

"No shame in that," the captain told his man.

The other crewman was obviously nervous, but he didn't speak up.

Kadorax gave the scared crewman a pat on the shoulder. "Go. Be quick about it and stick to the shadows. If we aren't there by nightfall, head for the priory."

The man nodded and turned, losing his footing for a second before taking off toward the center of Oscine City.

"Alright," Kadorax said to the four others, their hands wrapped tightly around their weapons. "If we're going in, we need to hurry. Ayers, figure out which side of the wall gives us our best shot."

The burly smith nodded, a determined expression on his face. There weren't many nearby buildings—most of them had been reduced to ruins after their foundations and walls had been scavenged into the jackal fortress—to offer much cover. Still, there was enough for the smith to move around without being seen while getting a view of the fortress from several different angles. Ayers waited a few seconds for the lookout dwarf to move his spyglass to a different section of the city before sprinting for the next ruins.

Kadorax held his breath as the big man ran. Luckily, the dwarven lookouts didn't catch him. Once Ayers was beyond the first section of ruins, there was nothing to do but wait for his return and remain hidden.

"Who do you think they're working with? Just the Miners' Union, or would the jackals have allies that we don't know of yet?" the bastion asked, not wanting to waste time before Ayers's return. He was thankful to have a bit of reprieve and to let his skills come closer to resetting.

"Jackals don't usually build compounds like that," Syzak stated.

"No, they do not," Kadorax agreed.

Percival let out a heavy sigh. "We need to find someone who's been to the north."

"Maybe one of the knights, if any of them are left," the bastion answered.

A loud sound came from the direction of the fortress, and Kadorax peeked his head over the rubble to take a look. "Some sort of weaponry," he said after a moment. "Looks like a ballista."

"Guess they're planning on staying a while," Syzak added. Fortunately for Ayers, the two dwarves with the spyglass had turned to help direct the installation of the ballista.

"There must be something in the city they're after," Kadorax stated. "We need to know what it is. Maybe a magical relic or some other artifact they need . . . for whatever it is they're doing."

The remaining *Grim Sleeper* crewman readjusted his belt. "If we catch a jackal alive, maybe we could find out."

The thought of torturing some answers from a jackal wasn't a bad idea, Kadorax knew. Capturing one alive, though, would prove difficult. "You might be right," he said. "If we get the chance, we'll try to take one alive."

A few minutes later, Ayers appeared in the next set of ruins, his face covered in grime. He waved to them but didn't call out.

"Ready to run for it?" Kadorax asked. The four of them crouched at the edge of their cover and waited for the dwarves on top of the fortress to turn their backs before heading for Ayers. They arrived at the smith's section and dove down behind a low wall, all of them more or less falling on top of each other amidst broken rafter beams and dislodged bricks.

"What's it like?" Kadorax asked quietly.

The smith wore a smile beneath the dirt on his face. "Like I suspected before, the eastern wall isn't finished. Problem is, they're in the process of finishing it right now. If we try to just rush up and bust our way inside, they'll see us coming."

"Damn," Kadorax cursed under his breath. "If I had another couple ranks of *Chaos Step*, I'd be able to teleport inside the walls. The range is only ten feet right now."

Lord Percival thought for a moment, his eyes flicking through the character sheet suspended in the upper part of his vision. Finally, he shook his head. "None of my captain abilities would be useful," he said.

"How much longer until you can use *Guardian of the Deep* again?" Syzak asked.

"Eight more days," the bastion answered.

"How . . . How about a distraction? I could draw their attention," the sailor next to Lord Percival asked. His shaking voice betrayed his lack of confidence.

Kadorax gave the man an approving nod. "I appreciate the sentiment, but you're not a fighter. You wouldn't be fast enough, and there's no safe place left in Oscine City to run."

Silently, the man cast his eyes toward the ground.

Kadorax rearranged his body to put himself in a position where he could see the wall under construction. The fortress's eastern flank was about six or seven feet tall, and a dwarven crew was busy laying a random array of salvaged bricks and beams to create the uppermost section. Farther off to the side was an area without even the lower part of the wall, but Kadorax knew they would never reach it unseen. That section of the fortress was too far from the nearest broken buildings. Even if it was night, which it certainly wasn't, they'd be charging across a hundred yards of open field without a hint of cover. The section nearest to them, however, was only about half that distance, and the angle gave them at least moderate protection from dwarven eyes.

"I don't know," Kadorax said quietly. "The dwarves are probably builders and craftsman, not fighters. I think we could take them."

"Problem is, we don't know what's on the other side of the wall. Could be a whole contingent of reinforcements waiting to finish sacking the city. Doing anything will be a risk," Lord Percival said.

Kadorax knew the veteran sailor was right. Still, he couldn't deny the spark of adrenaline he had been cultivating since the battle with the giant only a quarter of an hour before.

Deep down in the farthest reaches of Kadorax's mind, he knew that something else might have been at play. His *Bond* had fallen to seven the last time he had entered Ligriv's realm, and the memory of seeing a World War Two–era Jeep in the woods outside Skarm's Reach was painfully fresh. "I shouldn't be the one to make a decision," he said after a few quiet minutes had passed.

Syzak let out a sigh. "If you're worried about seeing things, just call out anything unusual," he told his friend.

Next to him in the rubble, Lord Percival wore a confused expression. Then the man's eyes jumped skyward, the tell-tale sign of reading another's character sheet, and the captain didn't bother to ask any questions.

Kadorax watched the dwarven work crew for another few moments before dropping back to conceal himself fully behind the ruins. "Alright, if we're going to go, someone else call it. I know we can take the craftsman. Maybe we won't have to fight more than them, and we can just take a quick look around the inside of the fortress before we retreat."

The shaman nodded, and his ophidian tongue flicked through the air in front of his mouth. "The longer we wait, the more established the jackals become. Let's kill them all."

"I'll lead the way," Lord Percival quietly announced, his scimitar in his hand. The man stood, then offered a hand to pluck his crewman from the ground.

"Ready?" Kadorax asked as he got to his own feet. They hadn't been seen yet, but he figured they would have a minute, probably less, before an errant glance toward the ruins would result in an alarm.

"Let drive and *Lay Her Course*, boys!" the flamboyant captain shouted with a murderous grin upon his face.

Kadorax had absolutely no idea what the nautical terms meant, but he felt the power of their magic at once. *Lay Her Course* had activated an aura of exhilarating fog, and in the corner of his vision, he saw little flashing notifications telling him that both his *Strength* and *Agility* had been temporarily boosted by two. His feet flew across the ground only a step behind the madly charging captain.

Empowered and emboldened by the spell, Kadorax, Syzak, and the two seamen crossed the gap from the outermost ruins of Oscine City to the exterior wall of the jackal stronghold in a sparse few seconds. Lord Percival, his scimitar in the lead, met the first dwarven craftsman before any of the work crew had a chance to yell for help.

Their surprise didn't last long, though, as the dwarf walking the top of the unfinished wall issued a cry of alarm before jumping down to take up a hammer and join the chaotic fray.

Percival struggled to remove a dead dwarf from his

sword. The magical speed and resulting crash had ended with his weapon buried to the hilt in an enemy chest.

On either side of the captain, dwarves were frantically trying to use their construction tools to ward off their attackers, though it was painfully obvious that none of them had a single combat talent to activate.

Kadorax cracked his whip across the front of the nearest dwarf's face, then immediately followed with another devastating laceration to the worker's unprotected ankles. As the dwarf struggled to retreat—his back trapped by the very wall he had been constructing—Kadorax ended his life with a third loud crack of his whip across the enemy's meaty dwarven neck.

Too late, Kadorax realized the error of his ways. The whip was loud. Though one of the workers had already called for help, there at least had been a chance that the plea had gone unheard. Three cracks of a heavy whip were far louder than the cry, and Kadorax could hear footsteps coming from inside the compound. Had the dwarf not died half on top of the wall and blocked his vision, he would have been able to see what was coming, but instead, he had to assume the worst.

"Be ready!" he shouted, dropping his whip and drawing *Assir's Edge* in the process. There were two more dwarves on his side of the melee, both barely holding their ground against sheer terror.

Kadorax lunged at the first worker and easily knocked away the dwarf's trowel before running his sword through soft skin.

The last remaining dwarf to Kadorax's left tried to flee. Unfortunately for the dwarf, it was too short to make it over the unfinished wall with any kind of speed, and Kadorax added its meager experience points total to his own with a single uncontested strike. He glanced to the side of his vision as the three others made similar work of their untrained opponents before grabbing the dwarf on top of the wall and throwing his bearded body to the ground.

On the other side of the barrier, a mass of jackals seemingly numbering closer to one hundred than fifty was approaching at full speed. "Syzak!" the bastion yelled. "What do you see?"

Kadorax desperately hoped his *Encroaching Insanity* was playing tricks on his mind. If the jackals were all truly there, they'd be upon him in an instant.

"Run!" the snake-man yelled after killing the last of the worker dwarves with a deft claw to the throat.

Sweeping up his whip as he sprinted backward, Kadorax growled through gritted teeth. "Toward the priory!" he yelled.

"*For* the priory!" came a heroic, bellowing response that Kadorax immediately knew had not been made by anyone in his party. He looked right, and there, amidst the ruins, was a small gathering of shining, heavily armored knights.

At the apex of the assembled steel stood two familiar figures: Lady Alexandrina Apos and Sergeant Reinhardt. Behind them stood about two dozen knights, though the contingent was so heavily battered and bloodied that their wounds could be seen from a good distance. Still, knights could hold a field against jackals for untold days—if not weeks.

Kadorax let his chest swell with a bit of unexpected pride. He felt his mind sharpening and his will being recast into unyielding iron. He knew the encouragement was magical in origin without needing to read the notification that blinked into existence in the bottom of his vision. "I will not fall," he growled without choice at the magical aura's behest. "For the priory!"

Kadorax's enchanted spats kept him from losing his balance as his body made the most severe turn and about-face possible. Finally, once he had fallen in with the charging knights, the compulsory aspect of the aura faded and returned his free will to his muscles. "I *hate* that priory bullshit," he mouthed, though his barely audible words were instantly lost beneath the crash of steel against stone.

As they continued forward like an inevitable bladed tide headed for jackal breakwaters, Kadorax saw the rest of his small party caught up in the charge as well. He feared for the others. They lacked metal armor, and one poorly placed foot would mean tripping. Falling underneath the magically accelerated mass of steel-clad knights was a worse fate than dying on a jackal sword or claw.

Luckily, the makeshift army reached the jackal wall without pounding any of their own into the ground. The resounding roar as the knights and jackals met was enough to shake loose some of the damaged rubble from the nearest buildings. Kadorax opted to match his steely comrades with his battered shield held in front of his face and *Assir's Edge* on his right.

In the center, Lady Alexandrina seemed to be the focus of the battle. One of the few knights not holding a shield, she swung her giant mace in a huge arc, scattering three jackals at a time.

Without any training or much of an idea of what to do when fighting in a coordinated line of shields and armor, Kadorax focused on defending himself until he found an opportunity to push away from the heart of the battle. It didn't take long for an opening to present itself, and Kadorax leapt to his side, planting one foot on a low section of unfinished wall. With his sword hand, he overbalanced himself forward, allowing the weight of his weapon to help him ascend the short bit of wall and elevate him above the mob at his feet.

With a view of the battle from above, Kadorax did what he had spent thirty years on Agglor perfecting: he searched the mass of enemies for a single target, a leader, to execute.

Near the back of the oncoming jackal horde stood a humanoid figure dressed in unique garb. It took Kadorax a few seconds to place the strange image in his memory, for "Louisiana voodoo priest" wasn't a trope that frequented his thoughts. The creature—generally human in stature and posture—was covered in an array of multi-colored leather, dangling bone ornaments, and little fetishes tied to its limbs.

A smile spread across Kadorax's face. He thought for a brief second to search for Syzak amidst the chaos, but he knew it would take too long. In his heart, Kadorax understood the simple fact that he was an assassin, class taxonomy be damned.

Kadorax jumped to a higher section of the wall, though he could feel the entire structure bucking and swaying with the momentous surges of the jackals and knights. The combination of his spats and his enhanced *Agility* allowed him to easily keep his balance as he sprinted away from the fight like a cat scampering across a narrow tree branch. When he was far enough from the knights to feel their emboldening aura fade from his body, he dropped noiselessly to the ground and shrugged his shield from his back. Even weightless, it wasn't the right tool for the job.

The great bulk of the jackal force was directed toward the broken gap in the unfinished wall. There were others near the back of the horde, their attention spread elsewhere, but none of them watched the bastion taking a wide arc around the inner wall of the compound. Kadorax positioned himself at a point dangerously far from his allies with maybe a hundred enemies between himself and safety.

Thirty feet—and a handful of jackals—separated Kadorax from his mark. The voodoo priest was deep in the throes of spellcasting, pumping bright waves of energy into the jackal army. Kadorax waited and watched, following the priest's movements to discern a pattern while simultaneously mapping an anticipated route through the jackals. Old practices flooded his mind from the depths of the past, and a familiar smile broke out on his face.

The battle seemed to wane for a moment, and Kadorax made his move. He sprinted forward, *Assir's Edge* held in a reverse grip so the flat of the blade was vertical and concealed against his wrist.

A split second before he would have collided with the priest, an invisible shockwave of powerful magic flung him backward.

Grinning, the strange voodoo figure turned to face him. She—Kadorax could finally tell—had a crazed look in her eyes, one that the bastion had never seen before, and it helped project a visage of deranged, murderous glee. The woman waved her hands, and one of the little voodoo dolls tied to her arm leapt forward of its own accord, running full speed for Kadorax's feet.

"What the hell?" he shouted. Kadorax skipped backward and swept his sword at the voodoo doll, trying to maintain his balance while figuring out what was happening at the same time. He summoned the priestess's character sheet to his vision. He couldn't see anything other than her level, name, and class:

Ock't'chu
Witch Doctor - Level 19

He'd never encountered the class before, but Kadorax had to assume a witch doctor operated at least somewhat similarly to a mystic, and that had been his multiclass as an assassin, so he knew more or less what to expect. Healing, dislocation magic, and illusions were the realm of the mystic.

Kadorax's first strike at the animated doll missed. He hadn't fully intended on scoring a hit, and the maneuver had been a simple tactic to buy some time while he repositioned his feet. Then, as he was about to lunge forward and begin a combination aimed for the doll's stuffed head, the little creation reared back and fired some sort of magical projectile from its mouth.

Jumping to his left, Kadorax dodged the incoming missile with ease. He didn't waste any time moving in for a killing blow. *Assir's Edge* slashed at the doll from its left before cutting back in the blink of an eye, but the quick little doll fell flat on the ground. Kadorax's sword cut through the air right above the doll's head.

Kadorax knew such a small opponent was going to be difficult to hit. With more *Agility*, he would have been able to position his weapon quicker and probably catch the doll off guard, but without more *Spirit*, he'd never be able to track the tiny creature with his eyes in the first place. Still, he swung again, aiming to chop the doll in half down its center.

The humanoid bundle of twigs and cloth rolled to its side. Kadorax kept up the chase, ramming his sword to the end of his reach—

—and a burst of violent orange fire erupted on his breastplate. The witch doctor had cast, and Kadorax had been too distracted to protect himself. He reeled from the force of the blast. *Cage of Chaos* activated again, but the response was electric in nature and didn't reach far enough to hit anything relevant. As Kadorax tried to reorient himself to include both enemies in his attack, the witch doctor cast once more. Bubbling quicksand appeared beneath the bastion's feet.

An idea came to Kadorax's mind. His enchanted boots prevented the quicksand from affecting him, but that didn't mean he couldn't sell it exactly that way. He yelled in mock terror and let his sword arm fall to his hip, pretending to struggle to break free. As intended, the voodoo doll took the bait and leapt for his torso.

Assir's Edge flew skyward with lightning speed. Two pieces of frayed, tattered doll fell on either side of the blade, and Kadorax took an unencumbered step forward. The witch doctor didn't look impressed. She still had at least three more dolls integrated into her clothing, and another burst of magic had already formed around her tattooed hands. She let fly, and a chaotic burst of incorporeal bats swarmed out from her palms.

Kadorax ran to his right to avoid the swarm, but he couldn't knock them all away, and they homed in on his body with startling precision. Each bat dissipated upon contact with his flesh. Wherever they hit, they hurt like hell. After the tenth and final bat sank through his skin, Kadorax saw a short debuff flash to life on his character sheet:

Haunted: Rank 4 - Ghostly energy swarms through your blood. All stats are reduced by 4. Additionally, the afflicted may not activate any talents. Effect: moderate. Duration: 24 seconds.

Instantly, Kadorax felt his reflexes slow to a grinding halt. His muscles burned from fatigue. Another powerful blast of fire erupted from Ock't'chu, and there was nothing the weakened bastion could do to avoid it. The fireball took him squarely in the chest. Before long, the heat inside his metal breastplate reached an unbearable level.

From somewhere behind him, Kadorax felt a refreshing wave of *Stitch Together* enter his body. "Too soon!" he growled in response to the healing magic. He stole a glance over his shoulder and saw that Syzak had battled his way to the front of the breached wall and was just in view through the throng. The knights, Lady Alexandrina still swatting jackals like flies with her giant mace, had pushed through and established a defensive half circle on the inner part of the wall.

Kadorax didn't have time to search for Percival or Ayers among the tumult. He turned back to the witch doctor just in time to *almost* duck out of the way of an incoming magical spear. The projectile caught his shoulder and scraped off a sizeable amount of his skin as it sailed past. With his stats crippled, Kadorax felt a pang of regret at having abandoned his shield. He should have known the mysterious commander would have been protected against physical assaults. He silently cursed himself and vowed to allocate his level fourteen stat bonus to *Spirit*.

Wracked with pain and barely able to move, Kadorax pivoted to get the witch doctor fully in front of him, and then he dropped low into a defensive crouch. "You can only cast so much," he said to himself, his mouth twisted in a snarl. Sure enough, the voodoo woman cast again, and a glowing blue circle appeared all around Kadorax's feet.

The circle, marked by familiar runes and gently floating particles of magic, was a spell Kadorax immediately recognized from the mystic repertoire. *Render in Stone* was a low-level incantation, and it had a slow timer before rank nine. Regardless of its relative weakness as a combat tool,

Render in Stone could produce absolutely devastating effects when cast on encumbered or immobile targets—like Kadorax. If the spell's rank was five or lower, Kadorax knew he would have about ten seconds to leave the circle before being petrified for upward of a minute. If the spell was a higher rank, he'd have much less time.

Kadorax yelled into the sky as he forced his body forward. He took one heavy step and knew he wouldn't make it in time against a high-rank version of *Render in Stone*. All he could do was hope the witch doctor hadn't improved the spell beyond the first few ranks. If she had, no amount of *Stitch Together* would prevent a fresh respawn.

Watching the few remaining seconds of *Haunted* tick by on his character sheet, Kadorax prepared to activate *Chaos Step* the moment he could. The timer hit zero. The amount of mental energy Kadorax forced toward *Chaos Step* was enough to activate the spell instantaneously, but the talent still required a full second to activate. Before he could think any further beyond his escape from the magical blue ring of runes, both *Render in Stone* and *Chaos Step* fired.

Kadorax appeared behind the voodoo witch doctor in the blink of an eye.

He couldn't move. His muscles refused to respond to his mental commands, and then the *Petrified* debuff flashed across the bottom of his vision. The number twelve blinked next to it.

All Kadorax could do was watch and tick off the seconds in his head. At first, the witch doctor clearly had no idea where he'd gone. She looked around frantically, then even took a step forward to test the area where Kadorax had been by waving her hand through it.

Eight seconds remained.

The witch doctor turned around, and another sinister grin found its way to her pierced lips.

Between Kadorax and certain death, a small cloud of rain suddenly appeared.

Kadorax felt his heart flutter in his petrified chest. Syzak was out of spells, but his trusted friend had just bought him another handful of seconds as the witch doctor leapt back, clearly expecting some sort of magical assault. Two more of her voodoo dolls dropped to the ground and came alive at the same time.

Four seconds remained.

A roar from somewhere off in the distance—muffled by the magical stone encasing Kadorax's head—made the woman's head jerk toward the breach.

Three seconds remained.

Just a little longer, the bastion silently pleaded.

The two new dolls leapt for his face and torso. Their little cloth and straw hands pummeled his breastplate, and there was untoward strength behind their small fists. His armor dented inward and screeched against the thin stone layer between his steel and flesh.

Two seconds remained.

Ock't'chu reared back another hand and let loose. Three spiraling bolts of congealed magic blasted through the air. As the final seconds ticked off the debuff, two of the witch doctor's missiles connected with Kadorax's body, imparting a monstrous amount of force on every joint and bone in his body.

Gritting his teeth and shutting his eyes to the pain, Kadorax was catapulted through the air for what felt like an impossibly long distance. When he finally crashed to the ground, he saw the experience points of two different jackal warriors flash into his vision for a split second. Their corpses were under his body, and they had likely padded his unceremonious landing.

His head swam with a concussion. Had *Render in Stone* still been active when he hit the jackals and then the ground, he had no doubt his physical body would have shattered into millions of tiny bloodless pieces just like a statue being dropped from a rooftop.

Another roar sounded from near the breach, but Kadorax didn't possess the mental fortitude to turn his head to see what was coming.

Above him, an armor-clad figured entered his vision and blocked his view of the sky. "Get off your ass!" Sergeant Reinhardt yelled in his direction.

A hand reached out from the blurry patch of rugged steel in front of Kadorax's eyes. Soon Kadorax knew he was being lifted from the ground, but then he tumbled back down and suffered another painful crack to the back of his skull. Reinhardt had one of his warpicks out and was busy bashing out the brains from a jackal soldier's fur-covered head. Then the hand returned, and Kadorax was successfully hoisted to his feet.

"The . . . dolls . . ." he said weakly.

Reinhardt, still keeping the bastion on his feet with a single arm, whirled just in time to see two voodoo dolls leaping for his armor.

Somewhere through the fog gripping his mind, Kadorax thought he heard the veteran knight laugh. Standing amidst a swarm of jackals, Reinhardt issued a wild, howling cackle that carried over their heads.

Then the knight was engulfed in blistering flame. The two dolls pounding away on his armor were instantly incinerated.

Despite the brilliant light, Kadorax took comfort in the fact that he was not burning alive. Somehow, the magic was powerful enough to distinguish friend from foe. Before the bastion could consider the awe-inspiring talent any further, he felt his mind slipping away and his brain succumbing to his wounds.

Still alive, he thought as his vision went dark. *Barely.*

Sergeant Reinhardt tossed Kadorax's limp body onto his shoulder like a sack of flour. To the grizzled veteran of forty years and forty-four levels, his *Strength* was so high that Kadorax might as well have weighed nothing at all.

A blood-soaked pick in his left hand, Reinhardt cleaved a path of destruction toward his fellow knights. They were winning handily against the swarm, but things were about to change—and he didn't want to be there when they did.

A third tremendous roar filled the sky. It was close enough by then to bring about an eerie calm over the jackal fortress as the dozens of remaining soldiers pulled back in alarm. The knights, holding their semicircle but suffering a constant bombardment they would not be able to withstand, fell back at the same time.

Behind them, emerging from the ruins of Oscine City like a great swamp monster rising from a bog, was a pallid Gar'kesh. Atticus strode next to the creature. The old man pointed toward the fortress, and the Gar'kesh appeared to understand. It lumbered forward with something akin to excitement on its hideous, horned face.

The knights barely got out of the way before the

Gar'kesh—not slowing in the least to preserve those in its path—would have trampled them.

Reinhardt roughly tossed Kadorax's limp form over the unfinished wall before pulling himself over and continuing the retreat. He formed up with the rest of the surviving knights, and Syzak offered a helping hand in bearing the bastion's weight.

"Full retreat!" Alexandrina shouted. "Let the beast work!"

Just beyond the breach, the Gar'kesh bellowed again, and jackal screams mingled with its deep, resonant voice. High-pitched and piercing through it all came Atticus's shrill laughter.

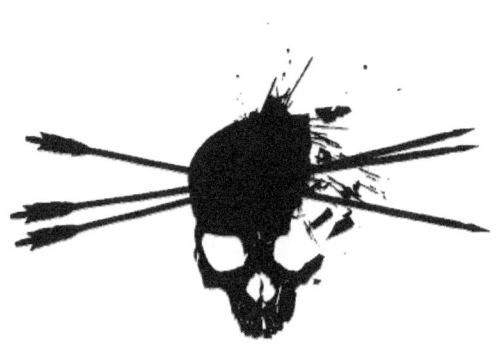

CHAPTER 6

Kadorax awoke in the priory, and the building was far quieter than he remembered. Once again, he found himself in a room full of low cots, many of which held injured knights or other members of the order. When he had pushed the weariness from his mind and checked the bandages wrapped around his head to make sure they were secure, he finally stood and stretched. Pain throbbed behind his eyes and in a halo around his forehead. Syzak and Brinna weren't with the other wounded, and that, he figured, was a good thing.

A nearby cleric was busy changing one man's dressings.

"Any idea where my snake friend might be found?" Kadorax asked. Speaking intensified the ache in his brain like a bad hangover.

Without looking up from his work, the cleric nodded and said, "Upstairs on the training pavilion, I think."

Kadorax thanked him and headed for the stairs that

would take him to the squarish stone area where he had earned his knight multiclass. Sure enough, both Syzak and Brinna were there, along with a handful of others practicing with weapons and what appeared to be newly acquired talents. Silently, his head throbbing even more from the recent movement, Kadorax decided to lean back against the parapet and watch.

Syzak was teaching Brinna how to grapple someone from behind, a common assassin and rogue technique. There were talents available to both classes that would make the maneuver magically accessible, but simply learning the proper form from a practiced master was always more efficient. Talent points were the most valuable possessions in Agglor—wasting them on moves that could easily be learned the old-fashioned way was practically suicide.

As he watched, Kadorax decided that the woman had a natural propensity for her class. He wondered how many lives she had used and how many different classes she had selected. Some people on Agglor, no matter where they had actually been born, tended to drift through dozens of classes as they aged, never really finding something that fit their natural inclinations. Given Brinna's lithe build and naturally graceful movements, he figured she had always been some sort of *Agility*-based class.

Finally, the two took a break, and Syzak noticed the bastion near the pavilion's entrance. "You're awake," he called, padding over on bare feet.

"Yeah, my head hurts, but I'll be fine. Did anyone grab my shield? Or my other equipment?" He realized *Assir's Edge* had fallen from his grasp during the fight and hoped it wasn't lost forever. The whip and shield, however, he could live without.

Syzak nodded. "Everything is in the storeroom below. Ayers took your shield, and they have a small workshop, so he's hard at work. Your breastplate should be there as well."

Brinna wiped a layer of sweat from her brow. She wore a smile, and Kadorax noticed a new swell to her arms that must have come from an increase to her *Strength* stat. "You leveled?" he asked, preferring polite conversation over pillaging her character sheet for easy answers.

"Level ten," she announced happily. The former mayor of Assir could barely contain her excitement.

Kadorax had to admit that he was impressed. "How many did you kill?" he asked.

She thought for a moment, a hand on her chin, though it was obvious she knew exactly how many it had been and was just savoring the moment. "There was an ambush, just like you predicted. We were supposed to follow their more obvious tracks, and thirty of them, including more than one spellcaster, were waiting in a culvert between an alleyway and a ruined potion shop missing a roof. I saw them, but they didn't see me."

"You killed thirty jackals by yourself?" Kadorax nearly yelled in disbelief.

The woman beamed. "They were all crouched together in the culvert and stacked on top of each other to remain hidden. The wall of the potion shop was easy to knock over. Several of them were crushed to death, and their bodies all pressing down on themselves made it impossible for them to escape. Once I had them trapped, it took me almost half an hour to figure out how to finish the job. Luckily, I was able to find a rain barrel and roll it down to the ditch."

"You . . . uh . . . drowned thirty jackals in a back alley by yourself?" Kadorax asked. He wasn't quite sure he believed the story, though her enthusiasm certainly added to her credibility. Still, the woman had been a mayor—a *civilian* mayor—just a few weeks ago. Kadorax wasn't even sure if some of his Blackened Blades had the mental fortitude required to slaughter thirty enemies all at once without a fight.

"Well, some of them were certainly crushed to death, but the rest drowned. Now I'm level ten!" She brushed some imaginary dust from her shoulders and struck a pose.

Kadorax, feeling a little dumbstruck, didn't have anything else to say, so he simply congratulated the woman and finally glanced at her character sheet to see which talents she had taken. Being level ten meant she was eligible for a multiclass as well, but she'd need to find someone at least level thirty in order to learn one. Around the priory, multiclass choices were limited. A rogue mixed with a knight would be interesting at best, a disaster at worst.

For level ten, the woman had predictably taken a fourth rank in *Sneak*, and she had also unlocked *Forced Entry: Rank 1*. The talent wasn't one Kadorax had ever used in his own lives, so he expanded the tooltip to see exactly what kind of bonuses it would offer:

Forced Entry: Rank 1 - From picking locks to smashing through doors and discovering hidden passages, the rogue becomes more efficient when trying to enter or exit secured buildings. At higher ranks, the rogue also receives a bonus to Fate and a bonus whenever attempting to locate or gain access to hidden valuables, no matter their location. Effect: minor. Passive.

"What do you think of the new talent?" Brinna asked.

"Not one I've seen before, and a *minor* effect level isn't going to be that useful," Kadorax replied honestly. Deep down, he knew he would not have made the same decision.

The woman was still implacable. "If I can put more

points into it, I'll be able to find all sorts of hidden treasure. Combined with *Sneak*, I'll never have to worry about gold."

For whatever reason, even though Brinna had been a rogue for as long as Kadorax had known her, she didn't strike him as a thief. Something in her had changed dramatically. He was starting to think that all of his original assessments of her had been wrong. He had tried to shield her and keep her from most of the more intense fighting, but perhaps that would change. Perhaps she was ready to stand on the front lines next to him.

"I take it you prefer to focus on a few core talents and take them as high as you can?" he went on. His own personal strategy only started to look like a concerted build once he had a dozen or more abilities to their first ranks. Especially in the beginning, having access to a wider variety was typically more beneficial than only having a couple of skills that were incredibly effective. No matter which path someone took, there were ways to make either strategy extremely successful. Some just took more skill or perseverance than others.

Brinna nodded, and then her eyes moved upward to her own sheet displayed in her vision. "I want to multiclass. I don't know what to do, though. As a mayor, I never really expected to get much past level five or six, and then I had anticipated multiclassing as a diplomat if I ever had the chance. Politics don't matter now, I suppose. I just want to get stronger in order to help."

"Well, I appreciate the sentiment. And the typical combinations would be either assassin or something magical that can also heal, like mystic, shaman, or druid. A few of the Blackened Blades preferred to take more heavy melee multiclasses, but it all depends on what you want to do. Sneaking around and breaking into houses would certainly

129

favor assassin, and I could teach you everything you need to know," Kadorax explained. He wondered if Sergeant Reinhardt's second class as a tactician wouldn't be the most useful to add to his party, but he doubted any of the talents would ever complement a rogue.

"Magic would be nice," Brinna mused, "but I'm not sure where to go to find it. I've already asked around the priory, and none of the multiclasses available here would fit well."

"Hey, what happened to Atticus? Did he make it back from the jackal fortress? And maybe pairing warlock with rogue would give some interesting results. You never know." Kadorax peered out from the edge of the open-air training pavilion, but he didn't see the old warlock anywhere below. For that matter, he also didn't see the Gar'kesh.

Syzak laughed. "The Gar'kesh did a number on the fortress, probably killed at least half the jackals inside, but they took it down. We left before too many knights could fall. Their fortress is heavily weakened. You'll want to see Lady Alexandrina about tonight's raid," he explained.

"What about the witch doctor?" Kadorax asked.

"Unknown," was the snake-man's response. "I would assume she's still alive. Never seen someone quite like that. Thought you had her for a second, but *Render in Stone* was just too fast."

Kadorax smiled at the prospect of a night raid and the possibility of ending the fight with the witch doctor. "Sounds good. If we can finish off the jackal fortress tonight, we might be able to rescue the princess and put an end to the whole war. Any other news of jackal incursions elsewhere?"

"No news coming in or out," Syzak said.

"And most of the knights on the dock didn't survive, if you were wondering," Lady Alexandrina said as she ascended the staircase to Kadorax's right. She wore comfortable clothes instead of armor, and several white linen bandages could be seen beneath them. "The raiding party will leave at dusk. I need someone to lead it. I was thinking of you."

Tipping his head in deference, Kadorax used the slight movement to hide his smile. "I would be honored, my lady."

"Good," she replied. "Sergeant Reinhardt will take a small contingent to their front door. The four of us will find a different way inside. When their leaders are dead, the knights will roll in to confront the remainder of their primary force. I suspect that kind of action is something you're accustomed to."

"You're coming with us?" Kadorax asked, eyebrows raised. He wasn't opposed to the idea of a singular knight tagging along, especially such a high-level one, but he had to wonder if all her armor would give away their position.

She nodded. "I won't slow you down. I know your history, and I know what you're capable of now. Be ready at dusk." She turned to head back down the stairs and to the interior of the priory. "Oh, and your captain friend is on the beach with Atticus. Not many civilians survived the docks. I think your friend is with the survivors looking for his crew."

"Thanks," Kadorax said as she left. He turned back to Brinna and Syzak with a bit of a bewildered expression on his face. "Ready to kill more jackals?"

Brinna's smile was devious. "Of course," she stated.

Syzak only flicked his tongue and flexed.

Kadorax elected to get some more rest before the raid. With about an hour until dusk, he got up from one of the cots in the priory and stretched his muscles. He knew he wasn't fully rested, but it would have to do. There simply wasn't time to waste. Ascending the stairs to the main part of the priory, he entered the storeroom and proceeded to the knights' forge to find Ayers.

The burly smith was covered in soot, and his exposed arms rippled with engorged veins, suggesting he'd been at an anvil for hours. Judging by the amount of armor scattered around the forge, he had a lot more work yet to finish before he'd get some sleep or even a few minutes of rest.

"How's the hammer treating you?" Kadorax said above the din of the forge. The room was enclosed on three sides with its rear open to the ocean. The fires of the forge didn't have any specific chimney to channel away the smoke, and while a gentle breeze coming in from the water helped, there was still a smoky haze hanging in the air.

Ayers dropped a piece he was working on into a cooling bucket next to his anvil. The metal sizzled for a few moments, and Ayers grabbed a water tankard from a nearby shelf and finished what was left inside. "Lot of work," he said between breaths. "The knights who survived the docks lost their weapons, shields, and most of their armor to the ocean. Turns out steel doesn't float. I could have told them that and saved the jackals a bit of trouble."

"Ha, no. It certainly does not." Kadorax picked up a freshly forged sword from a rack. It was crudely made, completely without ornament or even thought given to aesthetics, but it would get the job done when the time came. He suspected Ayers had been focused exclusively on quantity rather than quality.

"Your shield took a beating back there," the smith said. He hefted Kadorax's shield from a different shelf and set it down on his anvil. "I was able to pound out the dents . . . most of them, anyway. She isn't pretty, I'll tell you that."

Kadorax took the shield and struggled under its weight. Without his armor and the *Rune of Perseverance* socketed inside, he had to bear the shield's bulky mass the old-fashioned way. No matter how much he practiced with it strapped to his arm, Kadorax didn't think he'd ever truly get used to it weighing him down.

Taking a quick glance at the smith's character sheet just to confirm his suspicions, Kadorax saw that Ayers had progressed to level nine. All the work in such a short amount of time had been worth a ton of experience points. He had taken two ranks in *Repair Combat Device*. The talent would be useful, of course, but Kadorax had hoped to see more skills relating to magical item creation. At Darkarrow, his weaponsmith had learned all ten available ranks of *Masterwork Forgecraft*, one of the three *Superior Talents* available to blacksmiths. The skill covered all manner of forged items, both weapons and armor. The other two *Superior Talents* were *Exotic Materials Handling* and *Blessed Metallurgy*. Each was incredibly useful, but *Masterwork Forgecraft* was the only one specifically designed for outfitting soldiers and nothing else.

"One final thing," Ayers added. He grabbed an item draped with an oilcloth and set it down on his anvil. "You need a proper pair of bracers, especially with that shield. Take a hard enough hit, and the edge of the shield can really cut your arm. I think you'll like these." He pulled back the oilcloth to reveal a matching pair of gray vambraces.

"Oh, nice," Kadorax said. He picked up the vambraces and aligned them over his forearms. They looked like they would fit perfectly.

Ayers's smile reached from ear to ear. "Call up the stats. No need to be polite about it."

Kadorax nodded and did just that, focusing his vision on the vambraces until a translucent text box appeared in his vision:

Stalwart Bracers of the Forsaken Lady (Forsaken Lady Set 1 / 3) - Allows the wearer to fully resist all incoming cold and necrotic-based attacks. Additionally, the bracers grant +1 Strength and +1 Fate. Effect: Profound. Passive while worn.

"Holy shit, man," Kadorax gasped. He had to read the description twice to make sure he had read it correctly. "You're level nine! How the hell did you make a set piece?" Even though the set theme appeared to be a little strange or perhaps ill-suited to slaying dogheads in the open field, the bracers were still an impressive feat in their own right.

A deep, bellowing laugh came by way of Ayers's response. Finally, he tossed a small wooden tool haft from his pocket onto the anvil. "The knights had two enchanted hammers just sitting here. Since their smith hasn't been seen since the initial attack, I figured they wouldn't mind going down to just one enchanted hammer."

"Well done, Ayers, seriously. I mean that. We're raiding the jackal fortress tonight. I'll make it one of my priorities to find wherever they're churning out gear and see if I can't steal something for you. Maybe a schematic or two." Kadorax called up the bracers' stats a third time and shook his head in wonder. Set pieces were incredibly rare, usually only found in the lairs of high-level bosses. Enchanted hammers provided a shortcut to acquiring set pieces similar to the way a wand could allow anyone to use a certain spell even if it wasn't available to their class. To find either a set piece or a hammer was incredibly rare.

Ayers bowed. "Nathan, the blacksmith from the *Grim Sleeper*, didn't make it through the docks. He drowned out there. Kill some jackal scum for me, and that's all the repayment I could ask for."

"I certainly intend to do exactly that," Kadorax said with a nod. From the main part of the priory, he could hear knights strapping on armor and preparing for the night's raid. He extended a hand for the soot-covered, sweaty smith to shake.

"And Kadorax," the man added, his voice low, "make it hurt. Drown one of the bastards if you get the chance. For Nathan's sake."

A smirk found its way to Kadorax's face. "Talk to Brinna. Ask her about a few jackals and a barrel full of rainwater."

About a mile away from the jackal fortress, Lady Alexandrina Apos broke away from the others after exchanging a few words with Reinhardt and the rest of the knights under his command. They were positioned in the ruins making up most of the northern section of Oscine City and facing the jackal fortress. Sergeant Reinhardt had a dozen armored knights with him, most of them still fairly healthy, though the organization as a whole was running dangerously low when it came to unscathed members.

When she rejoined Kadorax, Syzak, and Brinna, the female priory commander wore a clouded expression of merciless anticipation. "It smells like death," she quietly stated.

Kadorax had to agree. "Lot of it lingering around here," he replied.

"How are we getting inside?" Brinna asked. She had

procured a black cloak from the priory, which she had pulled tight around her body. It wasn't enchanted, but it would make her harder to spot. Considering her fourth rank of *Sneak*, Kadorax wasn't sure she would need the cloak's added camouflage at all. At any kind of distance, any jackal without enhanced vision would almost certainly fail to spot her.

Alexandrina, her steel armor reflecting moonlight, drew a wand and a rune from a pouch on her sword belt. Shuffling the wand forward on her hand, she said, "I have a single charge of *Dimensional Door* to get us through the wall, and the rune will quiet my armor and make me much harder to see. We'll approach from the opposite side of the breach. They've likely reinforced that area in anticipation of another attack. Hitting them from the west presents us with our best opportunity."

Everyone gave their silent assent. Without any pageantry or even so much as a brief pep talk, the small party darted away from the other knights. When they were facing the tall, solidly constructed western wall, Lady Alexandrina didn't waste any time expending her charge of *Dimensional Door* and creating a shimmering, magical portal on the wall's face. If anyone was looking directly at the portal, they would easily see through to the other side, though the real beauty—and the reason they wouldn't just use a *Spike Trap* to make a temporary hole—was that from the side, the wall appeared unaltered.

Alexandrina took her rune next and placed it into a circular receiver on her chest piece. Since it was a consumable object and not a passive rune, she didn't need to be a smith to attach it to her armor.

"Wait, I have something as well," Kadorax whispered. He grabbed the *Jackal Slaying Potion* from his belt. "The potion master in Kingsgate gave me something that should come in handy." He uncorked the bottle and downed a mouthful. It tasted somehow slimy and ashy all at once. Then he unsheathed *Assir's Edge* and sprinkled a little on the blade. "Here. There's still some left. A full dose lasts an hour. I don't want to be inside that long. We can also use some on our weapons."

"What exactly does it do?" the knight asked, though she took the glass bottle and dripped an ounce or two onto the head of her club.

Kadorax had to wait for a moment to let a burst of indigestion subside. "I should be able to see the jackals through walls when we're close enough, and it'll add a fire buff to your weapons."

Syzak, being essentially unarmed, let Brinna use the last of the potion on her two daggers. The *Talon Dagger* didn't need any extra buffs to be devastating. When the potion bottle was empty, Kadorax tossed it behind him, into the ruins, where it shattered against a fallen bookcase that had broken through a residential building's wall.

"Shhh," Alexandrina said, a finger over her lips.

"Sorry," Kadorax whispered back.

The four waited for a couple of seconds to ensure no one from the wall was looking their way. Then, Brinna in the lead with *Sneak* making her nearly invisible, they ran for the *Dimensional Door* as quickly as they could.

The interior of the fortress hadn't changed much since the previous day. There were dozens of dead jackal bodies strewn near the breach, and the whole place reeked. Unfortunately, there was only a single entrance leading to the wood and stone building the walls protected. The whole thing was large, two floors, and judging by the changes in patterns, contained at least twenty distinct rooms.

Kadorax used his magically enhanced vision to see through the outer wall to the first two rooms on either side of the door. He held up a fist and pointed to the right of the door, then held two fingers and pointed to the left. Stealing a quick glance back to the guards on top of the wall, he smiled when none of them were watching the interior of the compound. So far, the group remained unseen.

The first thing Kadorax noticed about the interior of the compound was how hastily it had been established compared to the outer wall, which had a certain craftsman-like appearance. Inside, the walls were made mostly from boards sloppily nailed together or simply lashed at various intersections, and the whole thing probably wouldn't take much effort to bring to the ground.

"Jackal work, not dwarves," Kadorax said with a voice so quiet it was barely audible.

Syzak nodded and ran a finger against the wall to his right. "Meant to keep others out, not for living," he whispered.

Kadorax had the same notion. If the fortress had been designed and raised with the intent of jackals building a permanent stronghold in Oscine City, they wouldn't have slapped it together in a couple of nights. The dwarven construction of the exterior wall, something meticulous enough to not even be finished yet, told a different story altogether. "Temporary?" Kadorax asked, omitting as many words as possible to remain unheard.

Both Syzak and Lady Alexandrina responded with slight nods.

Second in the group's position, Brinna had her eyes fixed on the first room to their left, both daggers in her hands. Kadorax lifted two fingers, then pointed to the woman's chest and motioned to the left with his head. Pointing to his own soul rod, he jerked his head silently to the right. Brinna grinned her affirmation.

The former assassin was well versed in the art of breaking into buildings with a small team. Typically, he would have employed fast, loud tactics meant to shock the inhabitants into inaction, if only for a few seconds. With an unknown quantity of jackals still hiding somewhere in the fortress, he knew he had to stay quiet. Their goal, after all, was to eliminate the leadership and gather information, not rouse the entire force into another skirmish.

Holding his hand horizontal and low to the ground, Kadorax told everyone to crouch. He got down low and placed a palm flat against the flimsy wood of the door. Though he could see the magically visible outlines of the enemies within, he had absolutely no idea what they were doing. All he could tell was that they were standing.

Kadorax pushed the door open slowly, and Brinna darted inside without hesitation. In the space of a heartbeat, the two outlines Kadorax could see were reduced to one. He moved in after the woman and saw that the room was a storage area full of crude weapons and various bits of armor that looked—and smelled—like they had been salvaged from the fallen jackals the previous day.

Brinna was already leaping over a low table full of unstrung bows and poorly fletched arrows. The remaining jackal dropped a spool of string to the ground with a quick shriek, and then one of Brinna's daggers found its throat, and the surprised creature collapsed to the ground in a quiet heap. A little spurt of flame accompanied her strike, courtesy of the potion she had sprinkled on her blades.

The other two ducked into the armory and shut the door behind them, both wearing unbelieving expressions.

"I'll level again soon," the rogue said once she noticed the looks she was getting from her comrades.

Kadorax double-checked the first jackal to make sure it was dead, then casually inspected the items laid out on the table nearest to him. "Look for anything useful; don't move it," he said curtly. The last thing they needed was one of Syzak's claws accidentally knocking a mace from a table and alerting a barracks full of eager warriors.

Sadly, everything in the armory was essentially junk. The best of the gear was already damaged from use, and the worst of it was in such a state of disrepair as to be altogether useless.

Kadorax didn't wait to move back to the door and peek into the hallway. The room directly across the hall was blocked by another closed door, but the potion's magical effect on his vision revealed no jackals contained within. "Could be dwarves," he whispered to the others, pointing to the room in question.

Lady Alexandrina shrugged.

"Not here for dwarves," Syzak reminded him.

Silently giving a thumbs up, Kadorax pulled the door open wider and sprinted on the balls of his feet down the hallway and to a narrow set of stairs. The only way forward was down, and though Kadorax hated being in such a confined space without any easy route for escape, he also didn't see any enemies at the bottom, so he figured the landing would at least be safe enough.

He was right, and the four quiet intruders alighted on a small landing that split out like a pinwheel into five other passages.

"See any?" Syzak asked.

Kadorax scanned each of the tunnels in turn. "There,"

he said, pointing down a tunnel on his left. "Barracks is that way. Handful down each of the others."

Brinna made a move as if she was about to charge headlong down the path leading to the barracks, but Alexandrina stopped her with an implacable outstretched arm. Between the woman's impressive muscle, *Strength* attribute, and tightly secured armor, Brinna wasn't going anywhere. "No," the knight said calmly to the back of the woman's neck.

Stepping up to block her path, Kadorax stared her down. "We aren't here for the whole force, remember?" he growled through clenched teeth.

Finally, like something inside the woman had decided it wasn't worth fighting and gave up, Brinna relaxed. Alexandrina let go of her chest. "Right," Brinna agreed. "Find the leaders."

"Three in that direction," Kadorax said, turning the group toward a tunnel opposite the barracks. Light came from two of the areas and from the entrance to the compound above, giving them just enough to move without risking bumping into the walls.

About halfway down the tunnel, sounds of jackals approaching from behind made the group stop. Lady Alexandrina pushed herself to the rear of their little column, her huge mace held aloft above her head.

By the sounds of their gruff voices, Kadorax figured three of the beasts were approaching, and since the jackals were at home in their own territory, they'd likely be quadrupedal. Just as he was about to work his way next to the tall knight to tell her not to anticipate enemies at her own height, the first jackal came into view.

Lady Alexandrina's mace crushed its skull in a single blow. The two jackals behind lunged forward, still moving on all fours like their canine ancestors, their sharp teeth snapping for the knight's thick armor. One of them landed a bite, but its teeth grated against steel without so much as leaving a minor dent. Then Alexandrina's mace crushed its shoulders and swept all the way through to the final attacker's head, laying them both low in a single sweep.

Almost as quickly as it had begun, the fight was over. Kadorax stood awkwardly behind the woman, mouth open slightly as he had been about to tell her what to expect of the incoming foes. Shaking his head, he took his hand from the hilt of his sword and pushed back around the others to his position at the front.

"Someone might have heard that," Syzak whispered. "How many in the next room?"

"Four," Kadorax replied over his shoulder.

"Rush in. We don't have cover, and if they heard any of that killing, we don't want to give them extra time." Syzak urged them forward, his clawed fingers on Kadorax's back.

His hands at his sides to quickly draw either his sword or whip, Kadorax ran ahead, his magical vision focused on the group of four huddled jackals waiting for them in the room. As he neared, the light expanded until the bastion could see what he was approaching. There was a door on the far end of a relatively small chamber, and inside stood four jackal warriors in armor. The tassets dangling above their hips prevented them from going quadrupedal.

"Trap," Kadorax announced as he entered the room with a running flurry. He leapt over a low wire strung across the ground, and the three behind him all followed suit. Thanking his twenty-one *Fate* points for catching a faint reflection of torchlight off the wire, Kadorax smiled. He was still only level twelve, but he felt like he was starting to get enough talents and items to be truly useful, not just a hapless, freshly minted class searching for the right build.

The four jackals in the room each had weapons, and they drew them at once, though one of the beasts sprinted for the door. Without some sort of ranged magic, Kadorax knew he wouldn't be able to prevent the creature's escape.

So be it, he mentally growled. *Four against three.*

The first jackal met Kadorax head-on, swinging a heavy length of oiled chain at his chest. Kadorax's shield was still slung to his back, and there was no time to grab it. The odd chain weapon hit, wrapped itself around Kadorax's body like a grappling hook, and then the jackal pulled hard.

Kadorax was wrenched from his feet. With more *Agility*, he probably would have been able to dodge the incoming grapple or at least maintain his balance, but the jackal was clearly a superior level, and four-legged beasts always excelled in stats like *Strength* and *Agility*.

Behind him, Kadorax heard the rest of his party spilling into the room. Before long, the small, circular chamber was awash in the chaotic movements of unorganized combat. Syzak had pounced on the next jackal nearest to him, digging his claws through thick canine fur. A wild expression on her face, Brinna had the third beast pushed back against the door within seconds.

Two heavy, sharp jackal claws slammed into Kadorax's back and triggered *Cage of Chaos*. Kadorax smiled as he smelled burnt animal hair. The first blast of elemental fire was quickly followed by a second, similar burst of magic that sent the jackal reeling—giving Kadorax just enough time to scramble to his feet, though his arms were still uselessly pinned by the chain.

The jackal drew a knife and charged. Turning, Kadorax

tried awkwardly to get his trapped shield into position to deflect the knife blade headed for his gut, but he didn't need to. Lady Alexandrina's mace crashed into the jackal's side and sent it flying.

A faint black mist burst out in a gentle circle all around the knight. Some of it landed on Kadorax, and he immediately felt his muscles surge with vigor. The buff—flickering rapidly through his vision to ensure he remained undistracted—would only last a few seconds, but it was monstrous. His *Strength, Agility,* and *Spirit* were all raised by twelve, effectively giving him the raw stats of someone at least above level thirty-five.

The chain clattered to the ground at Kadorax's feet in no time thanks to the temporary boost to *Agility*. He glanced once toward the knight to make sure she had her jackal handled, then drew *Assir's Edge* and ran for Syzak. His jackal was restrained, though for every swipe of his claws, the shaman received an equally nasty bite.

Kadorax couldn't contain his *Strength*-fueled rage as he brought his weapon down on the side of the jackal's face. Skin and fur exploded in a rain of gore. *Assir's Edge* carved down to the jackal's collarbone, shattering it and then continuing another inch before coming to a halt.

Against the door, Brinna let out a stifled yelp. Something the jackal had cast was repelling her, knocking her backward with invisible force. Worse, the woman had dropped both of her daggers and was frantically clawing at her own eyes as though they were covered in insects and she were a terrified child.

Despite its magic, the jackal was outnumbered too severely to put up any fight beyond the single spell it had cast against Brinna. Lady Alexandrina arrived first, her mace catching the jackal fully in the stomach, and then Kadorax's blade sank through its kidneys.

When the last jackal stopped whimpering a few seconds later, Kadorax flicked the blood from his weapon and returned it to its sheath. "How's the cooldown on that aura?" he asked the knight.

She smiled, adjusting an armor plate that had been jostled slightly out of place. "Thirty-eight minutes. I probably didn't need it, but I also didn't want anyone to have to use any healing. Better to conserve the most important spells."

"Can't argue with that," Kadorax agreed. Healing, no matter what, was always the most important. Death meant respawning at level one, and respawning would all but ensure the jackals' victory over at least Oscine City, if not more.

More sounds of jackals came from the tunnel opposite the door.

"Can you open it?" Kadorax asked.

Brinna, closest to the handle, pulled it open. "Come on," she said, and the other three ran after her without a word.

"Two more ahead," Kadorax said as they arrived at the next room. He saw a pair of jackal outlines in his vision, though one of them was distinctly larger than the other. Fresh memories of the armored giant he had fought before flooded through his mind. Without a lucky bit of creative thinking, he would have been killed before ever even finding the fortress. He hoped—if it was another whirlwinding brute of a jackal—that having a veteran knight in his party would sway the balance in their favor.

Brinna burst through the next door without stopping to formulate a plan. Kadorax cursed her recklessness under his breath, but at the same time, he knew she was probably right not to wait. One of the jackals from the first room had escaped and presumably warned whatever awaited them, so maintaining speed was still likely their best plan of action.

Lady Alexandrina followed behind Brinna, fanning out to the right with her mace in front of her and her left shoulder lowered to tank any incoming blows. Behind the two women, Kadorax and Syzak hesitated for a second to figure out the general pattern of the coming fight.

The center of the room was dominated not by a gigantic, hulking jackal in thick armor, but a tall wizard surrounded by shimmering blue magical protection. In front of the wizard was the jackal warrior from the first room—already hard-pressed against Brinna's ferocious two-dagger assault.

"Go left," Kadorax said to his companion. The shaman nodded and darted for the left side of the room while Kadorax sprinted to the right, using Lady Alexandrina's imposing mass to hopefully hide himself from the wizard's view.

At once, Kadorax felt a growing magical presence under his feet. The sensation was strange, unlike anything he had felt before in his thirty years in Agglor, and the simple fact of the magic's uniqueness set Kadorax on edge. Whatever it was, it was coming from the wizard in the center, and it was spreading beneath him toward the edges of the room.

Lady Alexandrina swung in hard with her mace, the attack aimed for the jackal warrior's exhausted defenses. As she came forward, her feet slid out from under her, stealing her balance and sending her crashing to her back.

"Ice!" Syzak called from across the sparsely decorated room.

A cackle erupted from Kadorax's mouth. The magic he felt beneath him was a sheet of ice nearly invisible to his eyes—and completely harmless. The damage it would have imparted was negated by his *Stalwart Bracers*, and whatever unbalancing magic it possessed was denied by his *Steel Spats*. Still, that didn't mean the jackal wizard *knew* its spell wasn't effective.

Kadorax ripped the whip from his belt and cracked it twice at the wizard's head. When he had the creature's attention fully locked on him and no one else, he made a grand show of throwing his whip in the midst of losing his balance and falling forward, sliding up to the wizard's hairy canine feet.

The robed jackal took the bait. It instantly summoned another burst of magic, no doubt one of its most powerful spells, and sent the bolt rocketing expertly into Kadorax's skull.

The bastion didn't feel a thing. Instead, he slid his hand beneath his leather and to the hilt of *Assir's Edge*. When he launched upward with his blade aimed directly for the jackal wizard's lower gut, the creature reeled in surprise. The blue aura surrounding it crackled and reverberated, sending a powerful shock down Kadorax's arm that nearly made him drop his sword. *Nearly*.

Assir's Edge skewered the jackal where it stood. Thick canine blood flowed down the weapon's fuller. Even without a rank in *Bloodletting*, the hit would have been devastating.

Painfully muttering the words to a short spell, the jackal teleported away, but only far enough to remove itself from impalement. The wounded beast could barely stand. Blood cascaded down the front of its robe, and every ragged breath threatened to be its last.

Kadorax didn't relent. He glanced once to his side to make sure Brinna had handled the warrior, then dove in for the kill. Already on the correct side of the room, Syzak reached the wizard first. The shaman's claws wrapped around the wizard's torso, pinning it in place.

Another spell came to the wizard's furry snout. The ensuing words sounded more like an unrefined bark than language, and then everything in the room became instantly loud—deafening—and thrumming with force.

Kadorax closed his eyes to the power of the blast. His boots lost their purchase on the ground, and he was blown back several feet as if a hurricane wind had suddenly sprung up inside the small room.

When he finally opened his eyes once more, he was tangled with Alexandrina's armor, and they had both been more than dazed by the spell.

Kadorax could barely think. He tried to clear his mind and return his focus to the battle, but he simply could not remove the ringing from his skull long enough to do anything but stagger around like a drunken brawler in a pitch-black alleyway.

Somewhere else in the room, Brinna screamed. Kadorax managed to wrench open a single eye through sheer force of will. The woman had both hands clenched over her ears, and blood was coming through between her fingers. Looking for his shaman companion, Kadorax saw him standing alone, no longer holding the wizard at all, and his chest was drenched in gore.

"Sy . . . zak!" he tried to call. The sound of his own voice rattling between his ears brought a fresh wave of debilitating pain.

In the very center of the room, perhaps only two feet from where Lady Alexandrina was thrashing her body against the stone floor in pain, came a tendril of oily smoke. It was small, though the pungent smell of it further added to the torment of whatever spell had so thoroughly wracked everyone in the room.

"Get . . . Run!" Kadorax finally yelled.

The witch doctor from the previous day smiled at Kadorax. She wore a dozen or more voodoo dolls tied to her patchwork clothing. In her hand she held a long, slender needle the length of her forearm.

"I appreciate the return visit," she cooed, her accent reminiscent of northern Europe.

Kadorax wanted to smirk at the prospect of considering the witch doctor in Earth-born terms. It had been so long since he had seen the planet where he had been born that he wasn't sure he would even be able to tell one accent from another. Maybe his world didn't even exist, and Agglor was all that was left.

The pain in his head began to subside. Kadorax forced himself to his feet and tasted blood. It was coming from his nose and the bottoms of his eyes, running in twin rivulets down the inner lines of his face. Squaring his feet and preparing to take up the offensive once more, he couldn't think of anything witty to say in response to the witch doctor's unexpected arrival. A myriad of threats flickered through his consciousness, but none of them felt right.

"Good," he finally said. The word still brought a pang of fresh pain to his senses, though it was obvious that the effects of the spell were rapidly waning.

The witch doctor laughed. Two of her small voodoo dolls leapt from her clothing. One charged directly for Lady Alexandrina, still prone and struggling under the weight of her bulky armor. The second alighted on the witch doctor's outstretched palm like a dutiful pet awaiting a new command from its master. Using the slender metal needle, the witch doctor lanced the doll's midsection, pushing all the way until the pin burst through the opposite side.

Cage of Chaos erupted in a rapid flurry of random magical elements. Water, sprouting vines, and little bursts of congealed electricity fired out in all directions, each of them hitting nothing. At once, the spell was overwhelmed, and its day-long cooldown began ticking away seconds on Kadorax's character sheet.

Torturous pain accompanied the triggering of *Cage of Chaos.* It blossomed between Kadorax's pectoral muscles and cascaded through the rest of his torso, crushing him back down to the ground and his knees. He coughed, and blood splattered the stones in front of him.

Laughing all the while, the witch doctor removed her needle and struck again, burying it in the doll's left leg.

Kadorax screamed. The pain was relentless, unbearable, and it threatened to snatch away his consciousness with every passing second. Then, for a split second, it relented.

Syzak had redirected the woman's focus with a deep bite to her side, *Paralytic Envenomation* coursing from the venom sacs in his mouth and into the woman's veins. Then a violent thrust of repelling magic shot Syzak across the room, and the pain in Kadorax's body redoubled in strength.

The scream that came from the bastion was weak and muffled by blood, the action itself eliciting new ruptures in Kadorax's mind.

Encroaching Insanity: Rank 4 flashed across the very bottom of Kadorax's bleary, delusional vision.

"Run from this place," a soft female voice whispered into his mind. "Turn back! Leave! You are unworthy. Save yourself! Run!"

Another gentle voice joined the mutterings in Kadorax's mind, and he could not tell if the male newcomer was a result of his class-specific debuff or something the witch doctor was doing. "Escape while you can. Be gone. Leave at once! You will not survive!" the male voice said, its words overlapping with those of the female.

Both voices joined together, still barely audible: "Run! Get out! Do not sacrifice your friends for the sake of your hubris. There is nothing here but death. Run!" they whispered together.

The voices wouldn't relent. They repeated their mantras, though they separated from each other in pacing, so all their words jumbled together in a confusing auditory blur.

As Kadorax writhed on the ground, both Brinna and the Priorate Knight commander found their feet. Lady Alexandrina didn't hesitate to activate a talent. *Behold the Blessing of the Pure*, an eighth-rank spell, burst out of her like a golden nova of warm sunlight. Every ally it touched—all but Syzak, crumpled against the wall and out of the spell's small reach—felt a burst of healing magic cascade through their bodies.

Suddenly, Kadorax's mind was at ease. The restless chanting came to an abrupt halt. His muscles relaxed, and the pain that had laid him low subsided to something tolerable.

"For the priory!" the woman shouted, activating a personal buff that added a wreath of deadly magical spikes to her mace. The spikes were as long as swords, and they pointed out in every direction like a jagged pinwheel of death suddenly fixed to the top of her weapon.

When the mace head connected with the witch doctor, her image flickered twice before dissipating, and then it reappeared in a corner of the room farthest from the action.

The witch doctor's expression showed fear. Taking his time on unsteady legs, Kadorax got to his feet and grabbed his sword. Next to him, Brinna also recovered.

Before they could advance, the witch doctor flickered

again and reappeared behind the pair, a bolt of magic already loosed from her fingertips. The attack, a slender fireball coated in a ward-piercing yellow shell, hit Kadorax directly in the chest. Luckily, there was enough strength behind the magical assault to trigger *Rune of Perseverance*, and almost all of the attack's efficacy was wasted.

Kadorax lunged forward with the point of *Assir's Edge* thrusting horizontally as a fencer might, but the witch doctor was too quick. She leapt away again and rematerialized in another corner, more magic springing from her hands to fill the room. All the while, the woman laughed.

With a grin, Lady Alexandrina stepped into the path of the new bolts.

Kadorax knew he had to take a risk. If the witch doctor could keep zapping herself around the room and firing off magical attacks, he'd never land a solid hit. And a single solid hit was all he knew he would need.

Charging at the witch doctor's latest image, Kadorax swung wildly and activated *Chaos Step* at the exact same time. As expected, the voodoo woman flickered out of existence. When she appeared in the only remaining corner she had not previously occupied, Kadorax teleported into existence directly behind her.

Rallying Strike caught her in the left shoulder, and *Assir's Edge*—enhanced due to the damage Kadorax had already taken at the woman's hands—ripped through bone, muscle, and sinew until it came out from her armpit. The severed limb fell to the ground with a spout of blood.

Once more, screams filled the small room, though their only epicenter was the witch doctor's twisted mouth.

Suddenly, there were two witch doctors in the room. The one Kadorax had struck continued to teleport around, dragging a faint curtain of illuminating orange dust everywhere she went. Another one, still with both arms attached to her torso, appeared near the first door, crouching over a small collection of voodoo dolls and other arcane implements, a terrified expression on her face. *Rallying Strike* had exposed the true witch doctor, and the woman's best line of defense was gone.

"There!" Kadorax yelled, pointing to the huddled woman wreathed in orange.

Brinna was the closest, and she didn't waste a single second. In the blink of an eye, two daggers rammed down into the witch doctor's back on either side of her spine. Lady Alexandrina arrived with her mace, still encircled by giant steel spikes, and she swung the weapon with her whole body, adding every ounce of her impressive weight to the strike.

Kadorax watched as the brutal weapon connected. In one moment, the witch doctor was there, crouched over the ground and fiddling with her tools, and the next . . . she was everywhere all at once. Alexandrina's rotating mace had obliterated her body, and the spikes coming out of the sides had served almost as a kind of kitchen implement, scattering a handful of the shredded voodoo woman's chunks across the room.

Again resorting to Earth-born analogies to reconcile what he saw, Kadorax had to imagine that the devastation wrought by the knight's enchanted mace had resulted in a scene similar to a soldier stepping on a landmine. The witch doctor had been reduced to a vaguely human puzzle, and all the pieces had been equally distributed around the floor.

The original image, one Kadorax suspected to have been a decoy all along, was nowhere to be seen.

"Holy shit that hit hard," the bastion exclaimed.

Lady Alexandrina beamed. "The other knights might prefer their shields and their tactics, but nothing beats a good ring of metal to the center of a body. She won't be coming back."

"If that was the real witch doctor," Kadorax added. "Hopefully it was. And hopefully they don't have others."

Slowly rising from his crumpled position against the wall, Syzak cast one of his healing spells to undo some of his wounds. He had taken the brunt of the incoming physical damage, but Kadorax had a feeling that the mental effects of the voodoo attack he had undergone would linger for some time. In fact, his head still throbbed with pain whenever he moved, and spoken words sounded distorted and too close to his ears when he heard them.

Still, he had to press on.

"Only one way out," Brinna said, her eyes locked on the door leading deeper into the complex.

"Hold on a minute," Kadorax told her. He riffled through the dead jackal's remains, searching for loot. Fighting against such generally unarmed or poorly armed opponents meant he hadn't been able to enjoy the material spoils of war as much as he would have liked. In the glory days of the Blackened Blades, skulking through the shadows to fulfill contracts and eliminate wealthy, human targets had meant fat purses and magical items after every fight.

Sadly, Kadorax found nothing of value on the dead jackal soldier, and the voodoo witch's small collection of roughly made dolls didn't feel like something he wanted to take. "Alright," he said with a sigh. "Nothing worthwhile."

Brinna hadn't taken too many hits, and her spritely eagerness clearly overcame any sense of fear she might have had.

Something about the woman's movements simply wasn't right. She was reckless, and her violent determination was starting to skirt the border between bravery and idiocy. "Hey," Kadorax half shouted, still keeping his voice low. He grabbed the rogue by her arm and spun her back. "Hold on a minute. What the hell's going on? Just plan on running into whatever comes next without a single shred of strategy?"

Lady Alexandrina took a step forward, arms crossed over her breastplate.

Her eyes darting all across the room, Brinna didn't respond.

"What the hell is it? Possession? Some kind of mind control?" the bastion demanded. He called Brinna's character sheet to his vision. She was still regarded as friendly, so he could see everything that was there.

No debuffs. Any mind control or similar magic would have either hid her sheet or been clearly displayed as a negative magical effect, showing a name, duration, and a general description of the ability. Brinna's sheet showed nothing nefarious.

"I . . ." she said quietly. Some of the fire had receded from her eyes.

"I can purge any unholy spirits within her body, but I see no such evil," Lady Alexandrina stated.

The three of them stared at Brinna as if she was some sort of failed experiment.

One of the rogue's daggers fell from her hand. "I just . . . I can't," she muttered.

"What is it?" Kadorax asked, a hand still on her shoulder. Without a debuff present on her character sheet, his suspicion and anger had faded into concern.

"I just want it to end. The killing and the war. Think of

everyone who's already lost. My son . . ." Her voice trailed off, and her eyes dropped down to stare at the ground.

"Jackals didn't kill your son, Brinna," the bastion reminded her.

She nodded, then stooped down to retrieve her fallen dagger. "But we can save more sons, can't we?" She straightened and slipped both of her daggers into her belt. "Just need to end the fighting . . . to end the jackals. All of them."

Kadorax wasn't entirely convinced he believed the woman's sentiment. Time was running out, however, so he decided not to push the issue until later, preferably back at the priory and without the threat of a hundred enemies coming down on their heads. "Stay behind me. I'll take the lead," he stated, his voice leaving no room for argument.

"How many jackals in the next chamber?" Syzak asked from the rear of the group.

Focusing his vision, Kadorax counted twelve figures, but they were below, not in the next immediate chamber. "They're under us. Maybe the next chamber leads down."

"If the leader is dead, when should we return to the surface to rouse Reinhardt and his contingent? We could storm the whole compound," Alexandrina offered.

"Not yet." Kadorax watched the glowing outline of the jackals. They were standing in a circular pattern, moving somewhat, though not much. "They're doing something. I don't know what."

"Remember the temple? The first Gar'kesh?" Syzak asked. His voice wavered slightly as he spoke.

Shaking his head, Kadorax pushed the memories of his own death far from his mind. "If they're summoning a new Gar'kesh, we need to stop it. Let's go."

Kadorax pushed into the next hallway, the other three

following close behind. The final room, it seemed, was the witch doctor's personal quarters. A bed rested against one wall with a short table next to it, and scraps of food were scattered all around. "Alright," Kadorax said, more to himself than the others. "Search for anything useful. Find some clues. Maybe the witch doctor was their leader. Maybe she wasn't."

Within a few moments, the four of them had the witch doctor's quarters completely upturned. For their brief efforts, the group was sparsely rewarded. Kadorax held the only possible clue. "Any ideas what it is?" he asked.

Syzak took the small carved rectangle of wood from Kadorax's hand. "Not magical," he said, confirming the bastion's cursory conclusion. Had the item been an enchanted relic like a wand or a rune, its stats and information would have been readily available for anyone to see.

"Perhaps a ritual component?" Kadorax offered.

"Makes sense," the shaman replied. "We—"

Sounds came from the chamber they had just left.

Kadorax tossed the strange object to Alexandrina, who quickly dropped it into a narrow pouch hanging from her sword belt. "Take it back to the priory. I'm sure someone there knows a thing or two about ritual artifacts from the northern wilds."

The only remaining exit, hard to clearly see in the minimal torchlight available to the room, was a ladder bolted into the wooden wall. It led down through a roughly hewn opening without any trap door or other barrier that might have been used to lock it.

"Down?" Brinna asked, some of her previous vitality making a return to her voice.

"We need to make it quick," Alexandrina answered. She peered down the ladder, but the only light from below was coming from a side, not directly at the bottom. The heavily armored woman placed a foot on the first rung of the ladder. When she placed her second foot next to the first, the wooden rung snapped clean through at the middle. She let out a sigh, looked back to Kadorax standing over her, then pushed off.

She landed with a thunderous crash at the bottom of the ladder. Kadorax leapt after her, catching himself on the bottom few rungs before landing on Alexandrina's shoulders and skittering to the floor.

The chamber beneath the fortress was exactly what Kadorax had feared.

A ring of robed jackal magic users stood around a stone altar. Runes had been painted on one of the walls—and they were runes the bastion recognized well. Without *Guardian of the Deep* to fight another Gar'kesh for him, he knew a successful summoning would spell his doom.

"Hurry!" Kadorax called to the rest of his party. He didn't wait for Alexandrina to get up from the ground or for his comrades above to join before charging at the nearest jackal priest.

He caught the creature off guard, and *Assir's Edge* sent the beast collapsing to the ground with a single strike. Then the rest of the jackals turned, some of them holding wands, others casting with their own talents.

In the span of a few heartbeats, all manner of spells rocketed toward Kadorax, pummeling his body. Wave after wave of elemental attacks cascaded down on him. *Cage of Chaos* had already been consumed by the witch doctor's voodoo, so no magical retort met any of the incoming spells. A small patch of snaking liquid fire ran between his leather armor and his skin. Kadorax screamed and yelled, rolling to his side to try and extinguish the flames.

HEAVY ARMOR

In the small area where the ladder met the ground, a white light began to blossom and grow. Soon it enveloped the entire room, knocking back the jackals and forcing them to close their eyes against its brilliance, interrupting the relentless number of spells flying from their hairy paws.

Lady Alexandrina was hovering several inches above the ground. From her back, ethereal wings spread out to the very edges of the room. Her head was wreathed in light, and a shimmering beam of it lanced out from her chest like an arcane spotlight. Everywhere the beam touched, jackals burned. They shrieked and screamed—and then, one by one, they fell silent.

The woman had activated her *Knight's Superior Talent*, and it was one Kadorax had never witnessed before. Then again, he had to remind himself that Alexandrina was a bit on the unorthodox side when it came to the Priorate Knights. She didn't use a shield, and that fact alone made her an anomaly among her own kind.

On the rare occasions Kadorax had borne witness to other *Superior Talents* from knights, he had only seen one: *Exalted Shieldwall*. It was a talent designed to work with a cohesive unit, ringing the knights' shields together with magical force and creating a virtually impenetrable wall. The talent Alexandrina had activated was completely different in nature, obviously designed for single combat.

Kadorax quickly called the woman's character sheet to his vision to see what she had cast:

Holy Oath of Divine Cataclysm, Fulfilled: Rank 8 - Sheathed in pure light, you become a beacon of devastation, bringing world-ending annihilation to those who would stand against you. Allies caught in the tempestuous raiment's presence are healed and restored in proportion to the judgment they've brought to your foes.

Knight's Superior Talent. Effect: Profound. Cooldown: Oath of Divine Cataclysm Fulfillment.

In his three decades of near-constant training, learning, and fighting on Agglor, Kadorax had never seen a single skill that required an "oath" to be fulfilled, whatever that specific term meant. Watching the jackals fall so quickly—so *easily*—to the spell, he trembled in fear. For the moment, he knew he was considered an ally of the Priorate Knights, perhaps even a favored member to an extent . . . and if he ever found himself once more in their disfavor, standing toe to toe with Lady Alexandrina would certainly bring about his doom.

The small underground chamber was silent before Kadorax could fully come to terms with the power standing before him. Every jackal was dead. The woman, still hovering above the ground by the force of magical wings, turned back to regard him. Her eyes were vacant, solid white spheres of pure magic, and they radiated so much power that Kadorax found his muscles shaking as he tried to get up from the ground.

"Rise," Alexandrina commanded him. The inside of her mouth glowed with radiance as she spoke, letting out little wisps of energy with every word.

Slowly, Kadorax placed his feet beneath him and stood to his full height, *Assir's Edge* still in his hand. The jackals' magical assault had pummeled him, though he felt none of it. All the damage he had sustained had been washed away by the talent.

"What . . . how?" Kadorax incoherently stammered. His mind was still too awestruck to process the scene.

The woman reached out a hand, and two small puffs of light wafted through the air behind her movements. "You've witnessed more of the Priorate Knights' true power than anyone outside of our organization," she stated.

Kadorax nodded. He wanted to say something, to offer some words to hopefully solidify his position within the organization and ensure he'd remain on their good side, but nothing came to his mind. Only fear.

"Now you know certain things about our power. There's no going back." The woman's wings slowly began to fade from shimmering white to a grayish translucence until they were gone altogether. The light within her eyes and surrounding her head took longer to vanish, but then they were gone as well, and the armored knight stood as she had before: still formidable, but far from a god.

Kadorax nodded. "As you say, my lady," he said. He swallowed hard.

Behind him in the chamber, Brinna and Syzak stood still, mouths agape, both of them quiet and trembling.

"Alright," Alexandrina said with a heavy sigh. She turned back to the rest of the room. "We need to figure out what they were doing down here."

Stepping to the woman's side, Kadorax ran a hand along the stone altar that dominated the area. He struggled to switch his mind so quickly from awe and terror back to the mission at hand. "We've . . . uh, seen one of these before. They use them to summon Gar'kesh—or at least that's our best guess."

Alexandrina nodded. She wore a hard scowl that looked chiseled from stone. "Sacrifice feels like the likely method. I've heard of magic like that before. Dark priests sacrificing others to summon their demon pets. Do you think the jackals could be . . ." Her voice trailed off as realization dawned on her features.

"The princess," Syzak hesitantly finished for her.

Everyone was quiet for a long moment. Finally, Kadorax

heard noise coming from above and broke the silence. "Do you think the princess, by virtue of her station, would improve the quality of the summoning somehow?" he asked.

Though it was obvious that no one in the room had any definitive knowledge, they all offered their various assents in turn. It was the only logical reason for capturing someone that would bring down the full wrath of Kingsgate against jackal holdings. If the beasts had just needed random souls to offer to their spells, they could have remained in Agglor's shadows for centuries.

"We need to go," Kadorax said. The movement from above was getting louder.

Syzak glanced up the ladder for a moment, paused to listen, then turned back. "A handful above, maybe more."

Kadorax checked his character sheet. The potion from Kingsgate would have normally lasted an hour, but by spreading it between himself, his blade, and the others, it was already almost expired. Still, he had enough time left to map out their escape with his magically enhanced vision.

"Only one way out, I think," the bastion said. "Back up the ladder. They're coming."

Brinna, who had just a moment before gotten to the bottom, quickly spun and leapt to grab the rungs higher up. She pulled herself rapidly toward the top of the ladder, Syzak hot on her heels. Kadorax went next, and he could feel the old wood straining under his grasp. "Be careful," he said over his shoulder.

Alexandrina nodded. She waited to grab onto the ladder until everyone else was off at the top, and still it buckled. Her armor was threatening to bring it down. If she fell, there'd be no way out.

With a flurry of blades, Brinna erupted into the upper

room. She took half a dozen hits, *most* of them superficial, as she gave absolutely no thought to her own safety. A wild fire had taken hold of her eyes once more, though at least for the time being, she was winning.

Syzak tackled the next jackal waiting for them at the top. Knocking the beast to the ground, he activated *Paralytic Envenomation*, made sure he left a full dose in the creature's veins, then leapt to his feet to defend himself from the rest.

When Kadorax emerged from the ladder, there were only two jackals left for him to fight. The first he skewered on *Assir's Edge*, and tinges of flame leapt from the potion coating his blade. The second took a ragged swipe at Brinna's head. The woman ducked underneath the attack and then came up hard, lodging both of her daggers in the beast's abdomen.

The immediate battle quieted, but sounds of more jackals came through the tunnels.

Kadorax's enhanced vision timed out just as he thought to count the incoming enemies.

"Let's go!" he shouted, pulling on Alexandrina's breastplate to help her emerge from the ladder.

The four intruders ran for the exit, Kadorax taking the lead. He barely had enough time to swing his shield around in front of him before the first defender crashed into it.

Kadorax yelled and slammed with his shield, then stabbed over the top of the metal rim. Experience points flashed by his vision in bright yellow. A few more jackals— even the lowly, expendable warriors—and he'd reach level thirteen. First, he needed to escape with his life.

A line of jackals poured down the tunnel. As far as Kadorax could tell, they were all basic soldiers, but he couldn't be certain. And in the tight quarters, it didn't matter. Their corpses would pile up, blocking the only escape route, and all four of them would be trapped and easily killed. Images of Brinna drowning a score of trapped jackals flashed through his head. He didn't think it would be water the jackals would use to kill them if they became trapped, but smoke didn't sound any more pleasant.

"Sy!" the bastion yelled without turning back. "Both traps to the right! Make a hole!"

At once, *Snake Trap* bored a horizontal divot about a foot deep into the wall. *Rat Trap* followed quickly behind it, and then Kadorax made his own tunnel with *The Obsidian Well*.

The freshly minted passage wasn't wide, but with all three spells properly aligned, it connected to the first armory room right next to the main entrance. "Everyone in!"

One of the jackal soldiers landed a solid claw on Kadorax's shoulder as he charged into the makeshift escape route. Brinna and Syzak followed close behind. Encumbered by her armor, Lady Alexandrina was too slow getting to the tunnel. The first of Syzak's traps hadn't dissipated yet, but time was running out. The woman fought furiously, bashing aside jackal after jackal and slowly pulling herself into the tight squeeze at the same time. She made it entirely into the rock cavern as *Spike Trap* ran out of time. The wall at her feet suddenly reappeared.

An unfortunate jackal was caught almost perfectly at the waist by the reforming wall. Temporarily unaware of its missing legs, the beast kept clawing forward, slashing at Alexandrina's armor until its life force finally gave out. The woman kicked it brutally in the head, then turned onto her chest to continue the arduous climb before *The Obsidian Well* expired, leaving her forever encased in the bedrock of the jackal fortress.

At the end of the tunnel, Kadorax frantically searched

for whatever it was the spell had conjured for him to find. He thanked his luck that there hadn't been a scorpion—or any other magical creature intent on killing—lurking inside like before, but that meant the spell had brought forth a "wonder" according to the tooltip information.

Finally, Kadorax caught the dark glint of a jagged piece of metal that was not obsidian. It appeared to be brass, perhaps copper, though the dark and glittering tunnel made it hard to pick out amongst the broken rocks. Helping Alexandrina with his left hand, Kadorax reached in with his right and grabbed the small trinket from between a cluster of crystals.

The sounds of jackals pouring into the tight halls of the fortress pushed thoughts of the unknown relic far from Kadorax's mind. They had circumvented the main bulk of the horde, but they were still far from safety. "We need to alert Reinhardt and the others," he commanded, already heading for the exit not far away.

"Wait . . ." Alexandrina called, her voice pained and weak. Behind her, *The Obsidian Well* evaporated. Hard stone filled the tunnel as though it had never been there in the first place. The knight slumped against it, her legs out in front of her. Blood was pooling beneath a stump where her right boot used to be. The heavy armor had been shorn in half when *Rat Trap* had expired, leaving her with little more than a heel on her right foot.

"Shit," Kadorax growled and jammed a hand under the woman's armpit. He tried to pull her from the ground, but she was too heavy. "Syzak, help me with her armor. Leave her breastplate."

Weakly, Alexandrina nodded and began unstrapping the tassets from her waist.

"Jackals," Brinna announced. She held the only available tunnel by herself, a dagger in each hand.

"Hold them off!" Kadorax yelled.

Alexandrina's heavy breastplate clattered to the ground at her side. Kadorax and Syzak each took one of her arms, and they managed to pull the knight to a standing position, though she had no balance and quickly fell backward into the wall once more.

"Leave me. I'll only slow you down," she said through gritted teeth.

"More coming!" Brinna yelled.

Kadorax scoured his mind for a solution. None of his abilities were designed to hold back a mob of jackals. As an assassin, he would have been able to teleport the woman at least a short distance to somewhere safe, but a Bastion of Chaos Incarnate had no such talent.

Just then, a war cry sounded from somewhere in the darkness outside the jackal fortress. "For the knights!" quickly followed the bellowing cry, and Kadorax saw a buff to both his *Strength* and *Agility* flash across his vision.

Sergeant Reinhardt and his contingent were barreling toward the fortress entrance, the high-level knight-tactician leading the way with a curved pick in each hand. His face was wild, vicious even, a stark contrast to the rigidly determined corps of soldiers only a step behind him.

"Brinna! Fall back!" Kadorax yelled. He couldn't tell if the woman had seen the incoming aid or not, and judging by her relentless attacks, she wasn't checking over her shoulder very often. Finally, Kadorax grabbed the back of the rogue's shirt and ripped her from the jackal mass, allowing a handful of the hairy beasts to fully emerge.

Reinhardt and his crew smashed into the horde a

split second later. Against fresh knights and without their magic-using leaders, the rank and file jackal soldiers didn't stand a chance.

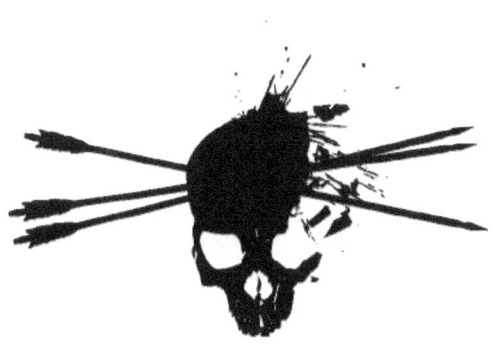

CHAPTER 7

Back at the Priorate Knights' headquarters, Kadorax was greeted by an unexpected scene. A few unarmored knights stood casually around an outdoor fire, and their company was rather strange: Atticus stood to one side with a wooden cup, occasionally taking slow sips without adding anything to the lively conversation, and across from him was Elise, a goblet in her right hand and an impressive array of daggers glinting in the firelight around her waist.

"We need a chaplain," Kadorax called before addressing his rival's unanticipated presence.

The fireside gathering turned as one, and then two of the knights rushed to Lady Alexandrina's side to bring her into the priory for proper healing.

"Well, well, well," Elise mused, smiling a sinister smile. A Blackened Blade dressed in dark leather stepped out of the shadows to join his leader at the fire.

An overt threat, Kadorax thought, but he also knew that

positions of power didn't remain in the same hands for long without extensive security measures. The assassin behind her was certainly adequate security.

"Elise," he stated flatly. "What brings you to Oscine City? Decided to join the war?"

The woman took another sip from her goblet and shook her head. "The war already came to Darkarrow," she cryptically answered.

"What do you mean?" Kadorax took a step toward the fire, and the others made room for him, Syzak, and Brinna.

Elise downed the rest of her drink and handed her goblet off to the Blackened Blade lackey waiting patiently at her elbow. "I take it you were unsuccessful? You failed to find the princess, yes?"

Kadorax nodded. "Not yet."

The woman let out a long sigh. Meeting Kadorax's eyes for the first time, she said, "We know why they need her. One of my crews captured a group of jackal priests. They need royal blood for a ritual. They're going to sacrifice her in the north to summon their god. It turns out the Gar'kesh are lesser denizens of the jackal hierarchy. Their god will make the Gar'kesh look like ants."

"And Darkarrow? There's been an attack?"

The woman's expression clouded. "Sacked," she stated. "Partially razed. What's left is in poor shape."

Kadorax waited a long moment as he considered the implications. The jackals knew who would be best positioned to resist their plans, and they had acted accordingly, eliminating the strongest threats before they could manifest. That explained attacks against both Priorate Knight and Blackened Blade strongholds.

After a while, Syzak was first to break the heavy silence.

"So what's the next move? Continue to hunt the princess here in Oscine City?"

Surprisingly, it was Atticus who responded. "The knights can continue the hunt here, I believe. More specialized skills are needed elsewhere. Your skills and mine. *Our* skills."

"Remember that temple you raided?" Elise asked, her smile absolutely devious.

Kadorax dipped his head, knowing full well what the woman was getting to. "The first Gar'kesh. The temple where we . . . met our ends."

"Exactly," Elise went on. "*That* is the temple where they're going to take the princess. *That* is where they need to be to conduct their ritual."

"And bring about the end of Agglor," Brinna added.

Her words hung in the air like poison suspended in a cloudy drink, marring the already dreary atmosphere.

"So . . . we're going back to Darkarrow, right?" Brinna asked.

"Clever girl," the leather-clad leader of the Blackened Blades answered. "You, Kadorax, Syzak, maybe a couple of the stronger knights. And me, of course. We're going to find that temple before the jackals can complete their ritual. It will be heavily protected, make no mistake about that, and there's a good chance we all die before we get close."

Atticus cleared his throat. "Do not forget about me," he offered before downing the rest of his drink and then throwing his cup into the fire, where it bounced off the burning logs.

Everyone's eyes found their way to the old man. "You're coming along?" Kadorax asked, though he didn't think he was opposed to the idea. He did, however, have more than a few lingering questions about the man's faculties.

Atticus beamed from ear to ear. "Of course, of course! So much to study, so much inquiry!"

Turning to Elise, Kadorax raised an eyebrow. "That a good idea?" he asked under his breath. If the old man across the fire could hear him, he didn't show any sign of caring.

Elise shrugged. "If he wants a ride, I won't stop him. And you heard him. He said his skills will be valuable."

"Speaking of our transport, any ideas?" the bastion asked.

"Your friend Lord Percival. I'm told his ship was destroyed, but there are others that survived. I suppose a little military requisition won't hurt anyone. Surely the esteemed citizens of Oscine City will not mind, will they?" Another member of the Blackened Blades, a young initiate by his looks, came hurrying out of the priory to offer Elise a full cup. Smiling, she took it and dismissed the recruit with a wave of her gloved hand.

"When do we head out?" the bastion asked with a sigh. He knew the trip from Oscine City to Darkarrow wouldn't be long enough to allow his aching joints enough time to recover. With the magical aid of one of the chaplains, he would recover much quicker, but he shook his head at the thought. They were needed elsewhere, he knew. Other men and women had suffered much worse injuries than his generally battered body had sustained. Alexandrina would require all of their efforts if her foot was to be restored.

With her drink in her hand, Elise turned from the fire to enter the priory. "We leave at first light. Be on the shore before dawn," she said over her shoulder.

She sauntered into the building as though she were the prior himself, exuding an air of utter confidence and authority. Kadorax wondered if he had ever been so arrogant during his years in her position, but he didn't know the answer. If he had, would Syzak have bothered to tell him? The snake-man's loyalty was unshakeable. Anyone else under his command at Darkarrow would probably have been too scared to speak up.

Shaking the notion from his head, Kadorax went to follow Elise, intent on catching some much-needed sleep before finding Ayers in the morning. In addition to the gear he hoped would be waiting for him, he had reached level thirteen and had several choices he needed to make with a clearer head. He fetched the little piece of brass from his pocket and inspected it as he walked, turning it over in his hands and feeling the smoothness of its surface. It didn't open or have any sort of ornamentation like a locket or amulet might have had, though it was essentially in the correct shape. Coming from *The Obsidian Well*, he knew it would be something extraordinary. Whether or not "extraordinary" would be synonymous with useful, he had no idea.

The next morning, Kadorax awoke an hour or so before dawn with a heavy hand on his shoulder. He opened his eyes, rubbed the sleep from the corners of them, and saw Ayers staring down at him, a smile plastered on his face.

"Heard you were heading out soon. Thought I'd get to you before you left," the burly smith said quietly.

"Yeah, just give me a minute," Kadorax told him. He rolled over in his tiny cot and stretched his back, yawning. When he finally got his neck to pop a third time and relieve the built-up tension there, he sat up and rubbed the muscles of his arms.

Ayers was practically giddy. "Hurry, Kadorax. You'll want to see what I've made," the big man said. He turned and scampered from the communal sleeping chambers without waiting to be sure the bastion was behind him.

Kadorax followed Ayers into the priory's smithy. His eagerness to acquire more loot served as a fine stimulant to push away all the sleepiness remaining in his body. "What have you come up with?" he asked, gazing around the small, smoky room. "I take it you rather enjoy having your own anvil and forge once more. I'd say the Priorate Knights have a lot more to work with than your floating station aboard the *Grim Sleeper*."

Nodding enthusiastically, Ayers brushed his hands clean on his oily apron. "I used that last enchanted hammer. I couldn't bear the thought of a war going on right outside the priory doors while a perfectly good enchanted hammer just sat on a shelf and rusted. It isn't right. And if anyone can put it to good use, that someone would be you."

"Truly, Ayers, I can't thank you enough. I'm sure there would be more than a handful of rather qualified knights within these walls," Kadorax said honestly. He thought of Lady Alexandrina. At level forty-four, he knew her gear must have been absolutely exquisite. He hoped Reinhardt and his crew had been able to bring most of it back, but those veteran knights had not returned by the time he had gone to sleep, so he didn't know.

Ayers, moving like a holy man reverently handling sacred relics, brought a breastplate, pauldrons, a gorget, and tassets up from the other side of his anvil. They were all wrapped in oilcloths, and the way the man gingerly pulled them from the armor made Kadorax think of a surgeon pulling blood-soaked dressings from a wound.

Apocryphal Plate of the Forsaken Lady (Forsaken Lady Set 2 / 3) - Grants the wearer Conjure Unholy Aberration: Rank 3, +4 Fate, and provides a significant reduction to incoming blunt, piercing, and magical damage. Effect: Profound. Passive while worn. Set bonus: Wearing two pieces of the Forsaken Lady's Armament grants the wearer the ability to curse enemies, causing them to temporarily forget their allegiance and fight the nearest living target.

Kadorax gawked as he read the armor's stats a second time. Still unbelieving, he read the description a third time, then finally met Ayers's beaming smile with one of his own. "You've outdone yourself, Ayers," he said. "Honestly, I mean that. I had cleared level seventy in my past life, and the armorsmith at Darkarrow had crafted some truly profound pieces . . . but such a set of armor from someone more accustomed to making nails and horseshoes than breastplates is truly remarkable. I mean that. You have my eternal thanks."

Kadorax flicked his vision to his pair of new abilities, eager to read their descriptions:

Conjure Unholy Aberration: Rank 3 - Produce a diabolical amalgamation of bones, dirt, and sinew at the target location. The golem will flail recklessly, destroying and distracting enemies along a random path before dissipating. Effect: moderate. Cooldown: 1 day.

Forsaken Lady's Condemnation: Rank 10 - If the target's Spirit is less than 20, they forget their allegiance and attack the nearest living target until killed. Effect: profound. Cooldown: 1 day.

Underneath the two new abilities granted by the *Forsaken Lady* set bonus, Kadorax had no new skills to unlock on account of attaining a new level, but he could upgrade *Chaos Shock, Bastion Weapon Proficiency, Bathed in Silence*, or *The Obsidian Well*. All four of the talents were still fairly low, so none of the next ranks brought about a whole lot of interesting boons. After considering the choice for a few moments, Kadorax unlocked *Bastion Weapon Proficiency: Rank 2*. Increasing the ability's rank would allow *Blade Training (Light)* to progress faster and unlock more powerful martial techniques, and he hoped something in the talent's path would be related to using a shield.

For the unused ability point, Kadorax discarded his previous sentiment and dropped it into *Strength*, instantly feeling his tired muscles swell with newfound power. He knew he needed more *Spirit*, but there simply weren't enough stat points to satisfy every deficiency. And Syzak would be focusing on *Spirit*, he told himself. He could keep pumping points into *Strength*.

"How many days do you think you'll be back at Darkarrow?" the smith asked, pulling Kadorax's attention back to the present.

Kadorax wasn't sure how long he'd been standing there, awkwardly staring at his character sheet and marveling over his new abilities. He shook his head and dismissed the information, meeting Ayers's eyes. "I don't know. Supposedly the jackals need a specific temple near there, one I happen to know from before."

"And you trust that woman?" Ayers went on quietly.

"Not for a second." Kadorax rubbed a hand across his chin as he thought of the woman running the Blackened Blades. She was ruthless, though that quality wasn't necessarily a bad one, but she was also inherently distrusting, and that made her unpredictable. "The jackal threat looms over everyone equally. She doesn't stand to gain anything by a betrayal . . ." Kadorax knew the words weren't exactly true as soon as they left his mouth.

The smith crossed his arms and huffed. "Be careful

around her. She's hiding something. I'm sure you know it just as well as I do."

Surprised by the bluntness of Ayers's observation, Kadorax called the man's stats to his vision. He had progressed rather quickly—likely in part to using two enchanted hammers in such rapid succession—and his *Spirit* was at an impressive nineteen. The stat's primary functions revolved around insight, foresight, and instinct, so it made sense that the smith could tell things about Elise that others could not so readily discern. Throughout his three decades in Agglor, Kadorax had never focused much on *Spirit* as it had not been a huge aspect of life as an assassin, and the most useful aspects of the stat came when assessing the motives of targets with a lower score. That meant Kadorax would have had to nearly specialize in it to gain the most benefit, so he had always let *Spirit* fall subordinate to things like *Strength* and *Agility*.

"What exactly did you notice about her?" Kadorax asked. He made a larger gesture than necessary when dismissing the man's character sheet to politely let him know he had checked his stats.

Leaning in close, Ayers kept his voice low despite few others being awake in the priory. "She arrived with a few of her goons, but there was someone else with them. A mage by the looks, but I couldn't be certain. Might have just been spell scrolls."

One of Kadorax's eyebrows arched in response. "Oh? You saw magic?" He thought of all the magic users he had employed at Darkarrow. Wizards, rare in general, had never been among the ranks, though more common classes with greater combat application such as mystics, shamans, clerics, illusionists, and theurgists had been great assets to the

Blackened Blades. If one such magic user was traveling with Elise, it would make sense. It also wouldn't pose any particularly new threat. The woman was the walking embodiment of a threat, with or without magical allies.

"When they landed, I was down on the shore, gathering some driftwood for the forge, and I don't think they saw me. A mirror, teleportation magic, and some kind of bird familiar: sounds like a wizard to me." Ayers looked around nervously as he finished, then stretched his back and moved about the room in an obvious attempt to appear nonchalant.

Kadorax nodded. "You're probably right. Mirrors are the domain of wizards and archivists, and I couldn't imagine Elise having need of someone to organize her books or copy scrolls. Thanks for the information. I'll keep an eye on her for certain. Oh, and one more thing." He plucked the small bit of brass he had taken from *The Obsidian Well* and placed it down on Ayers's anvil.

"Where'd you find that?" the man asked, inquisitively rolling it across his fingers.

"I said I'd look out for some new materials. Grabbed it after making a bit of magic. *The Obsidian Well* says it can summon 'wonders or terrors' when cast. I found that inside. Any ideas?" Kadorax watched with curiosity as the smith returned the brass to the anvil and grabbed a hammer. Ayers began lightly tapping on the metal, and it rang just like any ordinary.

After a few taps and no results, Ayers returned the hammer to a hook and shrugged. "I'll see if I can do something with it. Might be useful, but nothing comes up when I try to access it."

Kadorax always thought it odd when Agglor-born people referenced seeing character sheets and other in-game statistics. The way they mentioned the world's game-like mechanics was so bizarrely casual to him that it always reminded him that there was another world out there, the plane of his birth, and all the people he had known probably assumed he was dead. Some of his friends back home likely *were* dead, and he had missed it all.

The man extended a hand, which Kadorax eagerly took in his own, bringing his thoughts back to the forge, the priory, and his impending return mission to Darkarrow. "I've never made a complete themed set of magical armor before. Hell, only a couple weeks ago I was making horseshoes and pry bars, not breastplates and swords. I want to finish that set. You're the only one I want wearing it. That means you need to live. Wouldn't look right on a level one."

"Ha, I'll keep that in mind, my friend," Kadorax replied. "I just have one last person to see before heading back to Darkarrow."

He found Estelle down on the coast beneath the priory. She was sitting on a large piece of driftwood near the lapping water, a wool blanket wrapped around her shoulders. Lord Percival and a few other sailors were farther down the coast, already preparing for the voyage.

"Hey," Kadorax called. He stood about twenty feet behind her, waiting politely to be invited to join.

Estelle tipped her head gently to the side, and Kadorax could make out a faint hint of a smile on her face, and then she turned back to the ocean without saying a word.

"I'm going back to Darkarrow in an hour or so. We'll be hunting a jackal temple, trying to put an end to it all." He stood in front of the log and faced the ocean, still wanting more of a sign from the woman before actually sitting next to her.

Estelle took a long moment before replying. Finally, with a sigh, she said, "I know. I heard Elise was taking you back."

"You're . . . welcome to come along, if you wish," Kadorax offered. He knew what her response was very likely to be before she began shaking her head.

"No," she answered. "The army from Kingsgate will be here soon, probably today. I gave Atticus my word that I would help him, at least in this life, so that is what I shall do. He wants me here to meet with the king's alchemists and magicians." She waited another interminable length of time, the sound of the gentle waves the only noise hanging in the air. "I remember days when your word used to mean something. You told me once that you'd never leave my side, no matter what happened."

"Estelle, I'm—"

"Then you killed me, and you didn't look for me to respawn somewhere. You didn't keep your word. You left."

Kadorax turned from the ocean to meet her piercing gaze, but he couldn't hold it for long, and soon his eyes were scouring the sand at her feet. "I'm sorry. I never meant to . . . I never meant for things to happen that way."

She sighed and readjusted the blanket across her shoulders. "When you're finished with Darkarrow, where will you and Elise run to next?" she demanded.

"Wherever the war takes us," Kadorax answered flatly.

"So that's it then? Kadorax, the ever-vigilant soldier. I guess it comes with the life of a knight, doesn't it?" Her voice was tainted by contempt, a sneer that marred her beautiful Spanish accent.

For a few seconds, Kadorax entertained the notion of simply turning back toward the priory and finding Elise to begin his journey. But he didn't, and he stayed, shaking his head. "You liked it better when I was skulking through the shadows with a knife in my hands, didn't you?"

She nodded. It was a small movement, but it was there nonetheless. "I liked it better when I knew that if anything happened to either of us, we would find each other. Now you're . . ." Her voice trailed off.

Kadorax put a hand on her shoulder and sighed. "I'm sorry. If I don't go now, there might not be anything left to return to later. That's a world I'm trying to avoid. Perhaps . . . when I come back and everything is finished . . . we'll talk then?"

The boat Elise had secured wasn't quite large enough to make the journey back to Darkarrow comfortable, but the two-masted brig was certainly quick and got the job done.

Curiously, the crew the woman had put together to man the sails and navigate the waters wasn't composed entirely of Blackened Blades. One of the crew was a tall, slender humanoid somewhat similar to an elf in stature, though the being's mouth was something altogether different. The teeth were unnaturally long and jagged, like shards of glass dropped between a pair of lips and allowed to set wherever they landed. The thing, an intelligent creature Elise introduced as "Bazrath," served as the brig's captain.

Lord Percival and some of his remaining crewmen from the *Grim Sleeper* were starting to run supplies along the coast east of Oscine City. They were looking for survivors and any goods they could scrape together to return to the priory for the war effort. Their ship had left at the same time Bazrath's boat had departed for Darkarrow. Kadorax wasn't confident he would ever see the captain again. Sailing away from the priory felt like a death sentence. Part of that unease came from Elise, and the rest was brought on by the presence of the strangely mutated elf manning the helm.

When night fell on their second day out from the relative safety of Oscine City, Elise called Kadorax and his party to a meeting with the strange elf creature below decks.

"We're close," the imposing woman began, skipping any and all formalities.

Bazrath sat to her left, casually picking under his long, pointed nails with a crude knife. His upper lip was pulled back to reveal his jagged maw, and Kadorax didn't know if the strange creature was trying to intimidate him or if the expression was simply his natural resting state. Curious, Kadorax called the captain's character sheet to his vision.

Bazrath, Elf, Corrupted

Nothing else was visible under the elf's name. No level, no stats, no abilities. Even if the elf had considered Kadorax an enemy, his level would still have been visible, and *Corrupted* was a modifier the bastion had never even heard of, much less seen before.

"So . . . what's, uh, the plan when we arrive?" Kadorax asked, his eyes still on the corrupted elf.

Elise, clearly not holding back on account of decorum, snapped her fingers in front of the bastion's face. "Darkarrow or the elf?" she asked.

"What do you mean?" Kadorax pulled his gaze back to the leather-clad woman and could only hope he had not insulted Bazrath and earned the strange elf's ire.

"We've both to discuss. Which first?" Elise clarified.

A little surprised, Kadorax nodded. "How about we start with you, Bazrath? What happened?" He thought addressing his question directly to the corrupted elf would help ease some of the awkward tension permeating the small cabin. When the elf didn't respond for himself, Kadorax knew that his ploy had failed, and he nervously looked back to Elise for an answer.

"You may have more knowledge of his condition than you think," the cryptic woman began. "You've met the one who calls himself Ligriv, have you not?"

Kadorax rocked back in his chair. "Yes. I . . . How'd you know? What happened?"

Finally, the elf spoke. His voice was grating and low, and his tongue snapped around his jagged teeth as he talked. "I died about a month ago. Wasn't the first time. Not much to it. You know the inn, right?"

Nodding, Kadorax leaned in to catch every word of the elf's story.

"I woke up, got dressed, went downstairs, and the trainers attacked me. Not all of them, but enough to make me run for it. Bartender wasn't there, either. Turns out I had respawned in a little village high in the Boneridge Mountains. When I left the tavern without a class, I became *Corrupted*, as I'm sure you've seen. Turns out Ligriv wasn't too pleased." The elf set down his knife and folded his hands on the table, an oddly normal gesture for one who looked so grotesque and misshapen.

"What's Ligriv have to do with it?" Kadorax asked.

The elf twisted his already contorted face. "He's the one who's been bringing everyone back all these years. He made Agglor, according to him, and now he's ready for something new. He's purging the whole world as people die, I think. I could be wrong."

Kadorax waited for a moment for the elf to explain himself, but no such explanation came. "What do you mean by purging? He's corrupting everyone who respawns?" Kadorax asked after a moment.

"Not exactly," Bazrath replied. "I died with four others, part of my old crew. We drowned when one of our smaller ships capsized in a storm. They respawned in the same inn. I was the only one who made it out."

"And they . . ." Kadorax knew the answer as soon as he spoke. "They died forever, didn't they?"

"Exactly," Elise interjected.

The bastion didn't know how much information he should divulge. If what the elf said was true, there were grave implications. "Ligriv is searching for someone. Atticus told me as much, and he knew him from a different life. He's finally tired of waiting to find what he wants. He's going to speed up the process, eliminate everyone who isn't strong enough, and start anew. He wants to up the stakes." Kadorax pointed to the corrupted elf's misshapen features. "Those who are strong enough to survive the trainers and escape will serve as the next generation's natural enemies. He'll breed a new world of stronger adventurers, maybe finding whoever it is he seeks." He decided that mentioning the soul rod's still unknown yet important purpose was for the best. If Elise thought she could get ahead by taking the soul rod for herself, she would no doubt cut it from his chest.

A tense silence fell over the group, the sounds of the rocking boat among the ocean waves the only the noise. The corrupted elf cast his eyes downward at the table.

"All the knights who died at the docks . . ." Syzak added.

"Some of them will return, but they'll be corrupted." Kadorax shook his head. "And Ligriv will continue pulling more and more people into Agglor. If we could find him somewhere outside—wherever it is he lives—maybe we could get some answers. Maybe not."

The elf looked up from his dagger and his nails. "The new arrivals will hunt us. I do not know what will happen if I die again. I may be able to escape the trainers once more, but I am not confident. I fear the next death will be my last."

"Can you learn talents?" Kadorax asked.

"No. I have no class. I earn no experience." Again, the elf hung his head.

Kadorax knew it would be impossible for the Agglor-born elf to describe exactly what it was like to be "normal" since the classless designation was only "normal" to one from Earth who had never known a class.

"You said the corrupted will be the next natural enemy of everyone else," Syzak added, rubbing a hand on his scaly chin and looking at the strange elf. "You seem friendly enough. You haven't tried to kill us yet, if I'm not mistaken."

Bazrath's eyes flicked momentarily to Elise before settling on the table once more.

Surprisingly, it was the woman who answered. She held out her right hand to bring attention to a glittering amethyst ring on her third finger. "Bazrath was . . . an associate of mine some time ago. I was fortunate to have recognized him when our paths crossed once more." She shot him a sidelong glance. "Magic has placated his mind. Without the ring, he wouldn't be lucid enough to captain the ship."

Kadorax focused on the ring to bring up the details in his vision:

Umber Halo of Wine-Blood - Grants the wearer the ability to dominate creatures of level 21 or lower. +3 Fate.

The bastion shook his head as he dismissed the stats, silently marveling at the value of such an item. He also had to wonder at the specific text making mention of "creatures" and not "characters" as he might have expected. The minor difference in language was likely what allowed Elise to control the elf since Bazrath no longer had a character sheet. Agglor considered the elf a creature, and that new designation would be world-altering on a large scale. There were thousands of abilities and artifacts that relied on the difference between creatures and characters. Without such distinctions, certain classes would become walking catastrophes, slaughtering friend and foe alike with their spells.

"You have my thanks," Bazrath said meekly.

Kadorax leaned back on his chair. The ship rocked a little side to side, jostling some of the items strung up in rope braces. "If you don't mind my asking, how much, uh, damage would you be causing without the ring?"

The elf met his gaze with a vicious smile. "I don't remember anything before the ring besides my harrowing journey through the class trainers."

"He was terrorizing Virast south of Darkarrow. Had a family trapped in their home with two of them dead out front." Elise smiled as she explained the corrupted elf's previous nature, though Bazrath himself continued to appear downcast.

"Well, that answers my question," Syzak replied.

"The sooner we can figure out how to get things back to normal, the better," Brinna said. A visible shudder ran through her body. "I don't want to become . . . corrupted . . . Sorry."

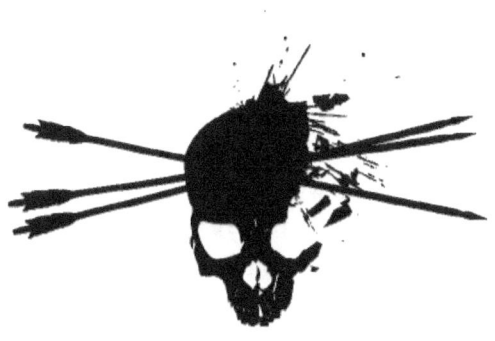

CHAPTER 8

When Bazrath's brig came to port at one of Virast's docks, the town was quiet. A heavy fog had settled over the rooftops, and the sun's rays only occasionally broke through here and there in irregular splotches. With no dockhands to greet the ship, the crew struggled to bring it alongside one of the docks, and several of the pilings suffered a bit of damage before the ship came to a complete stop.

"To Darkarrow first, yes?" Kadorax asked the woman at his side. They both stood at the railing as Bazrath shouted commands to his crew above the din. Behind them, Atticus paced back and forth on his cane. He seemed a little lost without Estelle, and Kadorax felt much the same.

Elise nodded, absentmindedly toying with the ring around her finger as she watched the docking process. "Well, maybe not so fast. You know the Nimble Cat, don't you?" She smirked, and her eyes said she knew the answer already.

"And what, pray tell, could you *possibly* need at the Nimble Cat?" Kadorax asked derisively. The tavern, or whatever the seedy establishment truly was, had a reputation for being one of the most dangerous places in all of Agglor. Being somewhat far from Kingsgate meant the port city of Virast didn't always feel the long arm of King Bennington's law in the same way that huge, important places like Oscine City did. With a lack of direct control and, Kadorax had to admit, Darkarrow being so close and so full of lawless assassins, the Nimble Cat had thrived as a den of thieves, murderers, and all manner of other unsavory types.

Elise snickered and shook a finger in front of Kadorax's face. "In the basement, the second sub-level, you'll find something we could both use to remove the jackal plight from these lands. Let's just say you'll know it when you see it. I trust you're up for the task."

"You know I'd probably have an easier time if I knew what I was looking for," Kadorax scoffed. He shook his head, knowing well that the cryptic woman would never do him any favors despite the added danger to the both of them. Her pride would always get in the way of a smooth mission, and there was no way to change her.

The woman gave Kadorax a final pat on the back before turning away. "You'll be fine," she said. "Meet me at the edge of town before heading to Darkarrow. I have some unfinished business elsewhere in Virast, and you do know how I hate the smell under the Nimble Cat. Wouldn't want any of it clinging to my cloak."

Kadorax didn't say a word as the woman left him to attend to her own group of Blackened Blades before walking down the gangplank and into the city.

On the docks, Kadorax surveyed his measly trio, himself included. Atticus had gone with Elise and the others, intent on studying Bazrath as they walked. Without the warlock, things felt more or less like the old days, and Kadorax remembered fondly all the missions he had carried out with his best friend by his side. He trusted Syzak with his life as he had for thirty years, though he still didn't really know if Brinna would be up for the coming tasks. In his mind, the woman was like a younger Blackened Blade out for her first dungeon run, and he and Syzak were the veteran instructors.

"Remember that building we passed the last time we were in Virast?" he asked the rogue.

She was toying with the hilt of one of her daggers. "The one you told me never to enter?" she replied.

Kadorax let out a sigh. "The very same. Elise needs something from the basement before we move to Darkarrow. I'm not very keen on spending time there, whether the city is abandoned or not. We need to get in and get out quickly."

"Which basement?" Syzak asked, his voice betraying a bit of fear.

"The second," Kadorax answered. "You know the Nimble Cat better than I do. What should we expect?"

"The sec—"

"Wait," Brinna interrupted. "The fearsome building I was never allowed to enter is called the Nimble Cat? Seriously?"

"Used to be a brothel before the damn Calloustry made it their home," the snake-man explained.

Brinna returned her dagger to its place inside her right boot. "What are they? Never heard of them."

"Not necessarily 'what,' but rather 'who' would be the more appropriate question. And they aren't a guild like the Blackened Blades, the Miners' Union, or the Priorate Knights," Syzak went on. "Just two of them. Brothers."

"Mimes," Kadorax added.

"With unusual tastes." Syzak led the three of them down the gangway a few paces behind Elise and her crew.

The Nimble Cat wasn't very far from the docks, and the building was conspicuous with its dilapidated exterior and lack of windows. With a little remodeling, it would have blended in as an average tavern anywhere in Agglor.

"So, what makes these mimes so dangerous?" Brinna asked, looking skeptically at the Nimble Cat's battered front door. No one else could be seen in Virast, though some of the houses and businesses had been boarded over, likely shielding families inside as fear of a jackal invasion strangled the city.

Kadorax was surprised. "You've met a mime before? They aren't a particularly common class choice," he asked.

"Not particularly useful, either," Syzak added.

The woman gave him a confused look. "We had one in Assir. He performed at all the festivals. I wasn't fond of his performances, but the children enjoyed it, and the city didn't have to pay him much."

"What level was the mime in Assir?" Kadorax asked. "Do you remember?"

"Not very high, maybe seven or eight, I think," she said.

Kadorax drew his sword before approaching the door to the Nimble Cat. "The Calloustry brothers were around level thirty-two the last time I had the displeasure of seeing one of them," he said.

"Mimes are never very combat-oriented like rogues and assassins. They're a performance class like the one you knew in Assir, but the *Mime's Superior Talents* are some of the most incredible abilities you've ever seen." Syzak readied his claws and stood to the side of the door as Kadorax opened it.

"And we're walking in just because Elise told us we needed to? We're taking orders from her now?" Brinna scoffed.

The woman's words gave Kadorax a moment of pause. Finally, his sword still in his hand, he nodded. "You're right not to trust her, but she needs to end the jackal threat just as much as the rest of Agglor. We're all on the same side. I just hope her hatred for me doesn't run deep enough to sacrifice her own allies."

Syzak just shrugged.

The inside of the Nimble Cat was as run down and musty as the outside. There were tables and chairs scattered throughout the main room like any normal tavern, though there was no long bar to prevent patrons from accessing the serving areas or racks of barrels lining the walls. Instead, the open floor plan allowed patrons to grab whatever they liked from the shelves on three of the square building's four sides.

"You said this place was a tavern?" Brinna asked quietly. No one was inside, but the tension was high nonetheless, and all three of them walked on the balls of their feet to limit the sounds of their footfalls.

"Not so much a tavern as an exclusive club," Syzak explained, his voice equally quiet. He cautiously stepped over a sideways crate that had been pushed from a table, its contents of squat brandy bottles shattered and spilled all over the floor. The pungent, fruity aroma filled the dark clubhouse air from wall to wall.

"What, did members just pay once and then come in and drink for free?" Brinna continued.

Kadorax held up a closed fist to stop them, and the other two froze in place. Syzak's foot was awkwardly hovering above the floor in mid-step. After nearly a minute, the bastion lowered his hand and brought a finger over his lips, then pointed directly down.

Syzak tapped his scaly right ear and waved his fingers horizontally to indicate he hadn't heard anything.

Whispering, Brinna chanced a few words. "Someone downstairs? The mimes?"

Two silent nods answered her question.

Toward the rear of the building, two doors were the only options for progress. One was closed and led to an alley bordering one of Virast's docks while the other, a trap door, led deeper into the bowels of the Nimble Cat. Kadorax led the way to the trap door and peered over the edge. "See anything?" he whispered to Syzak, hoping the snake-man's eyes could penetrate the darkness below better than his own.

"Ladder's broken. Not much else," Syzak answered after a moment.

"And what's in the first basement?" Brinna asked, swallowing hard. She and Kadorax both looked to Syzak for an answer.

"Mostly drinking and gambling, though the stakes below were *much* higher. You won't like the smell," he quietly explained.

Kadorax nodded and tested the first rung of the wooden ladder that would lead them into the darkness. When it held, he descended quickly the remaining rungs until he reached the bottom fourth, where the ladder had been broken off. He looked over his shoulder once before dropping onto his heels, muffling his landing as best as he could.

Brinna, utilizing her rank three *Sneak*, followed quickly behind the bastion without making a single sound.

At once, Syzak's prediction concerning the smell proved correct. The three stood at the entrance to the Nimble Cat's more violent and benighted gambling hall—where wagers were typically placed with blood and flesh rather than coins. Illuminated by two meager candles in metal lanterns at the opposite end of the hall, the empty room displayed a gruesome array of cages along one wall and tables of various sizes scattered about the floor. Opposite the cages, the source of the foul stench was displayed like trophies in a hunting lodge.

"The hands are from those who couldn't pay, and the heads are from anyone stupid enough to be caught cheating," Syzak said under his breath.

Brinna and Kadorax both had to cover their mouths with their hands. "You've been here before?" the woman asked behind her finger. "Why?"

A shudder ran through the snake-man's body. "Sometimes . . . people needed to be purchased. The Nimble Cat was the closest seller."

"We were assassins, not slavers. I won't tell you that everything we did was without fault, but know that the Blackened Blades will always be above the likes of those who congregated here," Kadorax was quick to add under his breath.

They continued on in silence until they reached the back of the room. Another ladder led deeper into the complex, and a bit of light shone up from it. Standing close to the edge, all three of them could hear voices below. Kadorax motioned back the way they had come, then scampered on the balls of his feet to get away from the open trap door.

"We need a coordinated plan before going down," he

said, shielding his voice with a hand and never taking his eyes from the trap door.

"I'll go first," Brinna stated.

For a moment, Kadorax considered talking her out of it, but he knew she was the best choice. Finally, he pointed to the dagger tucked away on her belt, the one he had given her from his private stash at Darkarrow. "If you have to, use that. Don't hesitate. Just drop down and look around. If you can avoid confrontation, wait for us."

"What kind of signal do you want?" she asked, her voice full of quiet confidence despite the little bit of shaking in her hands.

"Just come back to the ladder if you can. We'll be waiting." Kadorax gave the woman a stern nod he hoped would help bolster her nerves. He couldn't help but think of the bloodshed Brinna had wrought in Oscine City. He knew she could handle herself, but she was also reckless—maybe even bloodthirsty, though the term didn't *quite* fit—and those qualities could ultimately prove dangerous. They were qualities he would have trained out of any true Blackened Blades recruit.

The wait at the top of the ladder was a long one. After several minutes of silence, Kadorax was contemplating jumping down the ladder himself when he and Syzak heard a muffled yelp from below. The voice was female, and though they couldn't know for sure if it had been Brinna, they didn't waste any time rushing into the second basement.

Kadorax landed first, *Assir's Edge* in his hand before he even had time to take in his surroundings. Much less graceful due to his lower *Agility* score, Syzak landed with a heavy thud behind him. The second underground level of the Nimble Cat demarcated the gambling and drinking levels from the more private lair of the Calloustry brothers.

194

There was more light than above, most of it by way of candles in mirrored lanterns hanging from the walls, and an oily sheen of smoke hung in the air above rows and rows of strange, unrecognizable implements. Some of the glass instruments were similar to the alembics and other devices used by the alchemists at Kingsgate, though the vast majority of objects were things Kadorax had never seen before.

At the rear of the long, rectangular hall was the origin of the yelp they had heard. Brinna was there, her *Talon Dagger* flashing in front of her, and two slender, flamboyant fencers were pushing her back against a wall. Her assailants were dressed in bright, gaudy colors and feathered plumes, their doublets slashed from shoulder to hip with vibrant green silk. They each held a long, slender fencer's sword, and it was clear from only a glance that Brinna was hard-pressed.

Kadorax and Syzak sprinted past the rows of implements for the rear of the room. Maybe ten paces from the fencing duo, a shimmering yellow crackle appeared in the air. Kadorax and Syzak were caught, frozen mid-step, by a powerful magical net.

Flying through his character sheet, Kadorax desperately looked for a way out. Right in front of his eyes, he watched as Brinna deflected one slender blade with a downward parry, though the maneuver left her open to an attack from the second fencer, and she took a hit to her left shoulder that stained the first three inches of the man's blade with her blood.

Kadorax waited a split second before activating *Chaos Step*. His body sizzled, then teleported directly behind one of the swordsmen, *Assir's Edge* poised to decapitate the man where he stood.

Just as fast as the bastion had activated his talent, the

fencer's body transformed and spun, locking him in a grapple and sending them both to the ground.

"Stay underneath!" Syzak yelled, his torso still held firmly in place by magic. "Four seconds!" On his character sheet, he could see the timer on the debuff ticking away painfully slowly.

Two images of Kadorax rolled and thrashed on the basement floor, neither one of them able to get their sword lined up for a kill, and neither distinguishable as the *real* Kadorax. "Damn mimes!" one of the mirrored combatants yelled.

Against a solo opponent, Brinna was able to keep herself from being skewered again, though she still barely kept the edge of the fencer's sword from its mark, and her forearms were riddled with gashes. Still, she stayed on her feet, and *Dual Wielding Block: Rank 1* allowed her a little more surety once she found a fraction of a second to pluck another dagger from her boot.

The magical prison encasing Syzak finally broke free, and the shaman tumbled down to the ground. He was on his feet in an instant. A circular *Rat Trap* appeared beneath the feet of the fencer attacking Brinna, and the man lost his balance. When he fell backward, his neck tilted to allow him a quick glance at Syzak, and then his skin, clothes, and even his sword transformed to become a perfect mimic of the snake-man bearing down on him from above.

Brinna hesitated, her weapons wavering side to side in her grip. Before she could lunge for the mime once more, Syzak slammed into his mirrored counterpart, and she lost track of which one was which within the space of only a few heartbeats.

After another thirty seconds of ferocious combat, Brinna finally found her opening. One of the Kadorax-images trading blows in front of a broken set of shelves suddenly lit up with magical light.

"Kill it!" one of the images yelled.

Brinna had to assume the illumination came from *Rallying Strike*, and she dove forward. Both of her daggers sank into the back of one of the images' breastplates. The man howled in pain, and his image flickered slightly, appearing for a split second as the mime he had originally been. The mime pulled away and spun, running for the ladder at the far end of the room, Brinna's daggers still lodged in the top of its back. As it moved, it continued to shift in and out of focus as the illusion spell cloaking it struggled through all of the pain.

The two Syzaks were still tearing at each other on the ground with their claws. Brinna helped the real Kadorax to his feet, and then the two couldn't do anything other than watch.

"That's their *Mime's Superior Talent*," Kadorax panted between breaths. "They can take other forms, but they don't get any of the talents or other abilities. And like I said, they aren't terribly good at fighting. Just confusing."

Brinna nodded, though she kept her distance, still a little overtly skeptical of the Kadorax standing next to her. "Where did we find Ayers?" she asked, a hand on the hilt of her dagger.

"Rescued him from bandits outside Assir," Kadorax answered. In front of the two, one of the snake-men was starting to come out on top. Both of them were bloodied, though neither appeared mortally wounded.

"Syzak!" Kadorax shouted at the one he thought looked most like his friend. "Who captained the ship on our way here?"

197

Both of the images answered, and Kadorax couldn't tell which one gave which answer, though he knew one of them had said the corrupted elf's name.

With the flat of his blade, Kadorax slammed the nearest snake-man in the back of the head. The creature flopped off the other, and the bastion tackled it to stop the fight. He had one Syzak pinned to the ground under his knees. "Right now, name of the ship we took to Kingsgate. Say it."

The creature hesitated, then stammered out a confused jumble of words that most certainly were not the correct answer.

"Brinna, a dagger, please?" Kadorax said. The mime's eyes grew wide, and its form flickered at once to resemble Kadorax's own body.

Brinna knelt and slit its throat. "That wasn't so bad," she said. "I don't know why you thought Elise was sending us into a trap."

Off to the side, Syzak was clutching his head with both scaly hands.

"Just wait. We have no idea if these are even real copies of the mimes or just more facsimiles. We need to find whatever it is we need and get out of here." Kadorax shoved the dead mime away and turned to help the snake-man regain his feet. "Start looking through everything. Elise said it would be obvious."

Brinna began shuffling through all the scattered detritus covering the room. "I don't know what I'm supposed to find."

Syzak got to his feet and stumbled around for a few seconds, his balance still trying to catch up with his strong desire to leave the Nimble Cat as quickly as possible. "Thanks for bashing me in the head," he muttered toward the bastion.

"Any ideas what we're supposed to find?" Kadorax asked.

"I might know a few secrets around here," the snake-man replied. When he had shaken the rest of the grogginess from his mind, he began searching through the scattered debris with the others.

Brinna was the first to find something that appeared useful. "Got a potion," she said, holding up a small glass vial with a cork stopper. "Doesn't seem that good, but I guess it's better than nothing."

Kadorax called up the potion's stats to his vision:

Spirited Healing Potion - Drinking this potion heals minor wounds and also intoxicates the imbiber.

"Honestly, I'm not surprised you found something like that," Syzak remarked from his side of the underground complex. "Everyone who comes down here is either an absolute scoundrel, wildly drunk, or both."

Kadorax kicked over a pile of well-crafted poker chips that had fallen from an overturned table. They clanged to the floorboards, and one of them slipped through an irregularity in the wooden slats and fell to the basement below.

A soft, muffled noise answered the falling poker chip. Kadorax held up a hand to silence the other two, who still rummaged through their own piles of junk. Everyone froze where they were. As quietly as he could, Kadorax lowered himself down to one knee and brought his ear over the thin gap in the flooring where the chip had fallen.

The sound of gently shuffling clothing coming from below was so quiet it was nearly inaudible. Kadorax listened for a long while as his two companions struggled to maintain their poses and absolute silence, and finally the bastion rose back to his feet. "Something's down there," he whispered. "Is there another basement level?"

Syzak wore a grim expression. "There is, but just storage.

We probably don't want any part of whatever's down there. They used to run fights here sometimes. Three or four drunks against a huge alligator or some other wild animals. Bears, wolves . . . I heard of the brothers bringing a gorilla from the north once, but I don't know if I believe it. Whatever's down there is probably starving and furious."

"Best to leave it be," Brinna added.

Kadorax thought for a moment before making up his mind. "I just want to see what's there. We don't have to do anything drastic. Just look."

With a sigh, Syzak grabbed a bent piece of discarded iron and moved over the hole between the floorboards. He used the iron like a pry bar, and the old flooring came up easily enough to give all three a bit of trepidation regarding the quality of the subterranean building's construction.

"The whole place could come down any minute," Kadorax said once they had the first floorboard removed and cast aside.

"Here, use a candle," Brinna said. She handed the bastion one of the taper candles from a nearby lantern.

Slowly, Kadorax lowered the candle and moved it back and forth to illuminate the room beneath their feet.

A little girl, covered in grime and shivering uncontrollably, was huddled up with her knees pressed to her chest in a space about the size of an average room at a cheap inn.

"By the gods," Brinna gasped. "We have to get her out!"

"Wait!" Kadorax grabbed Brinna by her arm to stop her from prying up more of the flooring. "We have no idea if the girl's real. It could be a trick from one of the mimes."

"How would a little crying girl be a trick?" the rogue demanded, suddenly defensive as if the prisoner was her own child.

Kadorax pulled her back. "Just wait. We need to think it through."

Syzak was pacing back and forth a few feet from the missing section of flooring. "We only killed one mime, so the other could be anywhere. We don't know if he got down there somehow when he ran. It *could* be the mime laying a trap. Still, I don't think it is."

Shaking his head, the bastion let out a heavy sigh. "Little girl?" he called into the darkness below. "What are you doing down there?"

"P-Please . . . Don't . . . h-hurt me . . ."

"She's terrified, and you just wanted to let her rot." Brinna stood and joined the snake-man in his pacing. "We need something to get her out of there. Did you see any rope?"

Kadorax wrenched another floorboard away so he had enough room to stick his whole heel into the tiny prison cell. The candlelight reflected off something metallic wrapped around the girl's ankle. "I think she's chained to the ground. Hard to tell," he said to his two companions. He took one final look around the underground room before standing and stretching his back.

"What's the plan?" Syzak asked.

The bastion looked Brinna in the eyes as he spoke. "We'll get her out. I'll drop down and see if I can't get her unshackled. If we rip up enough floor, we can just drop a few tables and chairs down and build our own ladder. Check the dead mime for a key, too."

Brinna immediately set to work scavenging the mime's bloody corpse for any kind of key. Kadorax ripped up another pair of floorboards and then sat on the edge of the hole like a swimmer about to jump into the ocean from a dock. Before

201

he could push off, the boards he was sitting on gave way, and he fell noisily to the ground about eight feet below.

The girl shrieked and tried to push herself farther and farther into the stone wall at her back.

"Sy, toss me the candle," Kadorax called back up to his companion. A scaly hand lowered the candle a few seconds later, and the bastion held it in front of him to see exactly what was huddled against the corner.

As far as Kadorax could tell, the girl was just a girl. He accessed her character sheet to be sure. Her name was Gabi, and she was a level one chandler—a civilian class like the Calloustry brothers or the alchemists from Kingsgate. The girl didn't view him as friendly, so her sheet revealed almost nothing.

"What are you doing down here?" Kadorax hesitantly asked. As soon as he spoke, he knew the question had been a stupid one. He was in the Nimble Cat. The girl was chained to a stone floor in a subbasement some forty feet below the street surface, and she was terrified beyond words. Kadorax knew *exactly* why she was there. She was someone's property, bought and paid for and awaiting delivery.

He shook his head. As an assassin, he had seen some truly despicable things. In a world where death could actually be an easy way to restart a life down and travel down a different path, captivity and slavery were the worst things one person could do to another.

Kadorax kept the candle close to his body and held out a hand for the girl to stand. "We aren't going to hurt you. I promise. We'll get you out of here. Would you like that?"

Sobbing, the girl nodded. She didn't take the offered hand. Instead, she pushed back against the wall and kept her arms crossed defensively over her chest as she slowly got to her shaking feet.

"Gabi?" Kadorax kept his hand out as if he was trying to offer a scrap of food to a timid cat. "Come on. We'll get you out of here."

Brinna dropped into the pit behind Kadorax, startling him. Still, he stepped aside to let the woman have a turn coaxing the girl from her wall.

While the rogue spoke to the girl, Kadorax busied himself grabbing things from Syzak up above and making their makeshift ladder. After a few minutes, Brinna was holding the girl's hand and standing in the middle of the dingy cell at her side. Kadorax couldn't tell if the girl was old enough to even be eligible for respawn, and he painfully remembered what it had felt like to bury Brinna's son alongside the road. Now that the respawning system had been corrupted, he wasn't sure if the girl was lucky to be so young or not. Perhaps dying for real would be a blessing. At least in Kadorax's mind, things were starting to look that way.

"Come on, I'll help you out," the bastion said once the pile of rubble was high enough to take them to the floor above.

Brinna and Gabi made a painfully slow trek up the stacked tables, shelves, and chairs, but they reached the top nonetheless. "Think she's what the boss was after?" Syzak asked.

Kadorax gave a curt laugh. "I have no idea. And Elise isn't my boss. I suppose the old prior is, assuming he's alive."

With their rescued prisoner lagging behind a little, Kadorax and his party ascended through the Nimble Cat's system of basements until they reached street level once more. Outside, a small group of refugees had gathered on the docks, and Bazrath's remaining crewmen were busy fending them off.

"Looks like everyone who saw the boat is trying to barter for passage out of Virast," Kadorax remarked. He turned to Gabi and tried to put on a genuine smile to ease the girl's fear. "Where are you from? Did you grow up here in the village?"

Terrified and skittish, Gabi buried her head in Brinna's side.

"She, uh . . . She probably won't be much use," Syzak muttered.

Though he didn't say anything to the effect, Kadorax had to agree. "Alright. Let's go meet up with Elise and see what other errands she has for us."

The four began walking north, away from the docks and the refugees. "Still think she isn't your boss?" Syzak playfully jabbed. "I've never known you to go looking for work from a superior like some everyday soldier. You really think she can help turn things around?"

Kadorax sighed and placed a hand on his friend's shoulder. "I have no idea. For all we know, she could be in league with the damned jackals and sending us to our deaths. I'm more interested in Atticus. He knows more than he says, and I plan on staying close to him for the next few weeks. We need some answers."

"Answers? Or is it Estelle you want to *truly* stay close to?"

"If she was what I wanted, I would have stayed back in Oscine City." Kadorax forced his mind to think of the jackals and the temple he was destined to raid—anything to keep his mind from the beautiful Spanish woman he knew he still loved.

Syzak's scaly mouth grinned. "I'm a little surprised she didn't come along. I think she's avoiding you."

"You're probably right." Up ahead, something caught

Kadorax's attention. He held up a hand, and the other three all stopped at once. "What the . . ."

The others quick to follow his movements, Kadorax pressed his body against the side of one of the businesses lining the street. The smithy had been boarded over, but the front door was destroyed, flattened by jackals, looters, or panicked citizens. The interior of the shop had been thoroughly trashed. Backing slowly toward the open door in case he needed to hide, Kadorax motioned for everyone to crouch.

At the end of the street, Elise and her hodgepodge crew were standing in a circle and conversing. Their extra company made Kadorax grit his teeth.

"Should have chased the damn mime and cut off its head," Kadorax practically growled. Elise stood next to a perfect image of himself complete with a kit shield strung over its shoulder.

"Would you like the honors?" the snake-man asked.

Kadorax flexed his arms. "Make the girl look away. It won't be pretty, and she's certainly seen enough already."

The bastion drew his whip and started running for the mime's back. When he was within range, the others had all turned to question his sudden approach. He sent a powerful crack of *Torment* directly into the side of the mime's face.

Blood exploded under the whip's cruel touch. He began to run, but Elise was quick to discern the true nature of the situation, and she grabbed the man's arm to hold him fast.

Kadorax slashed another bloody line down the mime's neck. He could have pushed his whip just a little farther to mangle the man's throat and likely kill him, but he wanted to deliver a bit of suffering first.

"The others are down the street," Kadorax said curtly so

Elise would know beyond a doubt that he was the real bastion of chaos incarnate. He dropped his whip back to his belt and held out a hand. "Let me borrow one of your daggers. My sword isn't really the right tool."

With a smile, Elise dropped a silvery knife into the bastion's outstretched hand.

The mime screamed before Kadorax even brought the dagger to his flesh. "I never really liked the Nimble Cat. Never really liked you. And I *hate* chasing down damned shapeshifters."

Kadorax stabbed the mime in the bottom of his gut, right above his pelvis. Almost at once, the mime's image began to flicker and change until all semblance of illusion was gone. Kadorax stabbed him once on either side of his collarbone. The man's chest blossomed with crimson blood, and the howls of pain only got louder.

Finally, Kadorax slit the man's throat. Elise let him fall to the street and held out her hand for her dagger without a single hint of remorse or even pity. "Did you find what you were looking for? Something more than the Calloustry brothers, I hope."

Syzak, Brinna, and their rescued prisoner made their way to the others at the edge of Virast. "That what you were talking about?" the bastion asked.

Wearing a frown like she was checking out a horse before placing a bet at the track, Elise inspected the young girl. "You, Gabi, are from the north, yes?" she stated.

Timid and terrified, the girl tried to hide her face in Brinna's chest.

Elise grabbed her roughly by the shoulder to spin her around, and Kadorax found his own hand drifting close to the hilt of *Assir's Edge*. "Watch yourself, Elise. She's just a girl."

"You've been to the north, to jackal lands, yes? Answer me, girl!" the leader of the Blackened Blades shouted. She wrenched Gabi from Brinna's grasp and forced her to meet her eyes, eliciting an immediate and violent response from the rogue. The whole situation threatened to devolve into an all-out brawl within a matter of seconds.

Finally, Gabi nodded. Tears were streaming down her grime-covered face.

"Good. I paid a lot of money for you, and I promise to set you free eventually, but I need information first. We're walking to Darkarrow. You have about a day to tell me everything you know about the jackal lands, their leaders, their cities, and everything else you can think of. Is that clear?" Elise had the girl's chin in her hand, forcing her to look up and not turn away in fear.

"Y-Yes," Gabi muttered.

"Alright. Let's go. Once we take back Darkarrow, we'll hit the temple. Everyone ready?" Elise surveyed the small group, a fierce expression on her face that left no room for debate.

"Once we take down their temple, you plan on going north to the jackal cities?" Kadorax asked as he fell into step with the others. Moving north brought a bit of happiness that the bastion hadn't felt in some time. He knew it would be good to see his old home again, despite having more than a few reservations about the company he was keeping.

The small band of adventurers didn't slow down on account of the mud that plagued their boots between Virast and Darkarrow. Fear and desperation were fine motivators to encourage their speed. All along the trek, Brinna plied Gabi for information about the north and the jackal command structure, essentially creating a report for Elise and the others once they reached whatever was left of the Blackened Blades' compound.

As it turned out, Gabi had been a hostage in the northern lands. Her father was a member of the Miners' Union, one of the few humans to choose to go among their ranks, and the jackals had captured him during a raid in the Boneridge Mountains. According to the girl, that had been the very first of the jackal incursions into the mountains that divided the east from the west. Being so isolated from the rest of Agglor, the Miners' Union couldn't defend its subterranean positions, and it had capitulated quickly.

What was most interesting to Kadorax was the strange, tenuous allegiance between the Miners' Union and the jackals. After the dogheads had killed a few hundred, they had asked for a truce and struck terms. That wasn't something jackals were known for doing.

Much to Kadorax's dismay, the frightened girl didn't know anything about who was commanding the jackal army, other than a single doghead who had painted fur and appeared to be in charge. Kadorax knew there was more to it all. Jackals didn't just organize themselves into cohesive armies and negotiate hostage captures or treaties. Jackals swarmed, and anything that wasn't strong enough to resist them was cut down and trampled.

All Gabi knew of the jackal leadership was the face of the one painted creature she had seen several times. That particular jackal had commanded some authority within the mangy ranks, and Kadorax thought of him as a regional commander, a general in charge of a specific allotment of soldiers, though the level of organization it implied still made him shake his head.

Brinna had almost finished recounting the girl's tales to Elise when the group arrived within sight of Darkarrow. The compound hadn't been entirely destroyed, but it was close. Most of the front had been burned. A few ramshackle wooden defenses were toppled over and ruined, leaving Kadorax to wonder which side had employed them. Seeing the jackals building and maneuvering palisades would be just as unlikely as seeing Blackened Blades doing the same. Neither group had a history of pitched battles.

Kadorax shifted the weight of the shield on his shoulders. He knew he didn't have a history of pitched battles, either, but times had changed. *Everything* had changed.

"Was anyone alive when you left?" Kadorax asked the assassin at his side.

Elise smiled. "A handful held what remains of Darkarrow. If they still draw breath, perhaps they can be of some use," she replied.

"No sense waiting out here for another attack." Kadorax moved away from the group's position along the side of the road perhaps three hundred yards from the entrance to the estate. "Jackals are no doubt watching us. We might as well not give them any extra time."

Without any reason to remain hidden, the rest of the party followed quickly behind the bastion, their eyes warily scanning the forest beyond Darkarrow's ominous influence.

A lone assassin met them at the ruined front gate. The walls on either side of the wooden door had been bashed inward, scattering charred planks and other refuse across the foyer floor.

"What's the situation?" Elise asked her underling, all business as usual.

The assassin blanched under his leader's intense stare. "Four of us left. No jackals since the day before yesterday, my lady."

"Four? Were there not five when I left for Oscine City?"

The man gulped hard. "One of those . . ." His eyes wouldn't budge from Bazrath's corrupted visage. "One of those things attacked. We took it down, but it got Lark. It . . . ate him."

The corrupted elf issued a sound that Kadorax guessed would have been a snort of derision had his mouth not been a circular mess of jagged teeth.

"If you still have the specimen, I would very much appreciate a few hours with it," Atticus said from the back of the group, speaking up for the first time since leaving Virast. Without Estelle by his side to help him along and offer her steady companionship, the old man seemed lost, consumed by his own thoughts.

The Blackened Blade pointed to the back of the ruined building. "You'll find the corpse out there next to about a dozen jackals. I don't think anyone else is going to want them. They're all yours."

Balancing on his cane, Atticus muttered to himself as he hobbled down the hall toward the rear courtyard.

"So, when do we leave for the temple?" Kadorax asked Elise when the old man was gone.

"We can stay here for one day. Most of the rooms were burned or collapsed when the eastern wall came down, but there are enough left undamaged for our small band." The woman looked to Brinna and the young girl clinging to her arms. "You two will remain here to await our return. Once the temple is cleared, we will move north. Don't let our only guide escape."

Brinna looked incredulous. "If you think I'm staying here while the fate of Agglor hangs in the balance, you're out of your mind. I'm no stranger to battle. I'm going with you."

Before Elise could offer any more protest, shouts filled the air. "They're here! Attack!" one of the Blackened Blades deeper in the ruins was screaming.

Kadorax, Syzak, and Elise immediately sprang into action, running toward the panicked shouts. "Get her somewhere safe!" the bastion yelled back over his shoulder to Brinna. "And someone protect Atticus! Go!"

Wood splintered somewhere overhead. The distinct sound was quickly followed by a heavy thump as a large piece of furniture crashed into the floor on the second level. Kadorax was the first to see the incoming invaders. The group of four—Bazrath had joined them in the sudden tumult—arrived at a ruined section of Darkarrow that had previously stood three stories high. The wood and stone wall had fallen outward, creating a small field of debris and offering a fine view of the tree line a hundred yards away.

On the second story, two Blackened Blades were readying a pair of bows. "What should we do?" one of them asked. In his panic, he accidentally loosed an arrow that only traveled about twenty yards before falling to the dirt.

"They aren't coming just yet," Elise said under her breath. "Why are they waiting?"

A horde of jackals had assembled at the edge of the tree line. They weren't hiding in the foliage but standing just in front of it, clearly wanting to be seen and to instill fear in everyone left at Darkarrow.

Again, Kadorax had to wonder at the strange tactics.

Jackals didn't wait and bide their time, planning their attacks for maximum effectiveness.

"Someone has to be controlling them. A real jackal horde would have charged by now!" Kadorax paced back and forth at the edge of the rubble, wracking his mind for an answer. "Elise, take our two friends with the bows and use your *Assassin's Superior Talent*. Circle around the horde and don't let them see you coming."

The woman nodded and called up to the assassins on the floor above her. She was jumping into action, following Kadorax's plan without question or complaint.

"What will become of Darkarrow?" Syzak asked.

"When they come for the building itself, let them have it. Kill as many as you can with traps, then run. Find Brinna and Atticus. Protect them." Kadorax clasped his friend on the shoulder. "Meet me in Virast. If the horde goes there, escape to Oscine City. We'll find each other among the knights."

Syzak nodded and wrapped Kadorax in a tight embrace. "If not in Virast, I'll see you in Oscine City. I'll wait for you."

Kadorax didn't have time for any regrets or final words. He spun to Bazrath, and the corrupted elf looked blood-thirsty, bordering on deranged. "How far from the ring can you travel?" the bastion demanded.

"I do not know." Bazrath flicked his tongue over the jagged points filling his twisted mouth.

"We'll just have to find out. If you feel the control waning, just run toward the jackals. You're coming with me, and we're going to pull them away from Darkarrow. Understood?" Kadorax was pleased that everyone standing amidst the ruins was on board with his plan. He knew there wasn't really anything else he could hope to accomplish in the face of so many enemies, but he longed for Sergeant Reinhardt's counsel. The tactician would be able to see the battlefield in ways Kadorax knew he never would.

Setting everything in motion, Elise and her two Blackened Blades were the first to leave the relative comfort of Darkarrow for the open field separating them from the jackal formation. Perhaps ten feet from the ruined wall, a deep blanket of shadows fell upon them, and Kadorax could no longer make out their forms. He could only hope the jackals were equally blind to their plan.

Kadorax and Bazrath ran out from the rubble to the right of Darkarrow, forming a pincer with Elise and her group. The jackals nearest to them followed their movements, but they didn't come out from the trees to attack. They stood ready, some of them gnashing their teeth, waiting for a command to come from somewhere and begin the slaughter.

The shadow covering Elise and her companions melded into the forest a few moments before Kadorax reached the trees himself. The jackal mass was to his left, and it was impossible to tell exactly how many of them were there.

"Look for their leader. Anyone who might be in charge. Just don't get too close," Kadorax whispered.

Bazrath grinned. "I can feel the ring . . . getting weaker."

Kadorax pushed deeper into the thick woods, *Assir's Edge* in his hand and ready to impale the first jackal who got in his way. Everything about the eerie calmness of the doghead horde was out of place. Kadorax felt the hairs on the back of his neck standing on end. He motioned for Bazrath to keep a tighter pace with him. "Stay close. Something is wrong."

For a moment, Kadorax considered the possibility that *Encroaching Insanity* was playing tricks on his mind, but everyone else had seen the same horde waiting to charge. No matter the truth of the scene, the uneasiness brought on by the persistent debuff was enough to slow Kadorax's steps. "Tell me if you see anything stranger than what's already going on," he told the elf captain. "I can't always trust my eyes."

Bazrath gave him a slightly confused look, but he didn't question the request.

When they were deep enough into the trees to have moved beyond the rear lines of the jackal horde, Kadorax started to see what was controlling them. Several humans patrolled behind the doghead lines, each one heavily armed and armored, and they appeared to be in direct control of the lower ranks. Each of the humans, however, also looked to be waiting for a command to come from higher up the ranks.

Bazrath started moving toward one of the human leaders, and Kadorax grabbed him by the arm to hold him back. "They're just middlemen. We need to find whoever is in charge."

Just then, the two humans Kadorax could see straightened their posture, and their heads tilted back toward the sky. The strange, synchronized posture lasted for a few heartbeats, and then the humans began shouting orders to their jackal charges.

Rank after rank—easily over a thousand jackals in total—began rushing out of the woods toward Darkarrow. They howled and shouted as they ran forward, goaded on by their human taskmasters. "Let's go!" Kadorax shouted to the elf. He charged for the nearest overlord, doing exactly what he had prevented Bazrath from doing just a second before.

The first human fell to *Assir's Edge* before he even realized that an enemy was loose in his midst. The second taskmaster saw the brazen attack, and Kadorax materialized behind him with an activation of *Chaos Step* before he had a chance to raise an alarm for his comrades. *Assir's Edge* removed the back of the man's neck with a single stroke.

They moved deeper into the woods, away from the rear of the jackal horde. It didn't take long for them to spot a command tent decorated with fine embroidery and a few pennants fluttering from the top. Kadorax waited for a moment at the base of a thick tree to look for any signs of Elise pursuing the same target. When he saw no sign of the woman, he scampered to the front of the tent, Bazrath right on his heels. "We'll go in hard. No use trying to be stealthy about it. We rush in, kill everything that moves. I'll go left. You split right."

Bazrath growled and nodded, clearly starting to have some issues controlling his corrupted bloodlust.

After a single deep breath to steady his nerves, Kadorax burst through the tent flap, ready to kill whoever or whatever was inside. The scene within the tent was far from what he had expected. Unlike other war tents he had been in, there were no chairs or even carpets and pillows to accommodate a gathering of commanders before a battle. Instead, the entire tent seemed to be covering something—a portal of sorts—and it swirled with a sheen of dark, reflective magic.

No jackals or other enemies were in the tent, so Kadorax hesitantly approached the portal, staying back on his heels in case he needed to jump out of the way of anything quickly coming through. In the depths of the swirling, chaotic magic, he saw a figure growing smaller and smaller. It looked like a man, though it could have been a jackal wearing a wizard's robes, and the figure was running away from the portal. The odd perspective of the magic meant Kadorax saw the man running down rather than away, and peering over the edge gave him a quick wave of vertigo.

"You're seeing the portal, right? I'm not insane?" the bastion asked.

Bazrath laughed. "I cannot speak to your insanity, but the portal is there—I can assure you of that. I've never seen anything like it. Truly remarkable . . ."

Kadorax grabbed a stick from the ground and tossed it into the swirling morass. The small twig vanished behind the murky darkness, but it reappeared almost as quickly. It sat on the bottom edge of the portal's *other side*, gravity keeping it fixed in place on what Kadorax assumed was simply the ground.

"I can't see where they are. Whatever is controlling the jackals is beyond the portal, but I can't see where it is!" Kadorax paced in front of the magical doorway, a dozen different ideas flying through his mind.

"Wherever it is, I'd bet it is far enough to be out of Elise's reach. Tell her I ran off. Or tell her I died. I don't care." Bazrath offered a curt salute in the tradition of Agglor's more seasoned sailors and captains before stepping into the portal.

At once, the corrupted elf was lost to darkness, and then his outline appeared above the stick Kadorax had thrown through, and the corrupted elf was sprinting toward the robed figure far in the distance. For a moment, Kadorax contemplated doing the same in hopes of finding the jackal leader and ending the war once and for all, but he shook his head and left the tent before doing anything he would later regret.

Back toward Darkarrow, the sounds of a battle filtered through the trees. Men and jackals alike were screaming or howling, and the distinctive pop of magic accented the cacophony at random intervals.

Kadorax paused for just a moment to offer the long-departed elf a silent nod of respect before running back to the fight. Without any distinct leader to kill, he had his eyes set on the human taskmasters who were leading the charge. He would kill them all, and if he could capture and interrogate even a single one of them, he might have a chance to get some answers.

Approaching from the rear of the jackal horde meant Kadorax was completely unseen by the human masters. He moved methodically, slashing each across the neck with a single strike until every last one of them was dead. He started to smile at the efficiency of his success, but his happiness was short-lived. It felt too easy, and without a challenge, there was no real accomplishment.

In the middle of the throng, Kadorax saw a small pocket of wispy darkness that had to be Elise. A huge number of the jackals had already made it to the breach in the side of Dark-arrow, and they were clambering over each other to try to get inside. Kadorax dove into the back of the horde, slashing from side to side as quickly as he could. Jackal warriors fell like stalks of wheat before a scythe.

After a score or more of the jackals had fallen to *Assir's Edge*, the others finally began to realize that they were being cut to ribbons by an unexpected attacker. A knot of the beasts turned, claws and teeth bared, and rushed in at the bastion from all sides.

Kadorax swung his shield around to his left arm just in time to catch a snarling jackal mouth with a high-pitched screech of teeth against steel. He chopped down hard on the back of the creature's neck, and it collapsed under the bastion's feet.

More and more jackals were coming in hard at Kado-rax from all sides. He blocked a pair of them on his left with his shield, and *Cage of Chaos* reacted to several more claws scraping against his armor on the right. Everywhere he turned, all he could see were mangy, gruffy dogheads trying to rip him apart.

From the horde's western flank, Elise and her two assassin cohorts were turning the mud red with jackal blood. Despite the massive difference in ability between the basic jackal soldiers and the small group of people trying to hold Darkarrow, the sheer size of the horde was too much to overcome with superior weapons and talents.

Claws began digging into Kadorax's flesh from nearly every angle, and he felt his stamina and resolve fading together. He had never trained his body—in his current life or the last—to wade into a swamp of ferocious enemies and survive. Perhaps with more training and more experience he would have been better able to keep his feet.

When he hit the ground, Kadorax knew he didn't have long. He held the hilt of his sword high in front of his face to keep the clawing jackals from tearing out his eyes. *Guardian of the Deep* was still on cooldown for another couple days. Still, the bastion had one option to at least buy him some time.

Gritting his teeth against the constant onslaught raining down from above, Kadorax activated *The Obsidian Well* almost under his own feet. The nearest five or six jackals instantly fell into the depths of the glistening cavern, giving him a few precious seconds to climb back to his feet and escape.

Conjure Unholy Aberration came next to Kadorax's mind, and he summoned a twisted golem of bones and magic behind him. The creature erupted skyward from the dirt, scattering a handful of jackals as it appeared, and immediately the tides began to turn. Still relying on the set bonuses from his armor, Kadorax activated *Forsaken Lady's Condemnation* on the nearest jackal about to bite down on his shoulder. The creature stumbled and turned, its eyes alight with hazy white mist, and then it began tearing into its comrades with reckless abandon.

Kadorax finally had an opening. He ran directly across the top of the magical well he had created, suspended in air by his enchanted boots, and got free of the horde. The golem continued its rampage without a moment's thought given to any of the wounds it was constantly taking. The jackals had surrounded it and were tearing it apart with their claws and teeth, but the golem simply did not care. It stood taller than the largest of its attackers by at least a head, and its heavy bone arms were tossing broken jackals left and right like a tavern brawler scattering broken barstools.

As a whole, the jackals were starting to falter. Those who had fallen into the black pit Kadorax had conjured had been forever entombed at the spell's conclusion, and the golem had already slaughtered several scores of them on its own. To the bastion's right, Elise was still flinging tangible bolts of shadow into the air as she fought, though there were still too many enemies crowding the battlefield for Kadorax to see exactly how she was faring. At Darkarrow's broken wall, some of the jackals had undoubtedly made it inside—but even where the building was weakest, so many jackal corpses had fallen that the invaders were being bogged down by their own dead.

Kadorax could hardly believe that his meager band was managing to win. The pain throbbing throughout his entire body was a constant reminder to remain humble, but they were winning nonetheless. He ran to the side of the battle where he had last seen Elise, hoping both to distance himself from the golem he had created and to gain some modicum of protection by being in her shadow.

The leader of the Blackened Blades was practically covered in gore. Kadorax easily recognized all of the talents the woman had activated, and they were certainly effective. Her body was coated by a magical jacket of spikes protruding about six inches from her skin. Each spike pulsed with poison as the woman spun and slashed. Her feet were encased in golden energy as well, a talent Kadorax knew as *Stable Footing*, and it magically prevented any of the jackals from knocking her down. Around Elise's head was the most impressive of her talents. A black veil covered her head from her eyes to a place several inches above her hair. *Impossible Sight*, as the talent was called, gave her a slower-than-reality perception of the battlefield. Such an advantage allowed every one of her strikes to be perfectly timed, exquisitely placed, and flawlessly executed.

At least fifty jackals lay dead in Elise's wake. Perhaps only fifty more still held the field. Kadorax saw among the dead the bodies of the two Blackened Blades members whose names he did not know, and the sight of their corpses made him wonder what Bazrath was doing deep in jackal territory on the other side of the portal.

His shield ready, Kadorax charged into the fray on Elise's left. Together they pushed forward and crushed through the horde and to its very center. Unbeknownst to the assassin, Kadorax's uncontrollable bone golem was still there, surrounded by torn jackal corpses and looking for new enemies to crush.

Impossible Sight expired at the same time Elise and Kadorax reached the golem, and the woman barely had the reflexes to dodge a heavy bone appendage meant to take off her head. Kadorax slammed into the creature with his shield first. He only wanted to push it back into the rest of the jackals, not to cut it down altogether, though he realized at once that he lacked the strength and mass needed for the job.

The golem fixed its hollow, misshapen eyes on Kadorax before smashing him with a heavy fist that sent the bastion reeling ten feet backward. Luckily, Elise seemed to grasp the situation quickly, and she retreated at full speed before pulling any more of the golem's attention away from the jackals. She grabbed Kadorax under his shoulder, cursed his shield for getting in the way, and dragged him toward the last remnants of the back of the fight.

A notification was flashing across the bottom of Kadorax's vision. He focused on it for a brief moment simply to confirm his suspicions that he had gained another level, then turned his attention back to the fight. His fourteenth level talent choices could certainly wait until the battle's conclusion.

The bone golem so effectively thrashing the jackal horde only lasted a few more moments before dissipating. When it vanished, the remaining jackals seemed to realize how few of them were truly left. They scampered around in an unorganized fashion, clearly waiting for some new direction from their slain human overlords, but none came. "Finish the job?" Kadorax asked with a sly grin, still panting from exertion.

Elise returned his smile with one of her own. "Certainly."

Less than a minute later, the field of death was quiet once more.

"We need to find Brinna. I don't know how many made it inside," Kadorax said. He kept *Assir's Edge*—slick with blood against his hands—ready to kill once more.

Entering Darkarrow proved to be a difficult task. So many dead jackals had piled against the fallen stones of what used to be the exterior wall that they nearly blocked the path altogether.

"Brinna! Atticus!" Kadorax called into the dark, blood-stained hallways. "Syzak! Anyone alive?"

"And what happened to my adorable little elf companion?" Elise asked as they climbed over the gruesome barrier and into Darkarrow once more.

Kadorax offered her hand to surmount a particularly large stone. "We found a portal that presumably leads back to the jackal homelands. Bazrath decided he would rather be there than under the influence of your ring."

"Heh, so be it," the woman scoffed.

The first corridor beyond the shattered wall was just as littered with jackal corpses as the field outside the compound. Blood ran thick under their boots. Kadorax paused for a brief moment to inspect some of the wounds, and those he could identify looked to have come from Brinna's daggers, but still more of the ragged beasts had been killed by means he did not recognize.

The hallway split in two at its end. One path led into the burned part of Darkarrow while the other went back toward the main entrance and the primary staircase leading underground. Moving away from the more destroyed area of the manor, Kadorax turned left and made for the stairs. "Brinna! Syzak!" he called out again.

"Down here!" came a woman's voice.

Kadorax pushed through some fallen timbers from the ceiling and stepped over a dead jackal to get to the stairs. "You have a torch?" he asked Elise. She shook her head. The lower levels had no source of illumination built directly into them since they were seldom used.

"Atticus is a warlock. Perhaps he conjured some sort

of light," Kadorax thought aloud. He relaxed a little and sheathed his sword, careful on the damaged steps for fear of them giving out beneath him.

At the bottom of the stairs, there was indeed a little bit of light. Brinna held a splintered piece of wood that had part of an old tapestry wrapped around it. "Is it over?" she asked quietly.

"They're dead," the bastion confirmed.

Elise, cold as ever, didn't bother concerning herself with the well-being of anyone but the girl she had purchased. "Where's Gabi? Did she survive?"

The young girl poked her head out from underneath the rest of the tapestry that had sacrificed some of itself for the torch. "Yes . . ." she meekly answered. Brinna helped her up from the dirty, insect-covered floor.

"What happened upstairs?" Kadorax asked. "It looked like you killed some of them, but there were so many. I had thought the building itself was lost once they started pouring through the rubble."

From a side chamber Kadorax had entirely forgotten about in the darkness, Syzak and Atticus rejoined the group, both of their arms and clothing covered in blood. "Brinna and I killed a good number of them, but Atticus finished the rest."

"Ha, well that answers that." Kadorax wondered what kind of high-powered magic the advanced warlock was capable of wielding in combat. The Grim Sleeper was still fresh in his mind, and the abilities she had used were potent to say the least.

"There's nothing left in Darkarrow. Come on, we should leave in case more return. I want to see the portal you say you found," Elise interjected. She was already heading back up the stairs.

Kadorax led them all to the command tent he had found behind the jackal army. The entrance flap had been blown to the side by wind, and they could tell nothing remained of the portal before even entering. The only thing left was a loose collection of stones that had once been a circle.

"It was here, and Bazrath jumped through after what appeared to be a wizard. Whatever we were chasing, it looked human from the back. And I killed a dozen or more humans that were giving orders behind the jackal lines. There's something else at play that we don't yet understand." Kadorax walked around the ring of stones and nudged one of them back into place with his boot. Nothing happened.

Elise didn't look terribly convinced there had ever been a portal between all the loose stones, but she didn't press the issue any further. "Still remember the way to that temple? I'm betting the horde that came here was a distraction to keep everyone away from the real summoning. The jackals have no need to hit Virast."

"If the princess really was in Oscine City, they must have some way of transporting her quickly or else we'll beat them to the temple," Brinna added.

Hands on his hips, Kadorax let out a sigh. "You're right. Maybe more magic portals like this one. Perhaps we aren't early but already too late."

"All the more reason to make haste." Elise pushed past the tent flap and back into the fresh breeze coming from deeper within the forest that separated the civilized cities and towns from the wild, brutal lands of northern Agglor.

"Don't get ahead of yourself," Syzak cautioned. "We need supplies. A wagon for Atticus wouldn't hurt. He isn't the fastest member of our group."

Shaking his head, Kadorax had other ideas. "I don't

know . . . The temple isn't that far, maybe two days if we're moving quickly." He looked to Brinna, Gabi clinging to her side with shaking hands, and she instantly knew what he was suggesting.

"I'll stay to protect them," the former mayor of Assir stated with confidence.

"We'll be back soon." Kadorax placed a hand on her shoulder, but she pulled away.

Brinna held her head high and proud. "I've spent my entire life protecting civilians. I'll stay in Darkarrow for a few days to wait for your return. After a week, I'll take Atticus and Gabi to Virast. Look for us there. If you aren't back in two weeks, I'll assume you're all corrupted."

"Better to be off sooner rather than later," Syzak said quietly, breaking the tension that had quickly grown thick between them all.

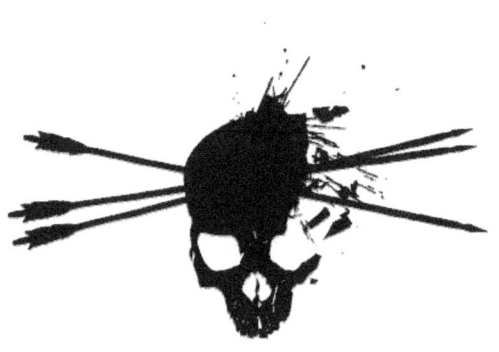

CHAPTER 9

Kadorax remembered well the path he and Syzak had taken from Darkarrow to the jackal temple that had seen both of their deaths. When they arrived at the temple's outskirts, a small number of fresh jackal tracks told all three that they weren't alone.

"I don't have my *Superior Talent* for a few more days. We'll need to get inside some other way," Elise said quietly from her position among a few trees.

Syzak and Kadorax crouched nearby in the undergrowth and watched. "If they moved an entire army here, we'd see them by now. The temple isn't that large inside," the bastion whispered back.

"Just a small group. Could be their elite warriors and the princess moving ahead of the rest." Syzak started inching forward, his tongue flicking out over his scaly lips to taste the air.

Kadorax rose from his crouch and waved to the others

to follow as he ran for the entrance to the temple. "Let's be quick about it," he whispered.

All three of them came to a stop just outside the doorway. The temple itself resembled a flat-topped ziggurat with only one way in or out, though the entrance had no actual door. Kadorax supposed the temple had existed for centuries before the jackals had claimed it as their own. The sides of the stone were decorated in worn, moss-covered reliefs, and art was not something the doghead species was known to employ.

Kadorax placed a hand flat against the ground and waited. "I don't feel any heavy footsteps. Hopefully no Gar'kesh inside . . ."

Elise turned the corner first, a dripping black dagger in her hand, and darted into the first stone corridor. On the ground level, there wasn't much light. The only room before the stone stairs leading down into the bowels of the temple wasn't anything particularly noteworthy, and the jackals hadn't placed any torches or candles inside it. What light reflected from the outside world was just barely enough to illuminate the uneven flagstones that made up the floor.

Stepping into the musty air once more, Kadorax couldn't help but remember the last time he was there. He and Syzak had followed a band of jackal priests and shamans in hopes of stealing some magical loot, and they hadn't expected to find the old temple the way they had.

Syzak gave a truncated snicker as the three moved past an old bloodstain on the eastern wall. The corpse the snake-man had made in that spot on his previous visit had since been removed, but the jackals hadn't bothered to scrub down the stone. Bits of doghead fur still clung to the jagged protrusions of the rock.

A pair of jet-black scorpions scurried across the blood smear and darted into an irregularity between two heavy stones. "Stairs are at the back. The jackals have a huge altar room down below, and there was a door at least three stories high at the end," Kadorax whispered.

They walked on the balls of their feet across the rough floor to the staircase that would take them down to the main room of the temple. "You remember the treasure room?" Syzak whispered so that Elise could not hear.

Kadorax subtly nodded. "I'm not sure I want to hit it with *her* alongside," he replied.

The three adventurers crept down the large stairs, and sounds of jackals moving about filtered up to them. "Doesn't sound like many," Elise whispered.

The stairs ended in a large chamber gently illuminated by holes and gaps in the ceiling overhead, where water and time had worked their way through the stones. "There," Kadorax said, pointing to a ledge he knew too well. "That rock shelf overlooks the main altar. If they're here with the princess, that's where they'll be."

Crawling to the edge of the natural platform on their bellies, Kadorax, Syzak, and Elise peered down to the jackals below. Six of the creatures, arranged in a small ring, were busy at work. "What do you think they're doing?" Syzak whispered.

Kadorax watched for a moment before replying. "Shackles over there fixed to the wall. And more than one cage. Looks like they're preparing for something big." He looked for any sign of the treasure room where he had previously lost his life to the Gar'kesh, but the stone wall behind the altar was as solid as ever. Memories of the great horned beast smashing through the stone and so easily slaughtering him made a shiver run through his spine. If another Gar'kesh was waiting behind the wall again, he wasn't sure the trio—as capable as they certainly were—would be able to survive.

One of the jackals below started to cast a spell. Elise lurched forward as though she would dive down to attack, and Kadorax caught her by the arm and held her back. "Wait," he said, shielding his voice with a hand.

The spell manifested as a swirl of black energy above the jackal, and then it shot into the ground at the creature's feet. Two of the other jackals began following suit. More and more bolts of dark magic entered the ground, forming no particular pattern Kadorax could recognize. He had never spent much time around necromancers and only had a cursory knowledge of warlocks, though the magic certainly evoked an evil feeling reminiscent of both classes.

"Raising the dead?" Syzak quietly hissed.

Both Kadorax and Elise nodded, their eyes transfixed on the unexpected scene.

After a few moments of casting, Kadorax knew what was going to happen. He inched a little closer to the edge. "Stay here. They're mine."

Before either Elise or Syzak could say anything in protest, Kadorax dropped the ten or so feet from the ledge to the larger cavern and drew his sword. "Hey!" he yelled at the jackal spellcasters. They turned at once and began readying their spells for a battle. "Filthy damn doghead scum. Time to die!"

Kadorax charged forward, and a hail of magical attacks spiraled in at his body. He didn't bother to grab his shield from his back or even dodge the missiles. They smashed into his breastplate and dissipated in small little puffs of frost. Kadorax's *Stalwart Bracers of the Forsaken Lady* completely negated every ounce of magic the jackals were throwing at him.

Assir's Edge tore through two jackal wizards before they could fully understand what was happening. Kadorax felt a deep, unsettling cold permeating the ground beneath his boots as he moved from enemy to enemy, cutting them to ribbons. He sensed the magical frost, but it did nothing. His balance held true, and all the physical pain the spell would have normally brought with it was reduced to a simple awareness that the cold was there, entirely devoid of pain.

Grasping bone hands started reaching up through the solid stone floor. The skeletons were clambering to the surface, and Kadorax was stomping them back down as quickly as they appeared. His boots, weighted by steel spats, crushed them to dust. Everywhere their hands touched his armor, the bones melted away as though they were nothing more than bits of darkness being scattered by the light.

Kadorax couldn't help but laugh as he cleaved through the jackal ranks. The wizards fell before him, and every last one of their necrotic spells was rendered inert before it could even slow the bastion down. *Assir's Edge* bit into the neck of the final wizard. The tall jackal stared down at Kadorax, its mouth agape and eyes wide, and it looked as though it was trying to speak one final word before heading off to the class trainers to either die for real or become corrupted.

Grinning, Kadorax twisted his blade and wrenched it free. He could feel the scrape of metal against bone as the weapon caught momentarily on some internal piece of the jackal, and then it was free, and the room was quiet.

"Quite impressive," Elise stated with actual admiration in her voice. "That armor you have is certainly fitting for the task. Well done." She was standing in front of the stone altar, surveying the images carved upon its surface and running her fingers in the ancient grooves.

Kadorax cleaned his blade on a patch of jackal fur and returned it to its sheath. Sadly, the casters hadn't been nearly high enough level to grant him any noticeable experience points despite their numbers. "They were trying to raise undead here, though for what I don't know," he said. He checked the jackals for any useful items, but their robes didn't have any pockets and they weren't wearing belts laden with gear.

"I think they might have been sent ahead of the main force to secure the temple or prepare it somehow," Syzak said.

Elise was still busy investigating the altar. "You were killed by a Gar'kesh, yes?" she asked over her shoulder. "I've only seen a handful of them myself, but I couldn't imagine one fitting too well into such a small space. How ever did it kill the mighty Kadorax, Lord of Darkarrow?"

The bastion growled, but he didn't respond.

Approaching the wall behind the altar, Syzak placed his hand against it and tasted the air. "Something still back there, Kad," he said. "The stones are hot."

Kadorax and Elise both placed their hands against it as well. The heat coming from the other side was too weak to be detected by anyone without the sensitive scales or infrared sensing organs of a snake-man. "What's behind the wall?" Elise asked, taking a step backward.

"The last time we were here, a Gar'kesh broke out from behind the wall. It looks like they repaired it. Maybe . . . incubation? They might need the wall in place to help the Gar'kesh grow, if that's even how they come into existence. I don't know." Kadorax took a step back as well and looked to the top of the remade wall. "My guess is that they need the wall to close in heat from something, but that feels like a stretch."

"Or they're afraid of the Gar'kesh just as much as we are. The wall keeps it from attacking them until it is fully grown and able to break out on its own. By then they would be far away," Syzak explained.

All three of them continued staring at the wall, straining their senses to try and glean any information they could from the other side of the rock. As expected, the stones yielded nothing.

"Any talents to see to the other side?" Kadorax asked the assassin.

Elise thought for a moment, her hand on her chin and her eyes directed skyward to her character sheet. "I can use *Detect Arcane* to see what kind of magic lurks on the other side," she finally said.

"I think we can assume that whatever is alive or producing heat in a sealed underground chamber is magical," Kadorax replied. He shared a quick look with Syzak that said both of them knew the real reason he did not want the assassin looking for magical objects in the underground chamber. The treasure room they had seen behind the Gar'kesh had been monumental, and it was bound to be laden with magical artifacts—perhaps even the items the pair of Blackened Blades had lost many weeks before.

"I can make a vertical trap to the other side to give us a window for a minute, maybe less. That might be the best we have," Syzak said.

Pacing in front of the wall, Kadorax started putting together a plan. "Make a trap and send me through. Put it in the corner and out of the way in case there's something waiting on the other side to break out. I'll see what's on the other side, and if there's some sleeping, incubating Gar'kesh, I'll kill it. When I need to come back, I'll pound on the wall."

Elise started to suggest that she go through the trap-made portal instead of Kadorax, but she quickly bit her tongue. "Just be quick about it," she quipped instead.

Syzak pointed his hands toward the bottom corner of the wall and cast *Rat Trap*. A dozen fetid little creatures scurried out of nowhere as the wall itself dematerialized in front of their eyes. A little bit of light was coming through from the other side. Kadorax crawled through the hole on his hands and knees. The chamber behind all the stone was much like he remembered it—full of treasure stacked from the floor to the ceiling.

"My God . . ." he mouthed to himself. He stood to his full height and stretched his back. Removing all the treasure would take a team of workers several days, and that would just be to get it up to ground level. Transporting it all back to Darkarrow or Oscine City would be another monumental task. There were chests brimming with golden coins stacked in groups of three, and between them were various paintings, silver and gold jewelry, and more artifacts than he could count.

Sadly, Kadorax knew the hoard of wealth would have to wait. He pushed through some of the chests and began climbing atop the pile to see what else might be lurking in the room, his mind anticipating the possibility of a slumbering Gar'kesh waiting to devour him. From the middle of the shaking, unbalanced pile, Kadorax could just see over the top and to the other side.

A pair of pale, translucent eggs slowly pulsed in front of what looked like a tight air shaft. The eggs were giving off light, and being so close, Kadorax could finally sense their heat. He carefully descended the back side of the loot pile to stand in front of them. Suspended beneath the skin of the eggs, he could see two Gar'kesh slowly shifting around as they formed in golden liquid. The eggs themselves were as large as wagons, and the creatures barely fit inside them.

All of Kadorax's preconceived notions of the Gar'kesh being magical god-like entities summoned by spells and incantation were wrong. The Gar'kesh were born, and that meant something was laying their eggs.

Something presumably much larger and far more terrifying.

Kadorax peered around the eggs to the air shaft behind them, and the sticky webbing coating the stone told him it wasn't designed to move air in and out of the chamber. It was a birth canal of sorts. A rut in the muck on the bottom of the shaft and on both sides meant that the eggs had slid down the canal at some point and come to a rest at the bottom. Whether they were laid by some monstrous beast on the surface or stolen from their nest and dropped down the shaft by the jackals, he had no way of knowing.

Before shattering the eggs to kill the fetuses within, the bastion quickly began picking through the vast mountain of wealth to find something he could easily take back with him to the other side. Most of what he pushed through was gold, and filling his pockets with money wouldn't help in a fight.

He tossed aside a few exquisite paintings and a wooden box full of non-magical rings before finding a necklace that caught his eye. It was silver, and hanging from it was a large pendant in the shape of an arrow piercing a skull. It generated a notification on Kadorax's character sheet the moment he touched it.

Selwyn's Eternal Brooch - When worn about the neck, this brooch imbues all of the wearer's weapons with longing and sorrow.

Those unfortunate enough to be struck are instantly filled with images of their deepest regrets. Effect: moderate. Passive.

Kadorax admired the detailed pendant for a few moments, watching as the light from the eggs reflected off a black gem in the center of the small skull. The gem wasn't symmetrical with the other side of the skull, however, and it looked like the gemstone that had perhaps once resided there had since been removed. With most magical items Kadorax had come across on Agglor, damage often meant reduced effectiveness or even being rendered inert. He wondered if placing a second gem in the skull would enhance the strange power already contained within the brooch.

Shaking his head at the bizarre, unexpected effect the necklace would have on his weapons, he slipped it around his head and dropped the talisman under his breastplate.

A few quick slashes of his sword later, the two Gar'kesh embryos were scattered all across the stone floor. Their deaths meant the light of the room had been extinguished, and Kadorax had to feel his way back across the loot pile. He pounded the hilt of his sword against the stone and called to his companion.

After only a few seconds, Syzak's *Spike Trap* appeared on the wall.

"Thanks," Kadorax said once he was standing in the main chamber of the temple once more. Elise had her legs dangling from the altar and was looking in the opposite direction as though she didn't care one way or another if the bastion returned at all.

"Did you find anything?" Syzak asked.

Kadorax gave him a wink and pulled up a few inches of silvery chain from his breastplate while Elise was still occupied. "Two Gar'kesh eggs and a . . . birth canal of sorts, I guess. Just a stone shaft where the eggs are deposited. There must be something massive out there to lay them."

"Let's try to avoid whatever makes Gar'kesh." Syzak hopped down from the plinth that held the altar and started moving back to the ledge that led to the outside world.

"Ready?" Kadorax asked.

Elise barely acknowledged him as she slid down to her feet. "I was expecting more, not a quick slaughter and no profit. Maybe our intel was wrong . . ."

Kadorax was wondering the exact same thing. "What's your next move? Head north with Gabi and kill every last jackal yourself?"

"Something like that," the woman slyly answered.

The three started back up to the surface, but a new noise coming from above stopped them in their tracks.

Kadorax held a finger over his lips and listened. A deep rumbling was coming from somewhere out in the forest. "Something's coming," the bastion whispered to his companions.

They crept up the stone stairs leading to the main room on the ground floor, and Syzak continued to the exit and peered outside. "Incoming," he said over his shoulder. "Two Gar'kesh. Maybe twenty jackals. Princess is with them in a cage."

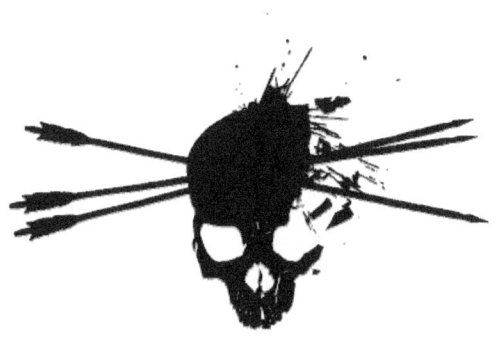

CHAPTER 10

"**R**un or fight?" Elise quickly demanded.

"Two Gar'kesh. Nothing we can do. Run!" Kadorax didn't wait for an answer. He ran out the front of the temple, sweeping Syzak up in his wake, and heard Elise's footfalls joining the retreat as well. When he emerged into the daylight, he dug in his heels as hard as he could. Syzak and Elise both crashed into his back and knocked him to the ground.

"Jackals are too close. They'll see us. Back to the altar!" he yelled.

Syzak and Elise didn't need any further prodding. They both scrambled back on their heels and lunged into the relative darkness of the temple interior as quickly as they could.

"Come on, downstairs. The birth canal." Kadorax led the way back into the bowels of the temple and the altar room. Without stopping for even a moment, he cast *The Obsidian*

Well, which had only been off cooldown for less than an hour since the fight outside Darkarrow.

A hideous screech came from the center of the jagged, glistening well. "What the hell is that?" Elise yelled. She had her daggers in her hand and was already throwing herself into combat.

The creature summoned by the well was almost as malformed and demented as the Gar'kesh outside. It was black and covered in sharp crystalline structures, but it didn't resemble any insect or other animal Kadorax had ever seen. It had three heads somewhat reminiscent of crustaceans' heads, and its legs were too numerous to count. The creature screeched and squealed, launching globs of viscous liquid from its mouths as it staggered backward under the ferocity of Elise's daggers.

Her wrists flared to life with blue magic, and she skewered the strange magical creation with one of her daggers. It screeched again, and she cut one of its heads off with her other hand. Blood splattered out of the insect's carapace, and judging by the speed at which the woman tried to shake herself free from the corpse, Kadorax assumed it didn't feel good against her skin.

The three of them scrambled through the well and into the treasure chamber, where they waited for the spell to dissipate, all eyes glued to the ledge on the other side of the wall.

"They're in the building," Syzak said in the darkness.

Sounds of the jackal retinue moving around were making their way to the altar room.

"Come on . . ." Kadorax urged. Still, the well painfully persisted. "Move back. Get as far from the well as we can."

All three of them pushed back against the far wall.

Someone's foot scraped against the side of a wooden chest, and the movement sent a handful of golden coins scattering noisily to the ground. Elise jumped on the errant coins to silence them, cursing under her breath as she hit the hard stones.

Finally, just as the first jackal was coming into view, the magical well expired and left a solid wall of limestone blocks in its place. "That took long enough," the bastion mouthed so quietly he could barely be heard.

No one moved in the pitch darkness. "How do we get out?" Elise whispered.

Kadorax wracked his mind for an answer. "There's . . . a pile of gold coins between us and the way out. If we crawl over it blind, we'll make too much noise. We're . . . stuck. Damn."

A deep, unsettling quiet squirmed in amongst the coins, treasure, and absolute darkness. The muffled sounds of jackals moving around the altar could just barely be heard through the stones. They were dragging something, and whatever it was made a loud, grueling noise against the uneven stone floor.

"Move now while they're busy," Kadorax whispered. He didn't wait for anyone else to respond before leaping onto the treasure pile and rushing for the egg shaft. The others followed behind him, and the noise they all made as the loot came tumbling down was certainly strong enough to be heard through the stone barrier.

Kadorax reached the escape route first. "Come on, not much time." He pushed Elise through, guiding her body in the darkness, and then did the same for Syzak.

Climbing out of the egg shaft was far from an easy task. The slime and muck clinging to the stones made them slick where they would have otherwise been rough and offered some traction, and the angle at which the tunnel pitched downward was steep. Kadorax, his enchanted spats offering him better purchase on the stones, had to constantly catch both Elise and Syzak multiple times to keep them from sliding all the way back down to the broken eggs below.

Eventually, the three reached the surface rather exhausted. Syzak had to double over to catch his breath.

"Will they come for us?" Elise asked, cautiously peering back down the tunnel whence they had come. The egg shaft ended in what essentially amounted to a mine entrance on the surface, though instead of being vertical for people to walk through, it was horizontal and flat with the forest floor.

Kadorax listened for a few moments, but all he could hear were the sounds of the jackal army on the other side of the temple. "I have no idea. If they do, they probably won't come up the egg shoot like we did. They'd just send their army to chase us through the woods."

The woman nodded. "We should climb the backside to get a look at how many they've brought. Maybe we can still take them unawares."

Despite a wave of reservations, Kadorax knew she was right. They had to stop whatever it was the jackals were doing with the altar, even if it meant going head to head with a pair of fully grown Gar'kesh. At least they'd be outside with more room to maneuver.

Kadorax and Elise started climbing up the back of the temple while Syzak crept around the building's foundation to provide support from the side. A horde about the same size as the one that had attacked Darkarrow was casually assembled among the trees and underbrush in front of the temple. In the small clearing right before the door sat two

Gar'kesh, their many arms resting on the ground at awkward angles. The lumbering beasts were too large to sit comfortably and looked strange just sitting on the ground instead of callously slaughtering enemies left and right.

"Any ideas?" Kadorax whispered.

The woman thought, her eyes moving upward through the character sheet in her vision. "I can take one of them, I think. *Rapid Execution: Rank 6* should do the trick."

"Has a long cooldown, even at rank six, right?" the bastion asked.

Elise nodded and readjusted her position on the stones to further hide her presence, not that any of the jackals were looking in their direction. "I can take one of them if you can take the other. And we don't have much time. They'll figure out how those jackals down below died, and then they'll be looking for someone."

A sinister grin spread across Kadorax's face. "Take the Gar'kesh on the left. I can handle the one on the right. Once it's dead, run back here. We won't want to be too close." He shimmied to the side of the temple and tapped his nails against the stone to get Syzak's attention. "Stay back, but be ready. Things are going to happen fast."

Kadorax and Elise exchanged a solemn nod, and the bastion felt like he was back in time with the Blackened Blades and about to fulfill a contract alongside a pair of his fellow assassins. Without speaking, the pair leapt from the top of the temple and each landed on their target Gar'kesh, instantly throwing the entire horde into rapid action. Jackal shouts and war cries rose up all around. The two beasts immediately thrashed and began rolling to free themselves of their attackers, but their huge size made them too slow.

Rapid Execution sheathed Elise's dagger in a deep cloak

of dripping shadows, and she rammed it deep into the creature's neck, severing its spine and pumping it full of fast-acting toxin that ate through its nervous system. Elise expertly rode the creature to the ground as it shuddered and died beneath her.

Twenty feet to her right, Kadorax was taking a much different approach. He held onto the back of the Gar'kesh's thick hide with his left hand while swinging hard with *Assir's Edge*. He bit through a few inches of the beast's flesh and then activated *Forsaken Lady's Condemnation*, one of the skills bestowed upon him by his armor's set bonuses.

The tenth rank talent activated, and Kadorax launched himself from the Gar'kesh's back, barely keeping his grip on his sword as he flew through the air and smashed into the temple's stone exterior.

The Gar'kesh roared. It flexed its mighty arms at its side and lowered its horned head. The jackals nearest to the beast seemed to realize what was happening, but they were too late. They couldn't scramble out of the way quickly enough, and they were caught beneath the heavy, crushing hooves of the beast as it charged forward.

Kadorax and Elise scrambled over the stone to the top of the temple. From their position of relative safety, they watched as the monstrous beast thrashed its way through rank after rank of the jackal horde. A few of the nearest jackals had taken notice of them and tried to attack, but they hadn't seen Syzak waiting along the side, and the snake-man cut them down as they tried to scramble up the stones after their attackers.

In the span of only a few heartbeats, the relaxed and organized jackal horde devolved into pure chaos. Jackals were trampled to death by the dozens, and those quick enough to run away didn't hesitate to turn for the cover of the trees and abandon their comrades.

"I don't think they'll be able to take down one of their own Gar'kesh," Elise casually observed.

"They don't have the coordination or the numbers to kill it," the bastion agreed. He watched the back of the beast as it slammed two of its arms into a small knot of jackal warriors trying in vain to mount a defense and save their lives. They didn't stand a chance.

Elise, hands on her hips, let out a contented sigh. "How long will the magic last?"

"Once the jackal army is dead, it will come back for us. It won't stop until we kill it."

"Oh."

"We need to make a plan before that happens," Kadorax said. "Running back to Darkarrow might work. I don't know if it would follow us or not. And the princess is still underground."

"If they haven't sacrificed her yet," Elise added. She flipped her dagger by the hilt, splattering tangible liquid shadows all over the stones.

They didn't have long to formulate any kind of strategy before the Gar'kesh came rumbling back into view. The beast was covered in hundreds of minor wounds, but the lacerations and burns covering its hide didn't seem to bother it or even slow it down.

"Distract it. I'm jumping on again," Kadorax stated. He readied his feet and got to the edge of the stone he was standing on, waiting for the Gar'kesh to turn its back.

Elise whispered a few words, and an image of her snapped into view to the Gar'kesh's left while she faded into the patchwork grays and greens of the temple's facade.

The Gar'kesh took the bait and slammed a fist down onto the illusion, immediately dissipating the magic but turning its armored back in the process. Kadorax leapt and landed on the creature's shoulders, sinking *Assir's Edge* into the meat under its collarbone and hanging on for his life. He pressed his palm flat against the back of the creature's skull and activated *Chaos Shock*.

Four heavy rods of reflective, shimmering copper shot out of his palm. They pierced the Gar'kesh's skull, and Kadorax ripped back his hand for a second element, leaving the metal firmly lodged in brain matter. The talent's second wave resulted in a short torrent of thick, sticky mud leaping from Kadorax's skin to coat the bloody wound on the creature's skull. The mud itself wasn't magical or even forceful enough to have any effect on so large an opponent, but the copper had done its job. The flat, circular ends of the metal had pierced the Gar'kesh's face.

The beast stumbled and tried to keep its footing, then attempted to howl, though its jaw had been effectively pinned shut by metal, so all that came out was a weak grunt. The Gar'kesh hit the ground with a mighty thud and moved no more. A new notification flashed across the bottom of Kadorax's vision at the same time. Hitting level fifteen meant he had two stat points to allocate and another talent to choose. It also meant he was closing in on his *Bastion's Superior Talent*, though he had no idea what his choices would be.

Elise's callous voice brought him back to the present. "Well played. I could use some magic like that myself," she said, moving to get a better view of the corpse. "Maybe when you're high enough I'll have you teach me a multiclass. Ha."

"The princess is still below," Syzak added. He shared a

covert look with Kadorax behind the assassin's back. "We can still save her. There's time."

What few jackals were left alive after the Gar'kesh's destructive rampage were either too injured to be of any concern or already running for their lives. Kadorax had to wonder if there had been any human taskmasters among the horde. The force that had assaulted Darkarrow had been prodded along by humans—and the bastion had no idea what any of it meant. The portal added yet another layer of complexity. His mind swam with possibilities, but without more information, he knew that guessing wouldn't do him any good. Saving King Bennington's daughter might be the best chance for some answers.

"Let's go." Kadorax led the way into the temple once more, running at full speed for the stairs that would lead them all back to the altar.

They reached the ledge overlooking the lowest floor, and the jackals around the altar were furiously scrambling to move into place all the pieces they needed to complete their ritual. Luckily, they hadn't bothered to station any soldiers inside the temple as guards, likely relying on what should have been an overwhelming force outside to deter any possible attacks.

The corpses Kadorax had left on the stone floor just moments before had been thrown to the side like discarded scraps after a meal. The jackals didn't care that their advanced group had been slaughtered, though the clear indication of intruders had certainly accelerated whatever it was they were preparing to do.

"Let me get a few, experience hogs," Syzak hissed as he pushed past Kadorax and Elise. The snake-man leapt down from the ledge and charged the back of the nearest jackal, clawing his way through mangy flesh and matted hair with all the pent-up fury of a seasoned adventurer who had just been denied a huge number of experience points.

The jackals were unprepared. They howled and screeched, chomped and slashed, but they were clearly not soldiers or even combat-oriented magic users. Kadorax figured they were the jackal equivalents of priests or shamans, and he watched with a smile as his companion made them die like helpless peasants.

"Come on. Let him handle the priests. Get the princess," Kadorax said. He and Elise leapt down from the stone ledge and ran for the metal cages at the back of the room. They had previously all been empty, but now they held two captives wearing dirty, torn rags. The female prisoner wailed at the top of her lungs, her voice as ragged as her clothing, while her male compatriot only sat on his own with his knees against his chest. What remained of his garb vaguely resembled that of a Kingsgate guardsman, though he was so disheveled that the red color of his clothes could have just as easily come from blood stains as dyes intentionally placed into the fabric.

The two shoddily constructed cages weren't locked. They had been tied shut with a few cords of leather, and Kadorax sliced through them with ease. He reached into the first cage to pull the princess free while Elise did the same with the man. The young woman clawed onto Kadorax's hand, falling over herself in her desperation to escape, and nearly brought him to the ground in her fervor.

Finally, when the princess was completely free of the cage, Kadorax pushed her behind in case any of the remaining jackals were coming near. Only two of the beasts were still alive, and Syzak was having an easy time herding them against the wall with his claws.

"You're the princess, right?" Kadorax asked the shaking woman still clinging to his armor.

She nodded meekly. "Yes. My name . . . is Lilly. Is . . . Is my father . . . alive?"

The last jackal in the temple died beneath Syzak's sharp claws. The snake-man slit its throat and then shoved it to the side after a cursory glance toward the two freed captives.

"I don't know. The last we heard, the king was heading toward Oscine City. I'm just glad we found you in time," Kadorax told the princess honestly.

The man Elise had rescued was barely strong enough to stand on his own two legs. He looked like he hadn't eaten in weeks and had been enduring constant beatings at the same time. "You're one of her guards?" Kadorax asked him. "What happened?"

The man's glassy-eyed expression showed nothing but despair. "We were headed toward Oscine City. Three ships. Forty guards." He hung his head in shame and coughed a bit, the movement wracking his frail frame. "There was a traitor. Samson was his name, I think. He set the ship on fire. Jackals were everywhere before we realized exactly what was happening."

"What happened to the other ships and the other guards?" Elise asked.

The man's vacant stare didn't waver from the stone floor. "Same thing. The ships burned, and jackals were everywhere. Only . . . six of us survived. Captured."

"How did the jackals board your ships?" Elise demanded. "I've never heard of dogheads with a navy."

Kadorax had to admit he held the same question in his own mind, though he silently chastised the assassin for her crass delivery.

The guard shook his head and ran a grime-covered hand through his shaggy hair. "They came from belowdecks. Some sort of sorcery. A portal perhaps. I didn't see it with my own eyes. All I know is that I failed to protect her majesty. I failed the king."

Elise's interrogation was implacable. "You said six guards survived. Where are the others?"

"They . . . They took them. I don't know where. Just . . . *away*. I don't know how long it's been. I'm the last one left," he explained while holding back sobs. He continued to stare at the floor and shuffle his feet.

"Come on, let's get out of here. We have some food and more supplies back at Darkarrow. You can stay there or go to Virast if you like," Kadorax said, reaching a hand beneath the man's shoulder to encourage him.

"My duty is to her highness, Princess Lilly. I'll stay with her," he said. Despite his gallant words, there was no strength or confidence at all in his voice.

Kadorax didn't feel like mentioning the man's weakened state and further diminishing what little honor he had left. "Let's get some food in you. We'll figure it out later."

Arriving back at Darkarrow once more felt odd. Kadorax hated seeing the estate in such ruin with so much death all around it, and he couldn't dislodge a nagging feeling in the back of his mind that rescuing the princess had been too easy. The jackal army had sent a horde with two Gar'kesh to ensure the princess's delivery to the temple, but they hadn't sent any powerful spellcasters. If the guard's story of portals was true—and the bastion had to believe it after what he had seen in the forest—they had more magic than he had previously thought common among the species.

Or more likely, the jackals had help. Human help. There was someone orchestrating the invasion from behind the scenes, and using Gabi to plunge northward into jackal territory would likely be the only way to find out exactly who it was.

Brinna, Gabi, and Atticus had salvaged what they could from the ruins of Darkarrow, and they had all of the palatable food spread out on top of several crates serving as tables. Lilly and her guard nearly leapt at it, eager as they were for a full meal after weeks of being transported in cages and treated like slaves. As the man had explained on the walk from the temple back to the outskirts of civilization, he had given all of his meager rations to the princess, electing not to eat a single morsel since being captured.

The meal consisted mostly of dried meats and old vegetables from the root cellar beneath the estate, though Brinna had discovered a rather copious amount of spiced mead in one of the damage barracks rooms close to the missing wall. One of the Blackened Blades members had been brewing it in a closet, and they had enough between two wooden barrels to get them all drunk if they wanted to.

Once everyone had a chance to finish their first round of food and drink and the appropriate introductions had been made between the princess and everyone else, Kadorax was eager to figure out the next step required to push the jackals back into their own land. "Our last message from Kingsgate indicated that the royal army was finally on the move and heading toward Oscine City. There's a contingent of Priorate Knights there as well. You'll be safe."

The princess bowed her head and continued eating. Though she hadn't fared nearly as badly as her companion, she still looked gaunt. Kadorax had to assume that she had been slight of build before starving for a few weeks, and the harrowing experience had taken its toll on her appearance in more ways than one. "Thank you," she said between bites.

Elise was standing behind the main group, a goblet of mead in her hand as she paced. "We need to combine the knights and the Kingsgate army. With a few thousand trained soldiers, we can plunge right through the heart of jackal territory. Wipe them from Agglor once and for all. Push their cities into the sea."

At the mention of returning to the north, Gabi's face paled.

"One step at a time, Elise," Kadorax chided.

The assassin scoffed. "If you're worried about the first step, we're going to need a new captain to take us back across the sea to Oscine City. Worry about that."

"I'm sure the rest of the ship's crew will be just fine without Bazrath." Kadorax turned back to the others still seated around the food. "Atticus, any progress figuring out the Gar'kesh?"

The old man was struggling to rip apart a piece of dried lamb with his fingers. He was missing the majority of his teeth, and though Brinna had offered to cut his food with one of her knives, he had insisted on struggling by himself. At the mention of his name, he perked up a bit. "Progress? Heh. Their secrets are easier to pry apart than this damned meat of yours!" Eyes wide, he stared at Kadorax as he spoke as though the bastion was also Darkarrow's head chef and the meal's poor quality was his fault.

"Well, what does that mean? Where are they from?" Kadorax went on.

The man's eyes lit up as he finally made a small enough piece of meat to drop down his gullet without chewing. "Where they're from? Agglor, of course. Did you think they were native to your world, hmm? Dinner first, then I'll show you what I can do!" He laughed as he began tearing another strip of meat from bone, rocking unsteadily forward and backward. Brinna wrapped an arm around his back to keep him from falling off his stool.

Content with his portion and not terribly eager to see whatever it was Atticus had in store for him, Kadorax got up from the crates of food to wander around the shattered halls of his former estate. He had two levels to negotiate, and he wanted some time by himself to enjoy the dark, shadowy halls of his long-lost home one more time.

Instead of going to his old room, Kadorax went to the southern section of Darkarrow, where sentries would typically store their gear and prepare for their shifts. He climbed a wooden ladder to the roof, and from there he could see just how badly the jackal damage was. More of the building's roof was burned than he had previously thought. The next time it rained—and it rained frequently in the area around Virast—the whole complex would be flooded. Anything left in the cellars would be ruined or washed away, and what furniture was left in useable shape would certainly meet its end.

He paced along the upper battlements skirting the edge of the roof and took in the sounds of dusk coming from the forest. Under normal circumstances, there would have been a dozen rogues and assassins prowling about the eaves, cross-bows in their hands. But that time had passed, and Kadorax was alone.

Stopping at a point on the northern wall to watch the

moon creep up above the trees, he called his character sheet to his vision.

Strength: 19
Agility: 15
Fate: 21
Spirit: 15
Charisma: 15
Bond: 6

A small flashing indicator beneath the *Bond* stat was patiently waiting for him to focus on it and select new skills. Before reading the new talents waiting for his decision, he placed another stat point into *Spirit* in the hopes of being able to put together the jackal plan a little better. Finding more clues and learning more information would certainly be key, but additional *Spirit* had tangible advantages as well.

Leaning back against the angled roof to get a little more comfortable, Kadorax called his new talent options to his vision. He had the ability to raise one of either *Chaos Shock*, *Bastion Weapon Proficiency*, or *Guardian of the Deep* to rank three, and he chose the summon spell without too much debate. The new rank reduced the cooldown to seven days and also opened up a sub-menu underneath the skill, where Kadorax could select one of three passives to enhance the minion: *Hardened Carapace*, *Enhanced Mind*, and *Additional Tentacles*. Again, the decision was easy to make. He focused on *Enhanced Mind* and unlocked it, already eager to get *Guardian of the Deep* to rank four so he could see what other passives would be available for him to unlock. The horrifying watery beast was already at least on par with a Gar'kesh in terms of strength, and each passive upgrade would mean more and more power.

Kadorax took his time reading the talents available for level fifteen:

Hunter through the Mists: Rank 1 - The bastion's senses commingle, allowing enhanced perception of his surroundings and enemy intents. Effect: moderate. Cooldown: 15 minutes.

Fires of the Void: Rank 1 - Born of flame, the bastion is no longer as strongly harmed by fire magic. At higher ranks, Fires of the Void also negates naturally occurring fire damage. At maximum rank (10), the bastion is healed by fire instead of harmed. Effect: minor. Passive.

Hungering Soul: Rank 1 - The void sustains all who have a strong enough connection to it. The bastion no longer needs to eat or sleep to maintain his physical body and presence of mind. Instead, the lives of those claimed by the bastion are absorbed through the flesh as fuel for further machinations. Effect: profound. Passive.

Battlefield Presence: Rank 1 - The knight's appearance in combat has a rallying effect on nearby allies, increasing their Strength, Agility, and Fate by 1 for 30 seconds. Effect: minor. Cooldown: 20 minutes.

Bring Together: Rank 1 - In times of desperate need, a knight's most valuable assets are his comrades. All allies within 50 yards of the knight are teleported together with the knight to one target location on the battlefield. Effect: profound. Cooldown: 1 day.

All five of the available talents looked interesting and effective enough to be worth unlocking. Kadorax mulled them over, thinking through each skill in the most likely scenarios they would be used, and slowly narrowed down his selection to just *Fires of the Void* and *Bring Together*. Of the other three, *Hungering Soul* was certainly the most unique and unexpected, but Kadorax hesitated to select it on account of his lack of prior knowledge concerning it. He didn't know if he would have to continue fighting and killing forever in order to survive, and that possibility wasn't worth the risk.

Fires of the Void held a particular attraction on account of the added survivability it offered, especially when Kadorax considered that some of the jackal magic users had used fire spells in the past. Unfortunately, it would take multiple ranks before it became extremely effective, and that meant the opportunity cost of unlocking the talent was simply too high.

With a smile, Kadorax focused on *Bring Together* and unlocked his second knight-specific talent. Being able to teleport Syzak to his side in the middle of a battle would provide a massive and immediate advantage, and even if he never progressed it even to the second rank, it would remain useful for his entire life.

Kadorax waited and rested on the rooftop for another hour or two, simply enjoying the pleasant weather before returning back inside to see what Atticus had learned of the Gar'kesh. He found the old man with Syzak, Elise, and Brinna in Darkarrow's northern courtyard. The four were standing around a corpse, and the beast's powerful smell hit Kadorax like a wall.

"About time you showed up," Syzak said playfully when he saw the bastion saunter into the courtyard.

"What's so special about the dead guy?" he asked.

Elise let out a subtle laugh. "I wouldn't get so close, and not just on account of the stench," she said.

Everyone other than Atticus moved back to the limits of the courtyard. The old warlock tapped his cane into the Gar'kesh's hide a few times, muttered a few words under his breath, and snapped his fingers.

The giant, lumbering monstrosity stirred and began to rise as though awakening from sleep.

"O-Oh . . ." Kadorax stammered. "Well. *That* changes things."

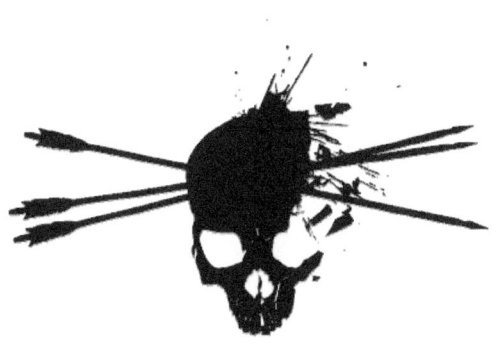

CHAPTER 11

The walk back to Virast was an interesting one. Atticus had looped a rope around the Gar'kesh's neck, which he held like reins, claiming that he *needed* to ride the beast to save his old legs the trouble. Everyone else kept their distance.

Every thundering Gar'kesh footfall kicked up enough dirt to send out a little mud ring for several feet. Perhaps once every ten minutes, the beast found the need to grunt, and the wind it pushed from its lungs would blow more dirt up from the path to splatter everyone's clothes. Kadorax stayed to the creature's right in what he hoped was part of its blind spot, though he didn't risk staying too far behind it as he didn't want to risk bearing witness to its backside when the time came for it to get rid of some waste. Speaking of food, not even Atticus had any real idea about what the thing would eat or how often. Just another mystery to be solved at another time.

Standing on the docks of Virast and looking at Bazrath's two-masted brig presented yet another mystery. "How do we get it on the boat?" Syzak wondered aloud.

The beast huffed, and one of the only civilians brave enough to open a shutter to watch the strange procession quickly ducked back below his windowsill in terror.

"I don't think the crew will *let* it on the boat, so that might not be an issue," Elise answered.

"Uh, can it swim, Atticus?" Brinna asked.

The old warlock gave a snort and then pointed toward the ocean. "In the waters, my pet! Mush!"

The rumbling Gar'kesh walked to the middle pier and nearly made it to the end before the wood beneath it gave way under the strain of so much mass moving so slowly. Two of the beast's huge legs splashed into the shallow waters of the shore. It continued on without giving the rest of the pier much notice, simply walking forward through water and wood alike. Atticus, now soaked from the waist down, laughed the entire time.

Eventually, the Gar'kesh was free of the docks and wharfs altogether, and it was swimming in the open ocean. Atticus clung to the creature's horns, and the waves splashed up against his chest, but he didn't seem to mind. In fact, he looked like he was thoroughly enjoying himself.

The entire crew of Bazrath's ship was assembled at the rail to watch the strange spectacle in rapt silence. Atticus turned his strange mount toward deeper waters and kicked it into speed. The beast turned out to be quicker than anyone watching could have anticipated for something so lumbering and colossal. It sped forward like a squid, its many appendages undulating behind its head and body.

"Well, it'll keep up with the ship. I guess we don't have to worry if it will fit onboard." Kadorax could barely believe the words as he spoke them. Everything he had learned about the warlock didn't comport with the other knowledge he had amassed about the class. Warlocks were supposed to be dark and brooding, full of secrets and enigmatic mysteries, not old men full of crazy ideas.

As Kadorax watched, a new thought came bubbling up in his mind. He sidestepped to get closer to Syzak. "The Gar'kesh is really swimming, right? I'm not nuts, am I?"

Slowly, the snake-man nodded. "We might all be insane. Atticus is riding a Gar'kesh through the water, and we're about to take it to Oscine City."

"At least I can trust my eyes," Kadorax said, slapping his friend's scaly shoulder.

"For now," the shaman replied.

The crew, led by the first mate, whose name Kadorax could not recall, demanded that Atticus and the Gar'kesh stay so far from the ship that the pair could barely be seen without the aid of a spyglass. Though Brinna had at least momentarily issued concern about sending the delusional warlock out to sea, she had been quickly out-voiced by everyone else aboard the ship. No one wanted the monster swimming alongside the hull like a harbor seal.

Princess Lilly was given as much of a royal treatment as the crew could offer, which meant she took over Bazrath's former cabin, and her lone guard from Kingsgate opted to stay with her. No matter where the woman went, he stayed glued to her side. One of the crew had given him an old saber as well, though he still lacked all the armor and pageantry of a true Kingsgate soldier. Kadorax thought he looked more like a beggar pretending to be a knight than a veteran soldier from the highest ranks of Agglor's formal military.

Other than stale food and a solitary squall that produced rough sailing conditions for about half a day, the trip from Virast to Oscine City passed without incident.

The city's expansive harbor was alive with activity. Many of the piers had been destroyed by the jackal horde—Kadorax shuddered when he thought of all the dead knights below the wreckage—but what was still serviceable was in heavy use. The fleet used to move soldiers from Kingsgate to Oscine City comprised mostly galleons flying the official colors of the king, and the largest of the ships had to anchor in deeper waters and send their retinues in by way of smaller vessels. At least two dozen carracks and twice as many brigs and schooners were lined up along the dock fingers like teeth in a giant leviathan. Priorate Knight banners could be seen along the shore, mingling among all the Kingsgate standards.

"My lady," the first mate began, his hat held in his hands, "I'm not sure there's anywhere to safely dock. We don't have a dinghy large enough to take everyone ashore at once. What should we do?"

Elise stood next to the helm as though she had appointed herself interim captain. "Bring us alongside that schooner. We don't have colors to run up the mast, but jackals also don't have boats. They'll recognize us as friendly." She pointed to a four-decked schooner that would probably be the first ship to spot them as they approached the city.

The first mate nodded and returned to the wheel, issuing orders to the rest of the crew that would prepare the ship for docking. Kadorax watched it all from the quarterdeck with Brinna, Syzak, and Gabi. Atticus and the Gar'kesh were about three hundred yards behind them.

"How do you plan on telling the king's men about our warlock friend?" the bastion asked.

Elise opened the ship's only spyglass and peered across the coastline. "Wave him in closer. He knows where the priory is up the coast. I'd rather have him land there and meet us later than risk the whole army turning their bows and catapults on the ship like we're the enemy."

Kadorax turned back to the sea and waved a large pole with a bit of old, tattered clothing attached to the top. The makeshift signaling system was the best they had worked out, and it took several minutes before Atticus finally noticed it and steered his monster in their direction. As planned, the old warlock directed the Gar'kesh to the rear of the boat as opposed to the sides in order to use the vessel as a bit of shielding in case any of the soldiers from Kingsgate happened to be looking in their direction. In all honesty, Kadorax had no idea what would happen if anyone on the ships happened to spot the swimming monstrosity coming their way. He had to assume they would attack, and then he'd get to pay a visit to all the drowned knights rusting in their armor at the bottom of the harbor.

Atticus brought his Gar'kesh into earshot, and Kadorax told him the plan. The man seemed a little delusional from the journey, perhaps more so than what was normally expected from him, but he understood the message nonetheless and turned for the priory farther east along the coast.

"Alright, let's see what's happened since we've been gone," he said, turning back to Elise and Oscine City.

Sailors aboard several of the ships noticed them coming

into port, but they didn't seem afraid. "There must be a hundred thousand troops . . ." Brinna said quietly.

Their small ship was dramatically dwarfed by the huge galleons and schooners as they pulled up alongside one of the king's transports. Sailors threw down ropes to facilitate the docking process, practically launching into a frenzy when they learned that the princess was aboard.

Within an hour, everyone from Bazrath's ship was standing ashore in Oscine City, surrounded by hundreds of troops from Kingsgate. King Bennington himself had not made the trip, but a man named Lord Ashcourt—Bennington's second in command—was somewhere in the midst of all the soldiers. Word of the princess's rescue had quickly spread, and the man arrived in short order, the old prior and a small retinue of knights trailing behind him. Kadorax was happy to see Lady Alexandrina among those guarding the high-ranking men.

A tentative air of celebration spread throughout the soldiers as Lord Ashcourt officially welcomed the princess back into royal protection. Some of the Priorate Knights joined the scattered cheers as well, though everyone kept an eye toward the north in anticipation of more jackals. While the princess was ushered into safer and more familiar hands, Kadorax, Syzak, Elise, and Brinna talked to Lady Alexandrina.

"You've secured the city?" the bastion began.

The woman's armor sported a fresh array of dents and scrapes, and she wore a cotton patch over one of her eyes. "More or less. When the army arrived, we were waiting at the docks to meet them. No one bothered to set up camp before charging north. We found two more fortress outposts like the one we raided together. The Miners' Union was helping build them. We managed to capture a few of them alive as we purged the jackal horde from the city."

"Oh, that must have been a fun interrogation. Learn anything useful?" Kadorax asked.

Alexandrina readjusted the cloak fluttering from her shoulders. "Miners are all cowards. They talked for hours before . . . expiring. They needed royal blood to open some kind of gateway to another world. The bastards we captured didn't know much about the gateway, but each of them mentioned it more than once. Seems the Miners' Union has built some sort of structure for the jackals to house their gateway, and they were paid a huge sum of gold for it. Everything is pretty far north, and none of the ones we captured knew exactly where."

"A gateway . . ." Kadorax quietly repeated. He mulled over everything in his mind, thankful for his recent increase to *Spirit* despite still not being able to put it all together.

Syzak flicked his forked tongue over his scaly lips. "A portal to another world? Earth?"

No one had any answers.

Finally, Kadorax broke the tense silence. "Whatever their gateway might actually be, I think we can safely say it has to stop. And they're working with powerful wizards, more magic than jackals have ever employed before. Whatever they're intent on accomplishing, we have to assume they're capable. They won't fail unless we stop them."

Alexandrina nodded. "We have a vague idea of where the rest of the jackals have retreated. Once we know that Oscine City is secure, we'll move against them."

"The princess said there was a traitor on her ship—a human implanted in her retinue. I wouldn't trust the army from Kingsgate with too much sensitive information. There could be a trap," Kadorax said.

"Trust no one," Elise added with a scoff. "Kill them all."

"But why would they need the princess at the temple by Darkarrow? Shouldn't they have taken her north?" Brinna asked, giving voice to the exact question bouncing around Kadorax's own mind.

"Either they needed her there to get the process started or that temple was just a small stop on the way toward their larger goal. We don't know." Alexandrina was starting to pace back and forth with her hands on the sides of her armor.

Back closer to the docks, a large section of the army was moving out, presumably to reman their forward outposts as the initial furor over the princess's return died down.

"The girl we brought with us has been north. She'll take us to the jackal cities. We can find their gateway and shut it down," Elise said. She nodded toward Gabi, and the girl shrank away behind Brinna like a frightened dog hiding from a pack of wolves. The rogue whispered a few words to her and then glared at Elise from behind her hair.

"We're having a war council tonight," Alexandrina went on. "All of you need to be there, of course. Meet us at the priory just after dusk." The woman nodded to each of them in turn before leaving to address other business with more of the knights.

"I'll see you all tonight at the council," Kadorax said. He stretched some of the weariness from his neck and back. "I need to go see Estelle and make sure Atticus hasn't destroyed the entire priory with his new pet. See you tonight."

Their goodbyes were brief, and then Kadorax left for the craggy cliffs overlooking the sea to the east of the main city.

The corpses littering the streets from the initial jackal invasion had been mostly removed. Blood stains still marked where many of the people had died, and it would take years to rebuild all the ruined businesses and homes, but the knights had at least removed the starkest reminders of death.

As Kadorax trudged alone through the vast city, he struggled to figure out what to say to Estelle. They had talked for several hours, but it hadn't been enough. Maybe it never would be. He struggled to come to terms with the thought that he would never be able to earn the woman's forgiveness, and he already knew there would never be anyone to take her place.

By the time Kadorax arrived at the priory's intricate driftwood doors, he still hadn't come up with any answers. The outside of the building was teeming with knights. They had several wagons of supplies and equipment parked to the side of their doors, and soldiers from Kingsgate worked to load and unload it all. Most of the gear being piled into wagons was food from the priory's reserve while items coming into the compound were mostly swords, armor, and other war material to replenish the Priorate Knights' reserves.

Kadorax pushed through the driftwood and past a pair of bustling knights carrying sacks of rice on their shoulders. He held the door for them, watched as they loaded one of the wagons, then went down the stairs into the barracks room and to the ocean cavern underneath the building.

Atticus and his enslaved Gar'kesh were frolicking in the sand. The old man was throwing a stick into the ocean waves, and the four-armed beast would bound into the water to fetch it like some overgrown, mutated dog. How the creature managed to pluck the stick from the waves with its mouth and return it to the shore undamaged was just another mystery that Kadorax added to a long list surrounding the Gar'kesh species.

Standing off to the side of the cavern and watching the playful spectacle with a slight smile was Estelle, her arms crossed over her chest. She was wearing a loose tunic the same shade as the deep blue of the Priorate Knights' banners. Kadorax found himself staring at the beautiful contrast between Estelle's chestnut brown hair and the rich fabric. She hadn't seen him, and in that moment, he felt like he could stand there for hours, just watching her breathe and laugh.

Then she turned, and the halcyon sight was lost. Estelle's playful, genuine smile soured, and her brows knit together.

"Hey," Kadorax said, walking to her and taking up a position at her side. He looked out toward the ocean as she did, unsure if he should meet her eyes or not.

"You came back."

"Of course I did. I told you I would. And it seems your adoptive father made a new friend," Kadorax replied.

"Yes, well . . . let's just hope it doesn't eat us all," she said. Estelle turned a little, and her shoulder brushed against the side of Kadorax's arm.

Kadorax moved closer, and when she didn't pull away, he finally let himself relax a little. "I know you probably heard already, but we brought the princess back to Oscine City. The jackals have nothing, and the war should be coming to an end soon. When it does . . ."

"I don't know, Kad. I don't know. The day for putting things back together was a long time ago, not today. What do you think you'll do once it is over? Restart the Blackened Blades?" she asked.

Kadorax stole a glance at her from the corner of his eye, and she was smiling. "No, Elise can have what's left of Darkarrow. There's going to be a meeting tonight to discuss the end of the war. I'm not sure what kind of role I'll be expected to play." He subconsciously rubbed the end of the soul rod lodged in his breast bone. "I think it's time I started trying to understand more about Agglor. Atticus knows some things, but I just don't know how much of what he says can be believed. His mind isn't really there, you know?"

Atticus threw his stick again and sent the Gar'kesh bounding after it. The beast made such a huge splash that saltwater sprayed back and splattered the warlock's tattered outfit, but he didn't seem to care.

"He told me things while you were gone," Estelle said quietly.

"What kinds of things?"

"About your soul rod. I think he knows exactly what it is." She turned to face him, and her hand reached out to take his.

Kadorax felt his breath catch in his chest for a second. Her touch was warm beneath his skin and reminded him of all the days and weeks they had spent together at Darkarrow. The ocean breeze mingled with her scent—lavender and honey and salt all blended into one intoxicating aroma— and Kadorax realized he was having trouble focusing on the words she was saying.

"—was always meant to be here. He knows the soul rod is only given to select people, probably the highest levels if I had to guess, and that's why you received yours. There's something Atticus said about returning it to where it was always meant to be, some final resting place perhaps, but I don't really know. He thinks the rod has something to do with Earth. He also thinks Virgil is a god, so who knows. It could be anything," she finished explaining.

"Does he know where I'm supposed to take the damned thing?" Kadorax asked.

Estelle shook her head. "Do you remember when you were trying to get back home before we met?"

Kadorax smiled as he remembered all those fruitless years of desperation and sorrow. "How could I possibly forget?"

"You told me that you tried to get into the library at Kingsgate, that you thought there might be answers held in their vault of scrolls. Atticus thinks that someone there knows more than he does." Estelle gave his hand a gentle squeeze and pulled away. "Father! Come here for a moment."

Atticus threw the stick once more, gave a sharp laugh toward nothing in particular, and walked over to the woman he believed to be his daughter. "What is it?"

"Tell Kadorax what you told me this morning about the library," she said.

The old man's gray eyes seemed to stare into the ocean. "Ah, yes. When Virgil brought me here, he took another one as well. Corporal Albin Hansson, one of my brothers in the trenches, you see. He was a real bookworm, and now he lives in the king's library. He knows things about things, that one."

"Now that you've brought the princess back to safety, maybe King Bennington will let you poke around the royal library for a few days," Estelle added.

Kadorax thought it over, and he had to admit the idea was better than anything else he had. Several times before he became an assassin, he had attempted to gain access to the Kingsgate library, only to be turned away for lack of standing and reputation. The concept of public libraries hadn't yet taken hold in Agglor, and that had led to many years of turmoil as Kadorax anguished over what he might learn if he ever had the opportunity to read what was stored beneath the castle.

Then again, maybe there was nothing.

"Whether Albin knows anything or not, I think it's worth seeing him. If we find the answer . . . do you still want to go back to Earth?"

Estelle smiled once more, and the ocean breeze tossed her hair around in front of her face. "I—"

A shout came from up above, and it was immediately followed by several more. When they didn't stop, Kadorax and Estelle raced for the stairs and sprinted back into the priory's foyer. Knights were running around everywhere, strapping on armor and grabbing weapons.

"What happened?" Kadorax yelled in the face of a young man struggling to tighten his breastplate with fingers made clumsy by scalloped gauntlets.

The man looked terrified, as if he had never fought before and didn't really know what he was doing. "There's, uh . . . There's been an attack, I guess. More jackals. Go outside. Some guy from the army just rode in yelling about it."

Kadorax pushed the man aside and ran out the doors. Most of the wagons he had seen before were gone, and in their place were a dozen or more armored men on horseback. They were shouting commands, telling everyone to assemble in Oscine City at some square that Kadorax did not know by name.

"You'll go and fight?" Estelle asked, her voice carrying sadness that betrayed her heartbreak.

"I'm not much use in an army. Never been too keen on taking orders. I'll go find Syzak and the others and see what's happening. You're going to stay with Atticus?" Kadorax asked.

The woman nodded and turned back to the doors. "I'll keep him safe. If you return, let me know. I . . . Just don't get yourself killed, alright?"

Kadorax wanted to give her a hug, to wrap her in his arms and tell her everything would be okay, but a dozen scrambling soldiers filled the space between them before he could will his feet to move. And then she was back inside, gone from his vision once more.

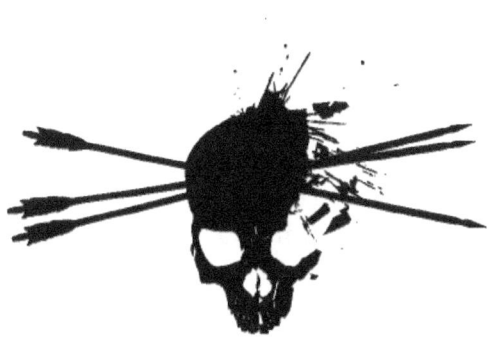

CHAPTER 12

The Founders' Square was at the very heart of Oscine City. The large area was surrounded on all four sides by towering marble statues of the two men and two women who had, according to legends that bore no proof whatsoever, been the first settlers in the village that had eventually grown into a sprawling metropolis.

Looking at the square now, Kadorax wasn't even sure if there was enough room for a single additional soldier. What men and women didn't fit between the statues were jammed into all the side streets, each of them eagerly straining to hear the orders coming down from the prior and the leader of the Kingsgate army.

Kadorax climbed up the legs of the nearest statue, a stone woman more than twenty feet tall with an axe in one hand and a bundle of three scrolls in the other. He searched the crowd for Syzak. Luckily, the snake-man was easy to find at the edge of the assembled troops. Being

271

one of the very limited number of nonhumans made him stick out.

The bastion pushed his way through the soldiers to where Syzak, Brinna, Gabi, and Elise were standing. "What's happened?" he asked, all business as usual.

"Most of the king's army is already fighting north of the city," Syzak answered at once. "The prior is organizing what's left to defend the rest of the city. Rumors said a big attack, more than before."

"We haven't seen anything with our own eyes yet," Elise added.

"Then that's our best plan," Kadorax replied.

Everyone looked to Brinna and Gabi. "Take her back to the priory. Estelle and Atticus are there. You'll be safe," Kadorax told her.

The woman nodded, though it was apparent that she longed to stay with the main group and fight rather than run away from the action to play babysitter yet again.

"Let's go find the jackals. We know our role." Elise twirled one of her dripping daggers on her palm, her expression doing nothing to conceal her vile intent.

"Find their leaders. Kill them," Kadorax said. "Are any of your Blackened Blades still in the city? Can they help?"

"Two dozen stayed. They should be mixed in among all the Priorate Knights. Most of them are probably still close to the priory itself. They'll know what to do." Elise didn't wait to discuss the plan any further. She took off toward the north, dodging incoming soldiers trying to get information from their leader in the square.

About a third of a mile away from the Founders' Square, the crowd of rushing men and women in heavy armor thinned to a mere trickle. "The first fighting broke out north of the docks," Elise said over her shoulder without slowing. "Let's go east. Outflank them."

Kadorax and Syzak followed without question. The three ran past several streets full of broken timbers, fallen stones, and ruined buildings lying half in the street.

They could hear and smell the jackal army before they actually saw any fighting. The bulk of the skirmish seemed to be concentrated to the west, more directly north of the docks, and only a small handful of battles were taking place in the streets above the Founders' Square. "Let's cut farther east," Elise said quietly, turning to her right to lead the trio through a section of destroyed houses that looked as if they had been pummeled by the Gar'kesh during the first invasion.

Kadorax paused for just a moment to make a mental map of the action. From what he could see, two main jackal forces were pushing into the Kingsgate army, though they weren't making much progress. The human soldiers had made the most of their several-day advantage by digging into the ruins and erecting fortifications where they could. They had turned many of the narrower streets into choke points and traps, and the raging jackal horde was falling into them with impunity. Kadorax pulled himself halfway up an exposed timber on the side of a business, using the gaps left by fallen bricks for handholds. "More are moving east with us," he told the others, pointing to a dark mass of enemies about ten or so streets away. He could barely see their heads among the ruins, though he could tell there was no Gar'kesh among their ranks.

"Hurry, we'll cut them off," Elise said. She darted over a collapsed roof, leading Kadorax and Syzak through a destroyed building that still housed the remains of its former occupants.

"How many could you see?" Syzak asked. "And where are they headed?"

Kadorax was thankful for his *Guardian's Enchanted Steel Spats* as they scrambled over splintered timbers and piles of loose shingles. "Looked like maybe forty. I don't know. They're moving east."

"Toward the priory?" Elise gracefully vaulted over two bloody corpses resting atop one another in the center of a cobblestone street.

"Could be," Kadorax answered.

About five streets farther east, Kadorax caught another glimpse of the group essentially shadowing their movements to the north. "Wait," he nearly gasped, pulling Elise back by an arm. "They're corrupted. Humans and jackals in chains with others behind them."

"You're positive?" the woman asked, her eyes wide. Her fearful expression betrayed a rare crack in her otherwise rock-solid air of arrogance and confidence.

"I know what I saw," Kadorax said. Then his confidence wavered. "Actually . . . one of you needs to go look. Make sure I saw something that actually exists."

Syzak nodded, offering him a sympathetic look. "Stay here."

The snake-man scampered away through the ruins, leaving Kadorax and Elise standing among the remnants of a thoroughly destroyed house. All four of the small home's walls had been brought down, scattering old food and glass jars all across the street. "Your . . . insanity. Don't get us killed, Kadorax."

"I know." For a fleeting moment, he almost considered killing the woman where she stood, but he knew his nerves were fried and the *Encroaching Insanity* debuff was starting to take a toll on his mind.

Thankfully, Syzak returned only a few seconds later, allowing Kadorax to let his thoughts return to the situation at hand.

"You're right. A whole group of corrupted humans and jackals. Maybe fifty or more," the shaman reported.

"Then we can't waste any time. We need to get ahead of them." Elise's stone-cold countenance had returned, and she didn't wait for any other plan before taking off on their original course once more, Syzak and Kadorax close behind her.

With only three compared to fifty, the group was able to easily outpace the corrupted mutants. "We can't fight them head-on," Elise said, crouching behind half of a wall to remain unseen. The corrupted humans and jackals were two streets north of them, noisily marching through Oscine City in the direction of the priory. Shouts from their uncorrupted overseers rose above the din, but they were still too far away for their words to be understood.

"If they're sending corrupted bastards against the priory, they're more organized than we thought. They know too much," Kadorax said, silently scanning his spells at the same time.

Syzak flicked his tongue and tasted the air. "What's the plan?"

Kadorax focused his mind on *Guardian of the Deep* and brought forth the monster's outline in his vision, ready to cast at a moment's notice. "When they get closer, I'll bring out my guardian. Then we run back to the priory. They have to be warned."

The time came less than a minute later. Kadorax leaned over the edge of a broken wall, lined up his guardian to break out of the earth in the very center of the corrupted mass, and let loose.

What followed was nothing short of pure chaos. Corrupted amalgamations of flesh, fur, and teeth screeched as they were thrown through the air by heavy tentacles. Salt water sprayed from the guardian's mouth, drenching everything within a hundred yards. Its body slammed through what was left of the nearest buildings, slaughtering corrupted soldiers by the handful.

"Kill the jackals and any they command!" He turned back to the other two at his side, hoping that the guardian's improved mental faculties as a result of *Enhanced Mind* would prove fruitful. "Come on, no time to watch," Kadorax reluctantly said. In truth, he wanted nothing more than to stay and witness the sheer destruction he had wrought, but he had to settle for watching experience notifications come rattling in across his vision instead.

As they ran toward the priory east of Oscine City, Kadorax read the notification for level sixteen flicker through his field of view. At level twenty he would be able to unlock a *Superior Talent* for his class, whatever that might turn out to be.

The guardian did its job, and Kadorax, Syzak, and Elise reached the priory before any signs of the jackals or their corrupted slaves. Out of breath, Kadorax felt like he was starting to know the path from the priory to the center of Oscine City and back a little too well. "Find out how many are left inside," he said between breaths. "We need to set up a defense."

Elise and Kadorax both pushed through the driftwood doors to the interior while Kadorax began trying to analyze the terrain to get an idea of how they would defend the building. The main approach was a wide dirt and stone road large enough for at least forty humanoids at a time, and blocking it would be difficult. Building a bottleneck might work, but

Kadorax didn't see anything large or heavy enough to move into place.

Atticus and his pet, he silently mused, remembering the old man's Gar'kesh and the sheer strength it commanded. He thanked his increased *Spirit* and ran into the priory, heading for the beach below.

The inside of the building was woefully unpopulated. A handful of knights had been left behind, and Elise had four of her Blackened Blades as well—and it wouldn't be enough. Kadorax hoped Syzak was still busy rousing others from deeper within the priory, though he feared Ayers would likely be one of the only ones left.

Trying to ignore their impending doom, Kadorax took the stairs down to the beach two at a time until he felt sand beneath his boots. Atticus, Estelle, and the Gar'kesh were still there, and it looked like they had already figured out that enemies were coming their way. Estelle was helping the old man get into more combat-friendly attire involving a thick leather vest with steel plates sewn into the shoulders and a pair of high boots designed for riding.

"I think the jackals know about the priory. We found a group of them headed here, and we slowed them down, but more will be coming," Kadorax said all at once. "Meet out front. Bring the Gar'kesh."

Kadorax bounded up the stairs back to the priory's foyer and took stock of everyone gathered there. Brinna, Gabi, and Ayers were crowded into one corner in front of the forge and workshop, and about ten knights were busy strapping on armor and sword belts in the center of the room.

"That's all we have?" Kadorax asked, yelling at Syzak above the commotion.

The snake-man looked sullen. "The knights are all

injured, left behind by the others," he said. "At least we have four assassins."

"And a Gar'kesh," Kadorax added.

Brinna stepped forward to grab the bastion's attention. "How many are coming?" she asked, her voice small among all the others in the room.

Kadorax slid his shield to his arm and drew *Assir's Edge*. He banged the weapon's hilt against the metal, and everyone gradually turned to face him. "We don't know what's coming against the priory or how many there are," he began, opting for honesty over a rousing speech as the knights were likely more accustomed to. "We need to defend the priory. If it falls, we'll lose an important position, but that doesn't mean retreat isn't an option. I won't throw our lives away. I don't expect anyone else to, either.

"By my guess, we'll have about an hour before any enemies arrive. I could be wrong. The jackals might be here in a minute, or there's a chance I'm wrong and no attack will ever happen. But we can't take the risk. We'll use the Gar'kesh out front to try and block the path, bottleneck them to use their greater numbers to our advantage." Kadorax tried to judge the expressions of the knights in the room. Most of them looked tired. Defeated already. They were all injured to varying degrees, some a lot worse than others, but they were Priorate Knights, and that meant their sense of honor wouldn't let them back down. If Kadorax told them to fight, that's exactly what they would do.

Outside, it didn't take long for some semblance of a defense to start coming together. Kadorax had the Gar'kesh start pushing boulders up from the craggy shoreline and roll them into place to create the bottleneck while Elise and her Blackened Blades went over the rest of the defensive plan with the injured knights. The priory had a few anti-siege supplies stored in one of the armories, and while most of it wouldn't be particularly useful against a land attack, they did find a few dozen sharpened stakes.

All the while, Kadorax kept seeing more and more experience points flashing across his vision in bright yellow. His guardian was still thrashing through jackals and corrupted somewhere in the city, though the rate at which the experience showed up was starting to significantly wane. Either the tentacled monster was running out of things to kill, or it was starting to lose ground.

Time slowly ticked by, and the priory defenses took shape. The Gar'kesh was able to haul several huge boulders up from the shoreline to block a good portion of the road, though the rocks themselves weren't really tall enough to stop an incoming army from going over the top of them. To solve that particular problem, they set rows of sharpened stakes directly behind the boulder wall and weighted them down with smaller rocks.

When they finally could prepare no more with their limited supplies, Elise sent two of her assassins out along the sides of the road to serve as advanced scouts. Then all they could do was wait.

CHAPTER 13

Less than an hour after Elise sent scouts to catch a glimpse of the jackal army, one of them returned at a full sprint. "They're coming," he reported. "Hundreds of them."

The steady stream of experience points coming into Kadorax's character sheet had ended some twenty minutes before, and he had reached level seventeen. The corrupted, it seemed, were worth far more experience than the regular jackal warriors he was accustomed to killing. He had taken ranks two and three of *Chaos Step*, increasing the talent's range to thirty feet and reducing its cooldown to only eighteen hours as opposed to one day. He wanted more points in *Guardian of the Deep* and *The Obsidian Well*, but fear had made his choice for him. If it came to it, *Chaos Step* would be his best talent for escape, and increasing the spell's range might mean the difference between life and death. Using the same logic, he had placed his sixteenth-level attribute point into *Agility* to bring his total to sixteen. Two more points and he felt he would be able to adequately dodge most attacks sent in his direction from rank-and-file enemies.

Still, despite all their preparation, Kadorax felt his heart sink when the scout returned.

"Any Gar'kesh among them?" Elise demanded from her underling.

The man gulped. "Two that I saw, my lady. And other things as well. Twisted, evil-looking things. I . . . We should run."

A few of the nearby knights looked around nervously as if they were searching for some kind of salvation to arrive all at once.

"We have a Gar'kesh of our own," Kadorax said with confidence he didn't quite believe. "We'll fight as long as we can, and then we'll run. Just remember the plan."

The assassin nodded and looked back to Elise for confirmation. "Go fetch Boristan. We'll need you both here, not out on the road," she commanded. The assassin left at once, and then the first sounds of the approaching army reached everyone's ears.

Kadorax wasn't sure if the two scouts would be able to return in time to save their own lives or if they'd be trampled by the oncoming horde.

"Brinna!" he shouted, looking for the woman near the back of the small bulwark. She was in front of Gabi, still desperately trying to defend the young girl. Against a smaller force, she likely would have been enough. "Get back inside the priory. Wait on the top level with Estelle on the training terrace, and be ready to run. Keep the girl safe."

Brinna nodded and ran for the driftwood doors, tears in her eyes.

There wasn't time to make any more changes before the fastest jackals started climbing over the boulder wall. A handful of corrupted creatures were mixed into their ranks as well, and they appeared more reserved, perhaps more intelligent, than their doghead counterparts. They watched as the first wave of jackals was butchered on the sharpened stakes behind the boulders. They didn't make the same mistake.

"Hold the gap!" Kadorax called above the small group of gathered knights. The men were heavily armored, and each one of them had a shield they knew how to use.

A deafening clash of flesh and weapons against steel heralded the start of combat, the knights filling the gap between the cliff on the left and the boulders on the right. One of the knights was bashed from his position closest to the sea, and he went tumbling down the side of the crags to his death among the waves and foam.

The battle had just barely begun, and they were down to eight knights holding the bottleneck. Luckily, the others were holding out. One of them activated a talent that cast a deep sheen of silvery magic over the entire area. More talents came from the jackals among the horde, escalating the ferocity of the fight tenfold.

Still unengaged, Elise held a dagger in each hand and waited behind the line of knights with Kadorax and Syzak. Ayers, a hammer in his hand, was behind them all at the doors, ready to open and close them as needed.

One of the corrupted humans vaulted off a jackal back and landed at the rear of the defensive line. It turned to slash with a curved sword at the back of one knight, and Kadorax leapt out to skewer it where it stood. The rest of the corrupted jackals and humans didn't need much time to figure out the same plan. They started running up and jumping, sailing over the knights. Many of them failed and collided with shields or swords, getting slashed and then pushed from the road to die among the rocks on the beach, but many of them succeeded.

Kadorax and Elise spun and whirled through the lunging corrupted soldiers. Syzak waited behind the pair, his spells ready and his eyes on the hiding Gar'kesh farther down the coast. Atticus sat atop the beast like a cavalier about to joust.

More corrupted came through the line, and two knights holding the gap between the boulders and the shore lost their footing. Kadorax tried to get to the pair in time, but another three corrupted jackals stood in his way. The two knights fell to their deaths before he could save them.

"Now, Syzak!" the bastion yelled as he slashed the jackal on his right and severed its head from its shoulders. Two more strikes came in from his left, and Kadorax could only catch one of them on his shield. The other scraped against the top of his breastplate—dangerously close to his head—and pushed him back a few inches on his heels.

The Gar'kesh came lumbering hand over hand up the side of the cliff. It roared as it crested the edge, and the remaining knights fell back right on cue, letting the huge beast fill the gap where they had just been. From the giant's back, Atticus launched spell after spell into the fray.

The horde started to sway backward. The jackals were losing ground in the bottleneck, and whoever was commanding them knew it. Kadorax pulled himself up to the top of the boulder wall, using two of the sharpened stakes as a makeshift ladder. "The Gar'kesh are coming in," he called back over his shoulder to the other defenders. Two huge four-armed beasts were trampling forward at full speed, giving absolutely no regard to any of their own soldiers mercilessly caught beneath their hooves. One of Atticus's magical bolts sailed out over the horde and struck the lead Gar'kesh in the chest.

"Warding!" Kadorax yelled, memories of his last respawn bubbling to the surface in his mind. The creature he had fought just a week earlier outside the temple had been magically protected, and Kadorax tried desperately to identify any kind of recognizable difference between the two that would tell him how to remove the beast's defensive wards. Without time to carefully scrutinize the creature up close, he found nothing.

Once Atticus was fully engaged on the front line, Elise ordered her Blackened Blades into the fray, sending the four assassins around the boulder wall to hopefully seek out any enemy leaders they could find. Whether they would be successful or not was impossible to tell from the front of the priory. As soon as they progressed a single row into the horde, all four of them were lost to sight.

The first of the enemy Gar'kesh reached the bottleneck, and even the jackal army slowed its relentless surging to watch the titans' slamming together. The brutal beasts pummeled each other, their fistfalls resonating like thunder.

"We can't take both of them," Elise said with a grimace, still fighting off jackals and corrupted that managed to make it over the boulders.

Kadorax knew she was right. "We have to kill it," he said. "Hold on." He moved his shield back into place on his back to let the woman grab hold of his left forearm, then waited a few seconds before activating *Chaos Step*, expending the talent he hoped to hold in reserve for the eventual retreat.

Kadorax and Elise appeared directly above the second Gar'kesh, suspended for a split second in midair. They came down on the creature's back, both scrambling for purchase, and Kadorax wrapped his free hand around one of the beast's horns. Elise found purchase farther down its back, holding tight with her fingers between two heavy plates of the Gar'kesh's natural carapace.

Chaos Shock surged through Kadorax's palm in the same way he had killed the beast outside the temple near Dark-arrow. His flesh erupted with shards of ice, and they re-flected off the Gar'kesh's magical warding like arrows hitting a smooth stone tower. The beast barely noticed.

A second wave of elemental magic came forth in the form of darkness, and it was just as easily repelled. Kado-rax growled in frustration and started swinging *Assir's Edge* down on the back of the creature's skull. A few feet below him and clinging to the Gar'kesh's hide, Elise was doing the same with her dagger. She had the auras of at least four dif-ferent active talents buffing her strikes, and her wicked blade had brought forth a torrent of blood.

"Kadorax!" the woman yelled, starting to lose her grip as the Gar'kesh thrashed. She slammed her dagger in with both hands, forfeiting her slick grip on the blood-covered cara-pace, and started falling to the ground—and the creature's heavy hooves.

Kadorax hadn't made much progress with his own blade against the Gar'kesh's neck and skull, so he leapt from the creature's back and landed with a roll a few feet behind it. The nearest jackals and corrupted instantly dove in on him before he had the chance to turn and try to help Elise. *Cage of Chaos* reacted violently to each incoming strike. His armor dulled most of the claws and teeth, but the corrupted enemies were more ferocious than the regular jackals by a huge factor.

Pain began to blossom throughout Kadorax's entire body. His left forearm was taking a beating, ringing with every impact deflected by his shield, and the pain was moving into his shoulder as well. His right arm, lacking the protection of a shield, fared worse.

Kadorax summoned his spells to his vision, desperate for some method of escape. He quickly focused on *Bring Together* but hesitated for a second before casting it. Instead, he switched to *The Obsidian Well* and cast it almost directly under his own feet. The nearest handful of enemies all tumbled downward through a jagged, pitch-black crystal cavern.

Getting back to his feet, Kadorax didn't have time to see what the talent had produced. He rushed back toward the Gar'kesh and saw Elise struggling on her back to dodge an incoming hail of thick, devastating hooves. Thinking quickly, Kadorax cast both *Conjure Unholy Aberration* and *Forsaken Lady's Condemnation* between him and the Gar'kesh. The nearest corrupted human instantly whirled around, slashing at its former allies and pushing two of them back into the rest of the horde. Between the Gar'kesh's hooves, a bone golem arose and pulled itself together from the remains of a dozen or more nearby corpses. "Kill it!" Kadorax yelled to his minion, pointing with his sword at the horned beast about to crush Elise to dust beneath its mass.

"Shadow Step!" Elise called, crossing her arms above her head to try and deflect an incoming hoof. Kadorax watched the creature's protective warding absorb her magic. One of its hooves smashed down, and Elise didn't manage to get out of the way in time. Her left arm was crushed into the ground, pinning her in place.

"Kad! Help!" she screamed at the top of her lungs.

Kadorax sprinted past the Gar'kesh and through several ranks of the horde. When he was about thirty feet away—far enough to hope the Gar'kesh would not pay him much attention—he activated *Bring Together*, his second knight talent.

Syzak and Elise appeared in a pop of gray smoke directly in front of Kadorax. Atticus and his mount arrived just behind them, and the jackal horde surged toward the priory. Nothing was left to stand between the army and the driftwood doors.

Unfortunately for Elise, the Gar'kesh had still been pinning her to the ground when Kadorax cast his spell. While most of Elise's body had teleported to the small patch of dirt in the midst of the jackal horde, her left arm had remained behind, mercilessly torn from her shoulder by the Gar'kesh's huge black hoof.

Kadorax heard a woman scream behind him—and the voice came from the wrong direction to have been Elise. He whirled backward, sword in hand and ready to cut down the first enemy he saw. Estelle was writhing on the ground, clutching her leg, blood seeping out between her fingers.

"No!" Kadorax gasped, suddenly rushing to the woman's side to lift her from the ground. As quickly as he hoisted her in his arms, he turned back to Syzak and the others. Behind them, he could see the first jackals reaching the knights in front of the priory doors. "Run! Retreat! The priory's lost!"

Balancing wearily in Kadorax's arms, Estelle pulled the cork from a small glass orb and drank the potion's contents. A bit of life returned to her muscles, and she pulled away to walk on her own. In front of her, Syzak had several jackals held at bay with his claws and traps, and Atticus's monstrous pet had crushed another dozen into a bloody pulp.

Kadorax stole a single glance back at Elise before pushing northward with the others, fleeing for his life.

"Atticus! Clear a path!" Kadorax shouted up to the old warlock, unsure if the man could hear him at all.

Syzak grabbed a fistful of a jackal's neck as it missed his gut by mere inches with an old spear. The snake-man hissed and tore, ripping the creature's Adam's apple from its body and throwing it aside. "You're leaving her?" he said to Kadorax, indicating Elise's prone and bloody body with his eyes.

Standing in the middle of so much war and terror, Kadorax wasn't sure what to do. Estelle was casting her arcanist magic furiously at the oncoming attackers to their left, and Atticus was using his Gar'kesh like a plow to trample a path to freedom. Kadorax couldn't see the priory doors through the battle. Perhaps they still stood, or maybe Brinna, Gabi, and Ayers were already dead inside, their bones being ground to dust against the stone floor.

Two more corrupted humans dove in for Kadorax's chest, stealing his thoughts away from his friends. He blocked one attack with his shield and slashed down with *Assir's Edge*, severing the twisted thing's hands from its wrists. The second one landed both jagged claws on Kadorax's armor, racking them across his steel bracers and splitting its own fingernails. Kadorax smashed his hilt into the corrupted human's face, then took off back toward Elise.

He skidded to a stop at her side, his knees kicking up blood and mud onto her armor. Her head lolled to the side. "You . . . bastard . . ."

Kadorax slid his shield to his back once more and started lifting Elise's torso from the ground. She groaned in his arms, and her already pained expression soured into anger. "You fucking . . . ripped off my arm," she growled, her teeth clenched.

289

With a sigh, Kadorax pushed himself to his feet and then dumped Elise's body in a heap to his side, eliciting another round of brutal screams from the dying woman. Her dagger had been caught underneath her back, and he plucked it from the ground. The hilt was ice cold to the touch, and the blade dripped liquid shadow.

Kadorax tucked the dagger into his belt and took off, deflecting several attacks with his armor as he ran.

Atticus's Gar'kesh mount didn't survive the escape from the jackal horde. It had taken too much damage trying to hold the bottleneck, and its spirit gave out not long after emerging alive from the battle. The old warlock seemed more displeased by the notion of needing to walk once more than by his pet's death. In the absence of his cane, Estelle had to help him keep his balance.

They stopped alongside a fountain in one of Oscine City's many opulent squares, and Syzak fished a dead body out of the water. "Think we can drink it?" he asked.

Kadorax stumbled to the fountain's edge and dipped a hand into the cool water. "Might as well," he said with an air of defeat.

For a long time, no one said anything.

Finally, Estelle broke the uneasy silence. "We can't stay here forever," she muttered. The sounds of a distant battle between the Kingsgate army and the rest of the jackal horde could just barely be heard coming from the docks and the Founders' Square.

"We need to rest," Kadorax replied. "Not just to reset our

skills, but we need to wait. If the king's soldiers win, we'll meet up with them tomorrow."

Estelle's eyes never left the ground. "And if the jackals take the entire city?"

"Ayers, Brinna, Gabi . . . they're all dead."

If you enjoyed this novel, please consider leaving a review at your favorite book retailer's website. Reviews from enthusiastic readers are vital to authors everywhere. Your support is greatly appreciated!

ABOUT THE AUTHOR

Stuart Thaman writes books. And he's written a lot of them. When not writing, he spends his days smoking cigars, listening to metal, and studying law, politics, and philosophy.

Check out all the latest books at www.stuartthamanbooks.com, where you can grab a free download just for signing up on the email list.

THE ADVENTURE CONTINUES IN
KILLSTREAK: KINGSGATE

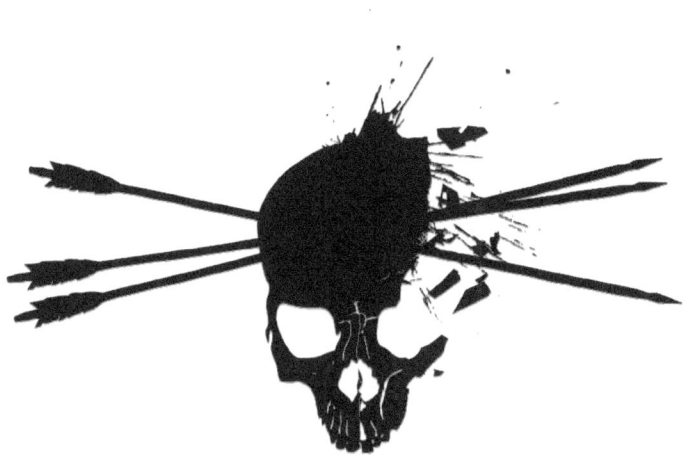

Get a free copy of *The Minotaur King*
by joining the mailing list!
https://dl.bookfunnel.com/lt2mw0eidx